Love Notes

By Susan Coventry

Cover Design: Woodchuck Arts
Edited by: FirstEditing.com

ISBN-13:
978-0692069080 (Coventry Industries LLC)

ISBN-10: 0692069089

Also by Susan Coventry

Chapter 1

"Oh no. Not again," Sophia said as she slid the wedding invitation out of the envelope. This was the fourth wedding she'd been invited to in the past two years, and she didn't expect them to let up anytime soon. Sophia and her friends were *of that age* where they were starting to settle down. Three years out of college, most of them had good-paying jobs, a place of their own, and a significant other.

"I guess two out of three isn't bad," Sophia said with a sigh as she perused the invitation. "Great! A destination wedding. Why can't people just get married at home already?"

Her college friend, Cassie, was inviting Sophia and a guest to attend her wedding celebration in Sanibel Island, Florida, on the third Saturday in May. She was marrying someone named Greg, whom Sophia had never met, but that was beside the point. She'd been close friends with Cassie throughout her four years at Wayne State University, and she felt obligated to go. Plus, they had mutual friends who would probably be invited too, and she would feel bad if she were the only one to decline.

If only I had a guest to bring, she thought with a twinge of self-pity. Six months ago, Sophia and her boyfriend, Jake, had broken up after almost two years together. She was over it now, but she missed having a date for weddings and special occasions.

Maybe I could say that I can't get away from work that weekend, she thought, but it was doubtful that anybody would buy it. Public libraries weren't like other businesses that had crunch times. Besides, there was always somebody who could fill in for her.

Sophia was wracking her brain to come up with some other excuse when her cell phone rang, and she smiled when she saw who was calling.

"Hey, Drew," she answered.

"Hey, Soph. What's happening?"

She glanced down at the wedding invitation and replied, "Not much. What's up with you?"

"Well, I was just calling to see if you wanted to meet for dinner this Friday."

"Friday? Really? No hot date?"

"Not until Saturday."

She should have guessed. Drew rarely went an entire weekend without a date. "So, you were able to squeeze me in, huh?"

"I always make time for you, Soph. You know that."

She couldn't argue with him, because it was true. No matter who his flavor of the month (or week) was, Drew always kept in touch with her. He was truly one of the best friends she'd ever had.

"It just so happens that I'm also available on Friday, so I would love to meet you for dinner."

"Great! I picked the place last time, so it's your turn."

"How about Alibi?"

"Adventurous as always!" he teased.

"Hey, what's wrong with pizza?"

"Nothing. I'm a big fan of it, as you know."

"I can't think of a food that you're not a fan of."

"Spinach. Popeye can eat all of it as far as I'm concerned!"

Sophia laughed, enjoying the warm, homey feeling she got whenever she talked to Drew.

"So, I'll see you Friday, then. Do you want me to pick you up, or should we meet there?" he asked.

"We can just meet there since I'll be at work until five and it's just down the road."

"Ok. I'll see you then. Bye, Soph."

After they hung up, she stared at her phone for a few minutes, the wheels spinning in her brain.

Maybe I should ask Drew to come to the wedding with me. It would be a hundred times better than going alone, and we always have fun together. Besides, he still owes me from that time I pretended to be his girlfriend back in high school. Drew had been trying to let a girl down easy, but she hadn't been taking the hint. So, he had asked Sophia to pose as his girlfriend at a party. They'd played it up big time, and even though Sophia felt bad for the girl, she had to admit that it was fun pretending to be Drew's girlfriend for a little while. They'd even kissed that night—the one and only time—and she still remembered how good it felt.

She shook her head to wipe the memory clean. *Don't be ridiculous, Soph! You're not a teenager anymore, and Drew has no desire to kiss you. But that doesn't mean you can't ask him to the wedding.*

Later that night, as she lay in bed, she thought back over their history. She had met Drew when she had moved from a small town in mid-Michigan to Waterford, a flourishing community located about fifty miles north of Detroit. At the time, Sophia had been going into tenth grade, and the last thing she'd wanted to do was change schools. However, her dad's job transfer necessitated the move, and there wasn't anything she and her two siblings could do about it. The one consolation was that her parents had bought a house on a lake (of which there were several in the area, thus the name Waterford).

She remembered the first time she'd seen Drew, who lived two doors down. He'd been outside shooting hoops in his driveway shirtless. She'd been admiring his buff physique when he had suddenly turned around and smiled right at her. *Holy cow. He's hot!* she remembered thinking as her face had turned beet red. And then he'd set down the basketball and started walking toward her across their neighbor's front lawn.

Her family had only moved in a couple of days prior, and Sophia was dirty from unloading boxes and cleaning her new room. She'd just stepped outside to cool off, when she'd been distracted by the sight of him. How she'd wished that she could have run back inside and freshened up, but the next thing she knew he was standing right in front of her extending his hand.

"Drew Kennedy," he said, "and you must be the new neighbor."

Sophia shook his hand, but she'd been rendered speechless. Up close, Drew was even better looking than she'd first thought. He towered over her petite frame, and he was muscular but not bulky. His neatly cropped hair was a brownish blonde, and his eyes were bluish gray. For some reason, she'd zoned in on his straight nose and masculine jawline and remembered thinking how it reminded her of the male models she'd seen in magazines.

Drew's laughter broke her out of her trance. "You going to tell me your name?"

"Oh. Right. Sorry. Sophia Russo. Nice to meet you."

"How old are you, Sophia Russo?"

"Sixteen. I'm going in tenth grade."

"Waterford Kettering?"

She nodded.

"I'm a year ahead of you."

She wasn't surprised that he was older than her. He had an air of confidence about him that made him seem older.

"Have you met anyone else in the neighborhood yet?"

"No," she said. "We just moved in a couple days ago."

"Well, I'll be glad to introduce you to some people once you get settled."

"Thanks," she said, still in disbelief over how hot he was—and nice too!

"I guess I'll see you around, then."

"Yeah."

Drew smiled and started to walk away, but when he was almost to his driveway, he turned back around. Of course, she was still standing there watching him. "Welcome to the neighborhood, Sophia Russo," he said.

And that had been the beginning of their friendship. Drew had made good on his word and had taken her under his wing that first year in high school. He'd introduced her to his friends and girlfriends (of which there were quite a few) and generally helped ease her transition into a new school. Once Sophia had made some friends of her own, they'd been dumbfounded and envious over her relationship with Drew.

She recalled one of her friends saying, "Seriously? How can you be just friends with a guy that looks like that? It doesn't make any sense."

Sophia had questioned it too at first, but it hadn't taken long for her to accept their relationship for what it was. Drew was a friend, but not just any friend—her best friend. And they'd stayed that way for all these years. Sure, there'd been some flirtations here and there, mostly from him since she was the shy one, but nothing ever came of it. At one point, she'd questioned herself, wondering if she wasn't pretty enough, interesting enough, or outgoing enough for Drew. But over time, she'd eliminated all those possibilities. He'd complimented her on her appearance, always noticing when she wore something new or changed her hairstyle. He never seemed to tire of her company, whether they were alone or in a big group. He'd always paid attention to her even in the presence of his girlfriends, much to their chagrin. And he'd often commented on how intelligent she was, soliciting her help whenever he had a writing assignment or an English test. (She was the language arts expert; he was the math whiz).

There was no doubt that they were opposites, but for some reason, that only served to enhance their friendship. She was an introvert who preferred reading to parties, while Drew was known by everyone as the life of the party. Everything about them screamed opposites, but it didn't seem to matter. They shared a connection that couldn't be broken, even when others tried to come between them.

With Drew being so popular, he'd never lacked girlfriends, and most of them had tolerated his friendship with Sophia. However, not all of them had been so accommodating. There was one girl, named Maddie, whom he'd seemed to be crazy about, but he'd broken up with her after she'd demanded that he stop being friends with Sophia.

"It's bullshit," he'd said when Sophia had asked him about it. "I'm not letting *anyone* tell me who I can or can't be friends with."

While Sophia had been touched by his loyalty, she'd questioned him at first. "Can't you understand where she's coming from? How would you like it if Maddie were best friends with some guy?"

Drew had studied her for a moment and then replied, "I'd accept it as long as I knew she wasn't into him *that* way."

Sophia was long past the point of feeling offended. She'd come to terms with the fact that Drew didn't look at her *that* way, and she was satisfied with being his friend. Well, most of the time, anyway.

Honestly, there'd been several times over the years that she had wondered about what it would be like to be more than friends with Drew. She already knew so much about him and his family and he was already such an important part of her life that she couldn't imagine him not being in it. The only thing that was missing, that had always been missing, was the physical aspect.

For some reason, over which she'd pondered and conjectured ad nauseam, they'd never crossed that line. But that didn't mean she hadn't thought about it. Oh, she'd squashed the feelings down and kept them in their place, but she wouldn't be human if she hadn't wondered what it would be like to kiss him, to touch him, and to have him reciprocate. They'd even talked about it a few times, albeit in a casual, jokey sort of way.

The only thing that held her back was her fear of jeopardizing their friendship, and she suspected that he felt the same way too. At least, she wanted to believe that was the reason rather than him not being attracted to her. Which was why it would probably be a bad idea to invite him to her friend's wedding on Sanibel Island. The sun, the sand, the bathing suits, the slow-dancing. It would definitely be a bad idea, but why did it sound so good?

Chapter 2

"So, I'm thinking about asking Drew to attend a wedding with me," Sophia said two days later to her co-worker and close friend, Eve.

Eve glanced up from the book cart and said, "Really? You're finally going to go after him?"

"What? No!" Sophia hissed, looking around to make sure there weren't any library patrons within hearing range.

"Well, if you don't, you're crazy!"

"How many times do I have to tell you that we're just friends?"

"You can keep saying it, but I don't believe you. He's too good looking to be any woman's friend."

Sophia sighed. "If I had a dollar for every time I've heard that..."

"I know—you'd be a wealthy woman, and you wouldn't have to shuffle library books around ever again!"

Sophia shook her head, her black curls bobbing around her shoulders. "I love this job, Eve, and so do you."

It was true. While most of her friends had gone into fields like nursing, accounting, and sales, Sophia had followed her true calling. She'd always been a bookworm, and she was proud of it. Even when she was a small child, she'd wanted to work in a bookstore or library someday. "But you won't make much money," her father had warned. "Why would you want to be around books all day?" her brother, Kyle, had said. But she hadn't listened, and now she was the proud owner of a library science degree. She worked at the Rochester Public Library, which boasted one of the best book collections in Oakland County, and she loved it there.

"When are you going to ask Drew to the wedding?" Eve said as she slid a returned book back onto the shelf.

"Tonight. We're meeting for dinner after work."

"Isn't he dating someone right now?"

"Drew doesn't really date. It's more like…"

"Wham, bam, thank you, ma'am?"

"Eve!"

"Well, that's what it is, isn't it?"

"I don't know all the details of his love life. I just know that he hasn't been serious about anyone in a long time." *If ever*, she thought.

"Don't you find it the least bit curious that he doesn't keep any woman around for long except you?"

"That's because we're friends. If he and I would have—well, you know—then we probably wouldn't still be together. Does that make any sense?"

"No. None of it makes sense," Eve said, but then she smiled. "But if that's what you kids are calling it these days…"

They were interrupted by a patron after that, so they never had a chance to finish the conversation. But it didn't really matter because Sophia had already made up her mind. Drew was her friend, and she was going to ask him to the wedding. The worst thing that could happen is that he might say no, right?

"Hey, hot stuff!" he said when she joined him at their table.

He'd called her that before, and she'd never given it much thought, but now, thanks to Eve, she was questioning everything.

"Hey...you," she said and slid into the booth across from him.

"You're still wearing your glasses," he said, studying her.

"Oh. I just forgot to take them off," she said, and then she slipped them off and tucked them into her purse. She mostly wore glasses for reading, and since she did a lot of that at work, she often forgot to take them off afterwards. "There. Better?"

Drew chuckled. "I think you look good in glasses. I told you that a long time ago."

Sophia recalled the first time he'd seen her in glasses back in high school. Those were the days when she had believed that "guys don't make passes at girls who wear glasses." Thank God she was past that now, and Drew had been the first guy to tell her that he liked her in glasses.

"It kind of gives you that naughty librarian vibe," he continued.

She had been perusing the menu, and suddenly, she jerked her head up. "Seriously?"

He nodded. "Yeah. A lot of guys have fantasies about that, you know."

Sophia set down her menu and waited for him to smirk or laugh, but he looked dead serious. For some reason, she was feeling bold, so she asked, "What kind of fantasy?"

"Well," he began, leaning forward, "it goes something like this. A guy walks into the library, and it's almost closing time. The only person there is a female librarian, who has her hair up in a bun and is wearing glasses."

"Continue," she said, subconsciously having leaned forward too.

"She has on a conservative outfit, like a long skirt and a white blouse buttoned all the way up so she's not showing much skin."

Sophia was intrigued, and she was starting to feel—oh my God—turned on! "And then what?"

"And then the guy asks for help finding a book."

"Instead of looking it up on the computer?"

Drew laughed. "Just go with me here."

She giggled nervously and said, "Ok. Continue."

"So, he follows the librarian down an aisle, and she finds the book he wants on the very top shelf."

"Is the guy tall enough to reach it?"

"No. Nobody but a pro basketball player could reach it."

"So, then what?"

"So, she gets a stool, and he puts his hands around her waist to give her a boost up."

"That's rather bold, don't you think?"

Drew laughed louder that time. "This is a fantasy, remember?"

"Fine. Continue."

"Once she gets the book, she turns around, and he helps her back down. Only this time, he doesn't remove his hands from around her waist."

Sophia swallowed hard. "What does he do next?"

"He tips his head down and kisses her."

"Does she still have her glasses on?"

"Well, yeah. That's part of the fantasy."

"Is there more?" Sophia's skin felt clammy even though it was early March and spring hadn't officially begun yet. She almost unbuttoned the top button on her blouse, but after his story, she thought better of it.

"Oh, there's more," he said, but he picked up his menu and buried his head in it.

"Hold on!" she huffed, pushing the menu back down. "You're not going to tell me the rest of it?"

Drew glanced around the restaurant, which had become much busier since they'd sat down. "I can't tell you the rest here. This is a family restaurant," he said, smirking at her.

Sophia shook her head at him, torn between feeling irritated, titillated, and confused. Why was he telling her all this? They'd talked about sex in vague terms before, but neither of them had gone into much detail. That was perhaps the primary difference between having a female best friend and having a male best friend. There were certain topics that felt off limits, and sex was one of them. Although, his little story was making her wonder...

"Drew?"

"Yeah?"

"When you said a lot of guys have that fantasy—does that include you?"

Just then, the waitress walked up to take their order, and appearing relieved, he ordered for them both. After that, he changed the subject, and she felt too uncomfortable to bring it up again. Instead, they ate pizza and salad and reverted to safe topics such as work and their families.

Drew was an only child, and his parents had recently retired to Fort Meyers, Florida. He was just telling her about how his mom was begging him to come down for a visit when it struck her.

"Speaking of Florida," she said after he'd finished talking. And then, just like that, she lost her nerve.

"What about it?" he asked as he polished off a second slice of pepperoni pizza.

"Oh, never mind," she said, flapping her hands dismissively.

His eyebrows knitted together. "What is it, Soph?"

"It's not important. Really."

But Drew wouldn't let it go. "It was something. Just tell me."

Feeling cornered, she looked into his blue-gray eyes and plunged ahead. "I was going to ask you for a favor that had to do with Florida."

He gave her his full attention. "Shoot."

"Well, I've been invited to a wedding on Sanibel Island, and…"

"Sanibel Island? Isn't that right near Fort Meyers?"

"Yes, it is. And I was going to ask if you'd go with me as my…my guest. But before you say anything, there's no obligation whatsoever. I realize that it's a long way to go for a wedding and you might have to work and…"

"Soph! Hold up!" Drew laughed as he held out his hands palms up. "Are you asking me to be your *date*?"

"Date? What? No! Not exactly." She felt the heat creeping up her neck and was glad she was wearing a high-collared blouse, kind of like the librarian in Drew's fantasy. *Oh God. Get me out of here!*

"Because I would love to be your date. I mean your *guest*," he was saying, but Sophia was still in such a state of panic that his words didn't register.

"It was a silly idea. Forget I even asked. We can go back to talking about—wait a minute. What did you just say?"

Drew chuckled again. "I said yes. I would love to escort you to the wedding. Whose wedding is it anyway?"

She started to relax when she saw the wide smile on his incredibly handsome face. "A friend of mine from college, Cassie. She's part of a circle of women I hung out with at Wayne State, and I would feel bad about not going."

"Of course you should go. Why wouldn't you? But I'm curious. Why me?"

Sophia shrugged. "I guess I feel like certain events, such as weddings, call for a date, you know? Sure, I'll probably know a lot of people there, but most of them will have dates, and I didn't want to feel like the odd one out."

Drew nodded. "I get it, but that still doesn't answer my question. Why me?"

Something about the way he was looking at her made her squirm. She debated her answer until she decided to step outside of her comfort zone. Heck, after he'd shared his fantasy, why shouldn't she?

"Remember that time in high school when I pretended to be your girlfriend?"

He nodded, peering at her intently.

"Well, I figured you owe me one."

Drew's eyes went wide. "Wait a minute. You want me to pretend to be your boyfriend?"

She plastered on a brave smile. "If you don't mind."

He sat back against the booth and crossed his arms over his broad chest, grinning at her like a Cheshire cat. "No, Sophia. I don't mind at all. In fact, I think this wedding could be a helluva lot of fun."

Or it could make me fall in love with you, she thought, but she just returned his smile, and they sat there grinning at each other until the waitress came with their check.

Chapter 3

Later that night, when Drew was lying in bed, he thought about Sophia's request. He'd been serious when he'd said he was looking forward to the wedding, not because he was the sentimental type who liked weddings, but because he would get to spend an entire weekend with her. In typical Sophia fashion, she'd outlined a plan for the weekend, down to the last detail, and she'd even offered to pay for his plane ticket!

"No way," he'd said. "I appreciate the gesture, but I make plenty of money. Besides, it'll be kind of like a mini-vacation, and I might even have time to visit my folks while we're there."

Sophia had perked up at that. Over the years, their families had become close, and they still got together whenever his parents came back to Michigan. It had been easy to stay in touch since Drew had bought his parents' house after they'd retired and Sophia's parents still lived two doors down from him.

He smiled, thinking about the Sophia he had first met when they were teens versus the Sophia of today. Some things hadn't changed, like her curly black hair, her sweet smile, and her large, expressive brown eyes. But what had changed was that she had grown more confident, more poised, more beautiful. Yes, he could admit that to himself. To him, Sophia was one of the most beautiful women he'd ever known, and a sweetheart to boot.

Too bad he would never be able to tell her that. Not without spooking her and risking the loss of their friendship. He laughed aloud when he recalled the look on her face as he'd told her his librarian fantasy. At first, she'd acted appalled, but then she'd seemed to really get into the story. It was obvious from the way she'd leaned forward in her seat, her full breasts brushing up against the table, her eyes wide, and her breathing shallow. He hadn't missed the redness that had crept up her neck, even though she'd been wearing a blouse not unlike the one he'd described in his fantasy.

At one point, she'd licked her full lips, and he'd become hard beneath the table. Good thing the waitress had arrived soon after that and he'd been able to change the subject. No. He could never let Sophia know how he really felt about her. Not unless he wanted to lose one of the best friends he'd ever had. How did he know that was what would happen? Because of his history with women. He'd only had two serious relationships, and both had ended in heartbreak—once for the woman and once for him. After that, he'd decided it wasn't worth the pain to get serious with anyone. It was better to just have fun—and yes, that included sex—and then move along.

Which was why he and Sophia had remained close over the years. They weren't in a position to hurt each other. Whenever they got together, it was light and easy—fun and flirty, without the sex. Although lately, he'd been thinking about her a lot more. Maybe it was because they were closing in on thirty and a lot of their friends were getting married and having children. Or maybe it was because no matter how many women he had *dated*, no one could hold a candle to Sophia.

Case in point, Lexie, the girl he was currently seeing. She was a model, literally, he'd met at a car show. She'd been standing there next to a red sports car, leaning all over it like it was a man instead of a machine, and he'd been instantly attracted to her. She was a tall blonde with big boobs and a killer smile, but there was something missing. Lexie didn't have Sophia's quick wit and charm. She didn't have that adorable dimple in her left cheek and that uninhibited laugh that warmed him to the core. He'd discovered that Lexie was a horrible listener, preferring to talk about herself most of the time, and when he was with her, he found himself zoning out. But the sex—now, that was good! And that was what kept him around, at least for now.

See? This was why he knew he was no good for Sophia. He sounded shallow even to himself. In fact, he'd always thought that Sophia was too good for him, which was one of the reasons he'd never tried to make a move on her, even back in high school, when his testosterone had been through the roof! She had been and still was so sweet, almost to the point of being naïve, and he hadn't wanted to tarnish her. It was like she saw the world through rose-colored glasses (or tortoiseshell glasses in her case), and he didn't want to spoil that for her.

He didn't want to be some guy who broke her heart, like that ass, Jake, who'd broken up with her six months ago. He'd never liked that guy, and he hadn't really tried to hide it. When Sophia had asked him why, he'd simply said, "He's not good enough for you." Funny thing, that was how he felt about himself too. He'd decided that he'd probably feel that way about any guy who went after her. But he also knew that she wouldn't stay single forever. He saw the way other men looked at her, or ogled her in some cases, yet she always seemed oblivious to it. He'd even pointed it out to her on a few occasions, and she had just giggled and dismissed it.

Which is why he tried never to ogle her, even though nothing about her escaped his attention. She was a conservative dresser, but he'd seen her in a bathing suit often enough to know that there were luscious curves hidden underneath her clothes. Living on a lake, they'd spent a lot of time swimming and boating, and he'd seen her body blossom over time. When he'd first met her, she'd been slimmer and flat-chested, but now, well...

Drew's hand drifted down beneath the covers, and he found himself hard and throbbing just thinking about it. The last time he'd seen her in a swimsuit had been this past summer, when he'd invited her over to go boating with him. It had been just the two of them, and it had been one of those glorious summer days where he felt so damned grateful to be living on a lake. Sophia had worn a cover up over her tankini until the last minute, when they'd decided to jump in and cool off. He'd tried to look away when she'd removed the cover-up, but he couldn't. As always, she'd chosen a conservative style swimsuit, but it hadn't hid her ample cleavage or the round curves of her bottom as she'd climbed over the boat and lowered herself into the water.

They'd swam around the boat just like they had in high school, and when they'd climbed back in, the wet suit had clung to her, the outline of her nipples clearly visible through the fabric. Of course, she'd quickly wrapped herself in a towel, and he had averted his eyes, but she might have caught him looking. He was a man after all, and she was a gorgeous, wonderful woman who meant the world to him.

Drew closed his eyes as he stroked himself and let his mind wander to his sexy librarian fantasy. He hadn't told her the whole thing because he'd been afraid to give himself away. But now that he was alone, he could indulge all he wanted to, and she would never know. In his fantasy, they were in the library after closing, with the doors locked and most of the lights turned off...

She took his hand in hers and led him back to her office, closing the door behind them. Her curly hair was tied back at the nape of her neck, and she took out the tie and shook it loose. He stared at her, mouth agape, palms sweaty, heart racing, as she slowly undid the buttons on her blouse. He was frozen in place, afraid to move, afraid to speak and break the spell. The next thing he knew, her blouse was on the floor, and then her bra followed. Drew sucked in a breath when he saw her bare breasts, full and round, her pert pink nipples beckoning to him. "I want you, Drew. I've always wanted you," she said and stepped toward him.

The fantasy stopped there because he was already so aroused that he was about to come in his hand. Tossing his covers back with one hand, he finished what he'd started, panting and groaning until he was spent. Afterwards, he reached over for the tissue box on his bedside table and cleaned himself off while his breathing returned to normal.

He felt guilty for a few minutes, thinking that Sophia might not like the idea of being the object of his fantasy, but then he thought again. Sometimes, he'd catch her looking at him with more than a friendly interest, especially when he'd been shirtless. And sometimes, when their eyes locked, he'd sworn he'd seen something there—something deeper than friendship.

But she'd never said or done anything to indicate that she wanted more than his friendship, and whenever the topic of sex came up, she seemed uncomfortable.

No. It was best to keep her in the friend zone. That was all there was to it. He'd have to keep his dirty little fantasies to himself from now on. The last thing he wanted was for her to find out that the star of his librarian fantasy was her.

Chapter 4

Two weeks later, Sophia and Drew were sitting in his living room eating Chinese take-out, which had been his choice for dinner. Chinese wasn't her favorite, but she had chosen the food last time, so it was only fair.

"Are you going to eat that?" Drew asked, pointing to her egg roll.

Sophia wrinkled up her nose. "No. If I can't identify what's in it, then I'm not eating it."

Drew snatched the egg roll off her plate and said, "Fine. More for me, then!"

"It's a good thing you work out so much with the way you eat," she teased.

"I didn't think you noticed," he mumbled.

"Huh?"

"Never mind. So, are you ready to go over your list now?"

"Yes," she said, digging a handwritten list out of her purse.

"Hit me," he said, clasping his hands behind his head and leaning back.

They were sitting close together on the couch because they had been sharing the food, but now that they were finished, Sophia scooted to the opposite end and turned so she could face him.

"Ok. So, the first thing on my list is wedding apparel."

"Well, the bride usually wears a gown, and the groom usually wears a tux..."

"Very funny. I'm talking about us. I think we should coordinate our outfits."

Drew raised his brows. "You mean so we match?"

"Well, not match so much as wear colors that complement each other."

He scratched his chin, which made a raspy sound against his razor stubble. Sophia liked seeing him like this, all relaxed and casual. Tonight, he wore a faded pair of jeans and a worn-in gray t-shirt that showed off his muscular arms. The last time they'd been together, he'd been wearing his work clothes, which he also looked good in. Heck, the man looked good in everything.

"You've given this a lot of thought, haven't you?" he asked, looking bemused.

She shrugged. "Well, if we're going as dates, I want us to look like we're a real—you know—couple."

"And real couples wear matching outfits?"

"Not necessarily, but they just look like they go together. Do you know what I mean?"

Drew nodded. "So, do you already know what you're wearing?"

"No. But I thought maybe we could go shopping together."

He rolled his eyes exaggeratedly. "Wow, Soph. If I'd have known that shopping was part of the deal, I might not have signed up for this thing..."

She scowled at him even though she knew he was teasing.

"What's the next item on your list?"

"Dancing. I think we should practice before we go."

Drew laughed. "I promise you that I can do the macarena with the best of them. And the chicken dance!"

Sophia giggled at the thought of him flapping his arms like a chicken. "Not that kind of dance. I'm talking about slow-dancing."

That made him sit up straighter, and he cleared his throat noisily. "Why do we need to practice? I know what I'm doing."

"I don't doubt it. It's just that. . ."

"What?"

"It's just that we have to look like a couple in love, and couples in love dance in a certain way. I don't want it to look like I'm dancing with my best friend."

"Hmmm. A couple in love, huh? Describe it to me."

She swallowed nervously, but she had started this thing, so she had to finish it. "Well, they hold each other really close so there's barely an inch of space between them."

"Go on."

"And they stare deep into each other's eyes."

"I'm with you."

"And they whisper things in each other's ears that might be sweet, or funny, or sexy. Only they know."

"Uh-huh."

"And they move together like it's the most natural thing in the world. Like they're familiar with each other's bodies, and they just fit together like puzzle pieces."

Drew scratched his chin thoughtfully. "I think you're right. We need to practice." And then he stood up and walked into the kitchen while she stared after him inquisitively.

He returned a few seconds later with his phone, and he scrolled through it with a look of deep concentration.

"What are you doing?"

"I'm looking for a song that we can practice slow-dancing to."

Sophia's eyes went wide, and she practically sprang out of her seat. "What? Right now?"

"Sure. It's never too early to practice. In fact, we'll probably have to practice several times before the wedding just to make sure we have it down. Ah-ha, here we go. They always play this song at weddings."

Drew propped his phone up against a table lamp, and the mellow notes of "Unchained Melody" rang out through the speaker. He turned around, held out his hand, and gallantly said, "May I have this dance?"

Sophia froze and stared at him like he she'd never seen him before. But that was kind of the point, wasn't it? They had to get to know each other in a whole new way. Slowly, she stepped forward until they were only a few inches apart. The music swelled, and he gently placed his hands on her hips.

"I believe step one was for us to hold each other close," he said, his eyes aglow.

This is just pretend, Sophia reminded herself as she took another step closer and looped her arms around his neck.

"Better" he said, smiling down at her from his six-feet perch.

She glanced between them, and in a tiny voice she said, "We could still be a little closer."

His hands left her hips and encircled her waist, and he pulled her forward at the same time.

"How about that?"

Standing this close, she felt every hard inch of him, and she was fairly certain that wasn't his wallet pressing into her abdomen.

"Good," she breathed.

They swayed to the music for a few beats and stared deeply into each other's eyes, just as she'd described. She had always admired his blue-gray orbs, and they were even more spectacular at this proximity. As the music hit a crescendo, Drew tipped his head down near her left ear and whispered, "You look stunning tonight."

His warm breath tickled her earlobe, causing a shiver to run down her left side. And then the music stopped, and the room was quiet again except for the ticking of a mantle clock and the pounding in her chest. *He probably can't hear that though*, she assured herself.

She took a step back, and he let go of her waist, albeit somewhat reluctantly. "Ok, then. Not bad for our first practice," she said, averting her eyes.

"Yeah. Hey, do you need something to drink? Because I could use some water."

"Sure," she called to his retreating back. He was almost in the kitchen by the time she'd responded.

Drew returned with two bottles of water. He handed her one and then sat back down on the couch. He drank most of his in a couple of gulps while Sophia studied him from across the couch.

"Drew?"

"Yeah?"

"Are you really ok with this? Because, if you're not..."

He swiped his moist lips with the back of his hand and said, "I'm good, Soph. I want to do this for you."

She nodded, unconvinced. For a few minutes, when they were dancing, she'd almost believed that they were a real couple—the way he'd held her, and when he'd whispered in her ear. *Does he really think I look stunning, or was he just practicing for when I'm dressed up at the wedding?* She glanced down at her jeans and sweatshirt, and decided it was probably the latter. But once the music had stopped, it had seemed like he couldn't get away fast enough.

"Ok. Well, we can discuss the other items on my list another time." She started to fold up the paper, but he stopped her.

"What? No. You're here now, so let's finish it."

She unfolded the paper again and scanned the rest of the list. The next item read: *practice kissing*, and the one after that read: *corroborate story of how we fell in love.*

"Soph? Why are you hesitating?"

"Ok, fine." She read off the next two items in a rush and then continued to stare down at the paper, refusing to meet his eyes.

Drew gulped down the rest of his water and then cleared his throat loudly. "Maybe we have done enough for tonight. What do you think?"

She nodded and stood up, grabbing her purse and jacket in the process. "Sure. Yeah," she said as she hurried toward the front door.

He pulled it open for her before she even had the chance, and she quickly went outside into the cool, fresh air. She had just stepped off the porch when she realized that she was being rude. Turning back around, she saw that Drew was still there, leaning against the doorframe, watching her.

"Did you forget something?" he asked.

"Um-hum. I forgot to say thanks for dinner. So, thanks."

He smiled at her then, and it was like all the awkwardness between them had disappeared. They were no longer a "couple in love." They were just Drew and Sophia—friends for life.

Chapter 5

After the dancing episode, Sophia decided to lay low for a little while. Even though Drew had agreed to go to the wedding, she didn't want it to turn into a chore for him. Truthfully, she needed the break. Dancing with him so close and pretending to be a couple had made her think about doing the next thing on her list—kissing him. She'd added kissing to the list because she thought that showing affection toward each other would add to the believability of them as a couple. Not that she expected him to dip her down and shove his tongue in her mouth, although that didn't sound half bad…

The sound of her cell phone jolted her out of her reverie, and she felt another jolt when she saw the name on the display.

"Hey," she said, trying to sound casual.

"Hey. What are you doing tonight?"

It was a Friday night, and Sophia had changed into her flannel pajamas after work. She'd planned to curl up on the couch with her latest read and a bowl of Peanut M&M's. "Um…"

"Am I getting you from something?"

"No. What did you have in mind?"

"Well, Lexie went out with her girlfriends tonight, so I thought maybe we could go shopping for our wedding clothes."

Why does hearing Lexie's name make me cringe?
Sophia had grown accustomed to hearing the names of
Drew's women over the years, yet none of them had
bothered her as much as this one. *Why her? Why now?*

"Soph?"

"Sorry. I'm just so shocked that you want to go
shopping. I kind of blanked out there!"

He chuckled, the sound of it warm and gooey in
her ear.

"Well, we should probably cross something off
your list, don't you think?"

How about kissing? When will we get to that one?
"You're right. Do you want to meet at the mall?"

And then there was a knock on her front door.
She glanced down at her flannel pajamas and panicked.
She hadn't been expecting any visitors. "Hold on,
Drew," she said and slipped the phone into the pocket
on her chest. She looked through the peephole and saw
his amused face staring back at her. And then, as if he
knew she were looking, he brought his left eye right up
to the peephole and stared back at her.

"I know you're in there," he said teasingly.

She flung open the door, forgetting about her
pajamas momentarily, and motioned him inside. "Why
didn't you just tell me you were here?" she asked,
feigning annoyance.

"I wanted to surprise you." His eyes perused her
from the top of her head down to her bare feet. "And it
looks like I did!"

She crossed her arms over her chest and said,
"Well, I wasn't expecting anyone."

"You don't say," he teased, eyeing the bowl of
M&M's on the coffee table.

"Make yourself at home, and I'll go change," she said as she walked away. Once she was in her bedroom, she hurriedly shucked off her pajamas and pulled on a pair of jeans and a purple crewneck. She tried to tame her riotous curls with her hands but soon gave up. She used to fight with her natural curls, but recently, she'd decided to embrace them instead. Her friends who had pin-straight hair claimed to be jealous of her waves, just as she'd wished she could trade with them. It was the ongoing dilemma of always wanting what you couldn't have. *The same thing applies to people too*, she thought as she strolled back into the living room.

Drew was sitting on her leather recliner, with the footrest up, her book propped open in one hand, and his other hand in her bowl of M&M's. He was so engrossed in the book that he didn't even glance up, which gave her an extra minute to admire him. He must have come over right from work, as he was dressed in his business attire—plaid button-down, dark slacks, and black dress shoes. He was a salesman for a company that sold parts to automakers in the Detroit area. She didn't pretend to understand exactly what it was he sold, but she knew that he made a good living at it. In her opinion, his profession fit his personality perfectly. He was outgoing, trustworthy, friendly, and a good conversationalist, which meant he listened as well as he spoke. If she were an automaker, she would buy from him. Speaking of parts…

"Enjoying my book?" She had left off on a juicy part of her romance novel, and based on his expression, he was enjoying it very much.

Drew quickly closed the book and set it down on the coffee table. "How can you read that stuff without getting…?"

Just say it, she thought as she waited.

"Turned on," he finished.

She smiled, glad that he was the one squirming this time instead of her. "I do sometimes, but that's part of the fun of reading it."

His eyes widened. "But then what? It seems like a waste if you don't have somebody... Oh God. Sorry, Soph. I didn't mean..." He stood up and walked toward her.

She put her hands out to stop him from coming any closer. The last thing she wanted was his pity. "Who says I need a man to get the job done?" she retorted, hardly believing she'd said it aloud.

Flabbergasted, he scratched the back of his neck just like he always did whenever he was uncomfortable. "Ok, then. We should go."

A few minutes later, while they were driving to the mall, he brought it up again. "I really am sorry. I didn't mean to insinuate that you needed a man for anything. You're an independent woman, and I admire that about you."

She turned to look at him for the first time since they'd gotten into his car. "Really?"

He nodded. "I admire a lot of things about you, Soph. Always have."

"Like what else?" She wasn't just fishing for compliments. She really was curious.

He laughed, which eased some of the tension between them. "Well, I like that you're so organized and detail oriented. Take this wedding we're going to. You've thought of everything, as your list proves."

She laughed. "Seriously? Some people would call that being anal."

Drew wrinkled his nose. "Not a word I would choose."

"Ok. What else?"

"I like that whatever you do, you do it with gusto, whether it be work, or play, or anything in between. You just have a zest for life that's very refreshing."

"Hmm. I never thought of myself like that before."

"Why not?"

She shrugged. "Maybe because, deep down, I'm an introvert who prefers a good book, cozy pajamas, and chocolate more than anything else."

He was at a stoplight now, and he turned and smiled at her. "You're authentic, and I love that. Don't ever apologize for being you."

The light turned green, and his eyes went back to the road, but the word "love" echoed in her ears. After a few minutes of silence while she took it all in, she said, "I admire a lot of things about you too."

"Do tell."

I probably shouldn't start out by naming his hot body. "Well, I like that you can go into a room full of people you don't even know and easily assimilate."

"Nice word."

"Thanks. But I'm serious. I've always wished I could do that."

"Maybe it's because I'm an only child. I always wished I had siblings, so get me around a group of people, and I go nuts!"

She laughed. "And I have siblings that make me nuts."

"What are you saying? Kyle and Gina are great."

"We're getting off track here."

"Please continue. My ego could use a few more strokes."

Got anything else that might like a few strokes? Ok, no more naughty books for me! "I like that you're a good listener. That's a very rare quality in this world."

"I agree, and I appreciate the compliment."

Drew pulled into a parking spot and shut off the car. One of the perks of his job was that he always got to drive cool cars. His current ride was a fully loaded Mercedes coupe. It was quite a step up from the seven-year-old VW Beetle that Sophia drove.

When they stepped out of the car, he shook out his arms and rotated his shoulders as if he were getting warmed up to play a sport. "Ok. I'm ready. Let's go shopping!"

Sophia had already given a lot of thought to how she wanted them to look at the wedding—more than was probably necessary. Drew was obviously not an experienced shopper, so she took the lead, guiding him through Macy's like the expert that she was. He followed her around, keeping mostly silent as she handed him the clothes she wanted him to try on. Once he was laden down with dress shirts, ties, sports jackets, and dress pants, she led him to the men's fitting rooms and let him loose.

"I'll wait right here, and you can model them for me," she instructed.

He disappeared into the fitting room, and a short time later, he reemerged in a navy-blue ensemble. She motioned for him to turn around slowly, and when his back was to her, he looked over his shoulder and grinned.

"Does this make my butt look big?" he teased.

"Very funny. Now, turn back around."

Sophia loved this. Here, she had a legitimate reason to ogle him without him getting suspicious. "It looks nice on you, but it's kind of boring. Try the next one."

He cocked his head to the side and said, "Aren't you forgetting the magic word?"

"Pleeeeese," she drawled.

When he came out in the next outfit, he took her breath away. She'd chosen a pale-gray suit, with a light-purple striped shirt and a tie in a deeper-purple hue. He'd balked when she'd first handed it to him, claiming that men don't look good in purple, but she begged to differ. It was the perfect shade to offset his eyes, and the suit fit him like a dream.

Drew looked at her expectantly, and when their eyes met, they both smiled. "This is the one, isn't it? I knew it the minute I put it on," he said solemnly.

She eyed him warily, and then they both cracked up. He'd obviously borrowed a phrase he'd heard women use before. "Yes. That's the one, and I'm so glad you like it, because it will blend perfectly with what I have in mind."

"I thought you hadn't picked anything out yet."

"Well, I might have been looking online a little. Hurry up and get undressed so we can go to the women's department."

"Geez, lady. I'd like a little foreplay first!"

"Such a joker."

"Is that something else you like about me?"

She smiled wide. "Yes. Now, hurry up unless you want me to come in there and undress you myself."

They both froze for a minute, and then a saleslady walked up. "Is there anything I can help you with?" she asked, perusing Drew a bit too closely.

He shook his head, never taking his eyes off Sophia. "No. I think we're doing fine all by ourselves," he replied.

The saleslady looked between the two of them and then walked away.

"Be right out," he said.

Once he was gone, Sophia slumped down on the bench outside the fitting room. *Wow! What is happening to us?*

She didn't have long to ponder it before Drew reemerged in his regular clothes. After he'd paid, he followed her to the dress department, but something felt off. Gone was their light, carefree banter, and in its place was something new—something foreign yet intoxicating. Was this how actors felt when they were filming a love scene? Did the playacting translate into real feelings, or did it end the minute the director called, "Cut"? Whatever was happening, Drew seemed to be taking his role just as seriously as she was. Just like when she read her romance novels, she thought, *I wonder what will happen next?*

Chapter 6

All too soon, Sophia and Drew were back in his car, driving toward home. The deep-purple dress that Sophia had seen online hadn't been available in her size, so she'd had to order it. At first, she'd been disappointed, but then she'd decided it might be better this way. She'd envisioned making a grand entrance when Drew saw her in the dress for the first time, and now she'd be able to.

"That was pretty painless," Drew said.

"I'm glad you thought so. Thanks for doing all this."

"It's no problem. Really," he said, shooting her a reassuring glance.

And then something struck her. "How does Lexie feel about you doing this?"

His hands tightened on the wheel, but his voice was even when he replied, "She doesn't know."

She stared at him incredulously. "Don't you think you should tell her?"

Drew shook his head. "I don't know that I'll still be seeing her in May."

She shouldn't have been surprised, but she was. He usually didn't stick with one girlfriend for long, but Lexie had lasted longer than the previous one, so she'd assumed they might be getting serious. "Are you thinking of breaking up with her?"

He shrugged. "I don't really know, Soph. Why so many questions?"

"Sorry. But if it were me, I'd want to know if my boyfriend was planning on taking another woman to a wedding—for an entire weekend!"

Drew sighed in frustration. "Look. Lexie and I aren't really like that, ok. I wouldn't define her as my *girlfriend*."

"How would you define her, then?"

They'd pulled up into her driveway now, and he shoved the gearshift into park with a little more oomph than was necessary. He was obviously rattled, but she wasn't sure why.

He angled himself in the seat to face her and said, "What would happen if you were to meet someone between now and May? Would you still want to go to the wedding with me?"

"Way to change the subject."

"If you can ask questions, so can I."

"Yes. I would still want to go with you."

"Ok, then. It's the same for me. I've said I'm going, and I'm going. That's all there is to it."

She nodded, although something was still nagging at her. "I have to make the hotel reservation soon."

"I'd expect that. I'll pay half of whatever it costs."

"It's not that," she said, looking down at her hands, which were clasped in her lap.

"What is it?"

"I was thinking that I should only book one room because that's what a couple would do."

"Naturally," he said, his voice warming.

"Are you sure you're ok with that?"

"Why wouldn't I be? It's not like you haven't seen me in my underwear before."

"That was by accident!"

"You call creeping around outside my bedroom window an accident?"

"We were in high school. I snuck out of the house and didn't want my parents to know."

"I remember," he said with a big smile. "That was the time we went for a late-night swim."

"Um-hum."

"I was just about to change into my swim trunks when you knocked on my window."

"That was the plan, remember?"

"The plan was to go swimming, not for you to see me in my skivvies!"

Sophia giggled at the memory. "Do you still wear tighty-whities?"

"You'll have to wait and see."

She swallowed roughly. "Just because we're sharing a room, that doesn't mean I have to see you in your underwear."

"Why? Is the thought of that disturbing to you?" he teased.

Yes! But not in the way you think! "No. It's just that..."

Drew chuckled. "You're cute when you're nervous."

"I'm not nervous," she argued.

"Oh, yes, you are. You're wringing your hands, and you haven't had direct eye contact with me since we started this conversation."

She purposely met his eyes and said, "It's kind of strange, isn't it?"

"What is?"

"For us to be doing all this. Acting like a couple, sharing a room, slow-dancing..."

"You forgot about the kissing."

No, I haven't! Suddenly, the air in the car felt very warm even though the blower wasn't on. "It's on the list. We'll get to it."

"Why not try a practice run right now?"

She couldn't help it. She had to unzip her jacket and let out some of the hot air. When she looked up, Drew was right there, mere inches away, patiently waiting for her response. *Me and my damn list!*

"Ok," she said, "but it doesn't have to be some big, elaborate..." Her words got lost because his mouth was already on hers, light as a feather, soft, gentle. It took her a moment to relax into it, and then she opened her mouth a little wider in silent invitation.

His lips were warm and full, and he proceeded cautiously, like he was exploring uncharted territory while fully aware of the danger. She wasn't sure when it had happened, but now her arms were looped around his neck, and her upper body was straining to get closer. If only the gear shifter wasn't between them!

"Mmmm. Nice," Drew murmured against her lips.

She wasn't up for talking, and she made her feelings known by pressing her lips against his with more pressure. They continued kissing like that (just lips, no tongues) for a few more seconds, until Drew pulled back.

"How was that? Do you think we can pull it off?" he asked.

Sophia nodded, trying to ignore the chill that swept over her when he'd pulled away. *This is just a game to him. Stop reading more into it!*

"We might need to practice again sometime before the wedding," she said, avoiding his eyes once more.

"Right. Because we want to make sure it comes across that we're a *real* couple. Got it."

Whatever magic had been between them a moment ago seemed to have disappeared, and Sophia zipped up her coat again. "Ok. So, I'll let you know once I've made the hotel reservation."

"Sounds good," he said as she opened the car door and stepped out.

She was just about to close the door when he added, "Sweet dreams, Soph."

"You too," she said and then quickly turned and walked away.

Chapter 7

Drew went through the motions of getting ready for bed all the while thinking about that kiss. He'd only kissed her one other time, when they'd been in high school, and he barely remembered it. But this time— wow! He'd wanted to do so much more, but he'd held back. He hadn't wanted her to think he'd been trying to take advantage of the situation, so he'd kissed her softly, gently, keeping his tongue locked down even though he'd wanted to tangle it with hers.

When she'd emitted a low moan and wrapped her arms around his neck, he thought he'd died and gone to heaven. The best part about it was that it seemed like she wasn't even aware she'd done it. She'd responded to him like a woman who was turned on, not like someone who was just playing a role.

When he'd pulled away, he'd witnessed the disappointment in her big brown eyes, but he'd kept himself from going back for more. Even though it had been her idea in the first place, after her comment about things being "strange" between them, he hadn't wanted to spook her. But damn if he wasn't already looking forward to the next time, and she had promised that there would be one.

He'd just crawled beneath the sheets when his cell phone buzzed on the nightstand. Hoping that it was

Sophia wanting to discuss something else on the list, he hurriedly picked it up, and he could barely contain his disappointment when he answered the call.

"Hey."

"Hey, baby. Whatcha doing?"

"I just climbed into bed."

"Want some company?"

"I thought you were out with your friends."

"I am, but it's getting dull, and I'd rather be in bed with you."

He could tell by the slight slur in her voice that she'd been drinking, but instead of responding to her suggestion, he asked, "Is there a designated driver?"

"Oh, how sweet. Are you worried about me?"

"Well, it sounds like you've been drinking, so I just wanted to make sure you have a ride."

"I do, but I'd rather take a ride on you," she teased.

In the past, he would have jumped on the invitation (literally!), but tonight, he wasn't feeling it. "Sorry, Lex, but I'm really beat. Rain check?"

"Oh. Ok," she said, obviously surprised by his rejection.

Just then, Drew heard one of her friends shout, "C'mon, Lexie. We're leaving."

"I gotta go," she said.

"Talk to you later. Be safe," he said and hung up before she could proposition him again.

"Damn!" he said as he set down the phone. "Since when do I turn down a sure thing?" But he already knew the answer—since he'd kissed Sophia. When he closed his eyes, it was her face he saw, not Lexie's, and that night, he had the sweetest dream. They were kissing, but this time, when he pulled away, Sophia whispered, "Please don't stop."

Chapter 8

"You kissed him?" Eve said loudly enough that an elderly patron glared at them.

"Shhh! This is a library, remember?" Sophia scolded.

They were sitting at the reference desk in the middle of the adult section on a rainy afternoon. Rain usually brought more people to the library because, really, was there anything better than curling up with a good book on a rainy day?

Eve lowered her voice. "So, how was it? Soft and sweet or hot and sexy?"

"All of the above," Sophia replied with a dreamy look in her eyes.

"You're in love."

"What? No, I'm not!"

"I think thou doth protest too much," Eve said with a smirk.

"We were just practicing for the wedding."

"Funny. I thought it was the *bride* and *groom* who usually kiss at weddings."

"It's just a precautionary measure. Couples often kiss each other spontaneously, and I want to be prepared. I didn't want it to be one of those sloppy kisses you sometimes see that make you cringe."

Eve rolled her eyes. "Like Drew would ever give a sloppy kiss!"

"You don't even know him."

"But I'd like to, especially if he can make a girl swoon without even using his tongue."

The elderly woman looked up again, and this time, she gave them a slight smile.

"Ok. This conversation is officially over," Sophia stated and stood up to leave.

"Wait. What's the next item on your list?"

Sophia waited until the elderly woman had drifted further away. "We're getting together tonight to corroborate our love story."

Eve shook her head. "If you can pull this off without jumping into bed together, you should write a book about it. I can see the title now—*How Not to Fall in Love with Your Best Friend While Pretending to Be in Love with Your Best Friend.*"

"Nobody would buy that," Sophia scoffed.

"Exactly!"

Sophia was stirring a pot of spaghetti sauce when the doorbell rang. "Coming," she yelled as she set the spoon on the spoon rest.

The minute she swung open the door, Drew started laughing. "I love it," he said, pointing to her apron.

"My sister gave it to me for my birthday. Real nice, huh?" The apron was black with white letters that read: *My cooking is so good even the smoke alarm cheers me on.*

"I have to say it makes me a little nervous. Is that a bubbling sound I hear?"

"Oh God. The sauce!" She ran into the kitchen, and Drew followed behind her. The sauce was bubbling on the stove, but she managed to lower the flame right before it spilled over. "Saved it!"

"Good. For a minute there, I thought we might have to go out to eat," he teased.

Feeling guilty for having asked so much of him, she'd decided to cook even though it wasn't on her list of favorite things to do. She'd chosen spaghetti because she'd thought that would give her the least amount of stress. Good thing she'd averted disaster.

"What can I do?" Drew asked as she began dishing spaghetti on two plates.

"You could pour us some drinks. I have beer, wine, and soda."

He poked his head into the fridge and pulled out a Miller Lite. "Wine for you?"

"Sure," she replied as she carried the plates to the table. She'd mixed a salad earlier and had bought a fresh loaf of Italian bread on her way home from work. She stood back for a minute, admiring her handiwork while Drew poured her a glass of wine.

"In all seriousness, this looks great," he said.

"Thanks. Despite what my apron says, I do manage to make a decent meal occasionally."

"I don't doubt it. Madam..." He pulled out her chair and motioned for her to sit down.

"Why, thank you, kind sir."

After he took a seat, he said, "We're getting pretty good at this, aren't we?"

"Good at what?"

"Acting. Maybe I should consider a career change."

She laughed as she handed him a slice of bread. "I wouldn't quit your day job just yet."

They ate in companionable silence for a while, and then Drew said, "So, what's on the agenda for this evening?"

More kissing, please! Sophia dabbed her mouth with a napkin and said, "We need to come up with the story of how we fell in love. You know. In case anybody asks."

"Do you really think someone will? I mean, won't most of the attention be on the bride and groom?"

"You don't know my college friends very well. They'll be dying to know how we got together. It's bound to come up."

"Ok, then. I suppose you already have some ideas in mind."

"I've given it some thought. More spaghetti?"

"Yes, please. But I can get it."

"No! Consider it my thank you for helping me out." She picked up his empty plate and went back to the stove to refill it.

"You don't have to keep thanking me, Soph. I'm enjoying this."

She returned with his second helping and set it down in front of him, oddly pleased that he was enjoying her meal. "I am too," she admitted. *Maybe a little too much.*

She took a sip of wine to bolster her courage while Drew ate heartily, even swiping another slice of bread through the spaghetti sauce on his plate. For some reason, she loved to watch him eat. *It must be the Italian in me—we love our food!*

"Ok, here's my idea. We met at the library when you came in to check out a book on…"

"How to please a woman in bed?"

She raised her eyebrows at him. "Um, no."

"What, then?"

"*Sales Management for Dummies.*"

He set down his fork with a clatter. "What? No way! That makes me sound stupid. Besides, I do my job very well. I wouldn't need a book like that."

"What would you suggest, then?"

"How about something like *Mastering the Kama Sutra*, if there is such a book?"

She took another sip of wine, and averting her eyes, she replied, "I wouldn't know."

He laughed and eyed her skeptically. "Don't tell me you never wander into the naughty section."

She picked up their empty plates and carried them to the sink. "I can tell that you're not taking this very seriously."

He had followed her into the kitchen with the salad bowl and the empty bread basket. "Ok, fine. I'll stop joking around."

"I guess it doesn't really matter what you came into the library for. Maybe it was a rainy day and you came in to relax and read the *Wall Street Journal*. How's that?"

"Better. Shall we take out drinks into the living room?"

"Sure, but let me top off my wine first. Another beer?"

"That'd be great." This time, he let her get the drinks, and then they moved into the living room. Setting the drinks on coasters, Sophia took a seat on the couch, and he sat a cushion's width away.

"So, you were reading the *Wall Street Journal* when I walked by and caught your eye."

"Stop right there. Why couldn't I be the one to catch your eye?"

"Does it really matter?"

"I don't want it to sound like I'm a creepy stalker trying to get laid at the library."

"Who said anything about getting laid? This story is about love, not sex."

"Bummer. Just kidding. Continue."

"Ok. We caught *each other's* eye, and it was like fireworks went off."

"I like that. Go on."

"I continued on about my business, but whenever I looked up, your eyes were upon me."

Drew shook his head. "Creepy stalker image again."

"What would you suggest?" she huffed.

"We both said hello at the same time and then laughed. We introduced ourselves, shook hands, and the minute we touched, BOOM, we just knew."

Sophia nodded. "I like that better. Keep going."

He leaned forward, his eyes lit with excitement. "We talked for a few minutes, but then your supervisor came looking for you. I quickly handed you my business card and asked you to call me sometime so we could get together for coffee."

"But I don't drink coffee."

"Well, if I said a drink, that would sound too cliché."

"And coffee doesn't?"

Drew shoved his hands in his hair and sighed. "Why does this have to be so difficult?"

She twirled a lock of her hair nervously. "I don't know. Maybe because it's hard to concoct something out of nothing."

He popped his head up and studied her for a moment. "What if we just said something that was closer to the truth?"

Tucking her legs beneath her, she said, "Like what?"

"Like that we've known each other since high school, but it took all these years for us to realize we were in love. And that the best things in life are worth waiting for." He reached out and stroked her cheek with his knuckles, and her body leaned forward, seemingly of its own volition.

Oh God. Are we going to kiss again? Please, please...

And just like that, he sat back, clasped his hands in his lap, and said, "How's that for a believable story?"

She nodded because her throat was too tight to speak. She picked up her wine glass and took a long sip.

"Ok, then. I should probably go," he said and stood up abruptly.

"Wait," she said. "I wanted to show you some pictures of the hotel." She'd already booked the room and had sent him a copy of her email confirmation, but she wasn't ready for him to leave just yet.

"I can just look at home," he said, already walking toward the door.

"Oh. Ok." Why the sudden urge to leave? And then it dawned on her—Lexie. He was probably going to meet her, although he hadn't brought up her name recently. "Hot date?" she asked flippantly.

Drew turned toward her with one hand on the doorknob. "No. I just have some things to do. Thanks for dinner. I really enjoyed it."

"You're welcome," she said, missing their camaraderie from earlier.

"Next time, dinner is on me. I'll call you," he said with one foot already out the door.

She nodded and watched him walk out to his car, slip inside, and drive away without so much as a backward glance.

Chapter 9

"Here he comes," Eve whispered.

"Here who comes?"

"That single dad who always stares at you during story time."

And just like that, Eve slipped out from behind the reference desk, leaving Sophia alone with the single dad.

"Can I help you with something?" she asked politely.

Single Dad cleared his throat and said, "Forgive me. I'm not used to doing this, but I wondered if you would like to have coffee with me sometime?"

"Oh. Well...um..."

"I've made you uncomfortable. Sorry about that."

Truthfully, she was flattered. She'd seen the man in the library on Saturday mornings for the past few months when he'd faithfully brought his adorable five-year-old daughter in for story time. He was handsome in an unassuming way—cropped dark-brown hair, brown eyes, and a nice smile. Today, he wore a blue t-shirt with the Detroit Tigers logo on it and a pair of Levi's. He basically looked like an all-American dad minus the all-American wife and the minivan (she'd seen him pull up in a bright-red Jeep once).

"Don't apologize. It's just that when someone approaches the reference desk, they usually need help finding a book."

Single Dad smiled, looking grateful that she hadn't taken offense. "My name is Jake Owen."

Sophia tried not to cringe as she reached over the counter to shake his hand (he shared the same first name as her ex) and said, "Sophia Russo. It's nice to meet you."

"It's taken me two months to get up the courage to ask you out, Sophia. I hope I didn't flub it up too bad."

She shook her head, but then another patron came up to the counter. Jake noticed too, and pulling a business card out of his back pocket, he handed it to her. "Call me anytime," he said and walked away.

Sophia laid the card face down on the desk and proceeded to help the next patron. After he walked away, she turned the card over and stifled a laugh as she read it. Jake Owen worked for Rent- A-Husband, a company who rented out handymen! She'd seen their trucks on the road, and the name had always made her chuckle.

Wait until she told Drew! Oh boy. Drew. What would he think of her going out with Jake? Then again, why would he care? After all, he was still seeing Lexie. Sophia looked across the library at the children's section, where story time was wrapping up. Jake was standing nearby, hands in the pockets of his jeans, smiling at his little girl.

That's it. I'm doing it! Sophia walked over to him and tapped him on the shoulder. He turned around, surprised to see her there. "I'd like to go out for coffee with you. What day is good?"

"Oh. Great! How about tomorrow morning?"

"Ok," she said.

"Starbucks ok?"

"Is there any place better for coffee?" she asked like she was a coffee aficionado, even though the last time she'd tried it was in college. She never had acquired the taste for it.

Jake chuckled. "You're right. Ten o'clock ok?"

"Sure." And then Sophia realized that he probably lived nearby, while she lived twenty miles away. "Um. I don't live around here, but we can still meet at the Starbucks downtown."

"Where do you live?"

"Waterford."

"Hmm. Well, I hate to have you drive all that way if you're not working. How about if we meet in the middle? Say, Auburn Hills?"

Sophia smiled. "The one by Great Lakes Crossing Mall?"

"That'll work."

Just then, Jake's daughter came running up to him and threw her arms around his legs. "All done, Daddy," she said in a sweet little voice.

"Ok, baby. Alissa, this is Sophia. She works here at the library."

"Hi," Alissa said, looking up at Sophia. And then she immediately turned back to her dad and said, "Can we go now?"

Jake laughed uncomfortably.

"That's ok," Sophia said, shooting him an understanding look. "It was nice to meet you, Alissa."

Alissa started to drag her dad away, but he looked back over his shoulder and mouthed, "See you tomorrow."

Eve suddenly appeared as if she'd been hovering nearby. "So? What happened?"

Sophia motioned her away from the parents and children who were still lingering in the children's section. After making sure that nobody was around, she whispered, "He asked me out."

Eve's eyes widened. "And?"

"I said yes. We're meeting for coffee tomorrow morning."

Eve studied her closely. "But you don't drink coffee."

"I know, but it sounds so immature to admit it. I'll just order something chocolatey."

Eve shook her head and smirked.

"What?"

"I'm kind of surprised you said yes."

"Why? I thought you said he was cute?"

"He is, in a non-threatening sort of way. Personally, I prefer somebody who looks more like…Drew!"

Sophia scowled at that, but Eve motioned wildly over her shoulder. "It's Drew. He's here."

Sophia jerked her head around so fast it hurt, and sure enough, there was Drew, sauntering toward her with a huge smile on his face.

"Two in one day. Lucky lady," Eve whispered before she disappeared.

"Just the librarian I wanted to see," Drew said, stopping in front of her. "I was wondering if you carry the *Wall Street Journal?*"

Sophia laughed at the reference. "I'm sorry, sir, but we don't. Could I interest you in the book *Sales Management for Dummies?*"

"Good one," he said, eyes twinkling.

"What brings you in?"

"I was in town shopping for a birthday gift for my mom, and I thought I'd stop by."

"Oh. I forgot that your mom's birthday is coming up. Did you have any luck?"

"I could use your help. Are you free for lunch?"

Sophia glanced at her watch and realized it was already eleven thirty. She usually didn't take lunch that early, but she hated to turn him down. Besides, Eve could cover for her. "Sure. Sounds great. Let me grab my purse and jacket, and I'll meet you out front."

"Or I can just wait inside, and we can walk out together."

Sophia nodded. Once she was in her office, putting on her coat, Eve sailed in. "Another date?"

"Shhh! We're going out to lunch, and I need you to cover for me."

"Are you going to tell him about Single Dad?"

"I don't know. Maybe."

Eve smirked. "Enjoy your lunch," she said and strode away.

Drew ushered her into the jewelry store first. "I couldn't make up my mind between two necklaces, so you can be the tiebreaker."

"Your mom's lucky her birthstone is a diamond," Sophia said as she admired the necklaces. One was an initial pendant with a small diamond embedded in the letter "D" for Diane. The other was a heart pendant with a diamond suspended from the point at the top of it.

"I suggested the initial pendant," the salesman said. "The heart pendant seems more appropriate for a girlfriend, don't you think?" He winked at Sophia as he said it, and she realized what he must have thought.

"Oh no. We aren't..."

"Well, our relationship is still new," Drew said, slinging his arm around her shoulder and pulling her close. "Right, sweetheart?"

Wow! He's really taking this acting thing seriously! "Yes. Too new to warrant a diamond necklace," she said, playing along.

"Should I box up the initial pendant, then?" the salesman asked.

"Yes. Thank you," Drew replied.

After Drew handed over his credit card and the salesman left to ring up the purchase, Sophia turned to Drew and said, "I never thought about practicing our roles in public."

"I'm surprised that wasn't on your list," Drew teased.

"It's a good idea. I'm glad you thought of it," she said as the salesman returned.

The salesman handed Drew the bag and said, "I have a feeling you two will be back for the other pendant."

"It's quite possible," Drew said, smiling down at Sophia.

Once they were back out on the street, he reached for her hand. At first, she was startled, but then she realized what he was doing. They walked hand in hand down the street until they reached the restaurant Drew had suggested for lunch. It was an old-fashioned-looking diner, complete with a black and white checked floor, chrome and black tables and chairs, and a jukebox. Sophia had been there several times with her co-workers, and the menu was right up her alley—burgers, fries, and shakes!

After they'd placed their orders, Drew leaned across the table and asked, "So, what's the next item on your list?"

"Honestly, I think we've covered just about everything," she said, wishing that weren't the case. They had a month left to go before the wedding, and other than shopping for the wedding gift, there wasn't anything more to be done.

"Shouldn't we practice slow-dancing again? Or kissing?"

The waitress appeared with their food and smiled knowingly as she set down their plates. "Anything else I can get you?" she asked.

"No. We're good," Drew said.

Sophia eyed him across the table and shifted uncomfortably in her seat.

"What's wrong?" he asked.

"It's just that...well, I..."

"Spit it out, Soph."

"It's just that I don't feel right about kissing you when I know Lexie's still in the picture. I know how I would feel if my guy were kissing somebody else, and I'd hate it. I don't feel right doing that to Lexie."

"I thought you hated her."

"What? I never said that!"

"You didn't have to. I could tell the first time you met her."

"Our burgers are getting cold," she said, desperate to change the subject.

Drew reached across the table and placed his hands atop hers. "Would it help if I told you I'm not seeing Lexie anymore?"

Her heart leapt, but she tried to contain her enthusiasm. "Really? Since when?"

"Since yesterday."

"What happened?"

"Well, I took your advice and told her about the wedding. And you were right. She didn't like it very much. In fact, she forbade me from going."

"Uh-oh." The last time a woman had given him an ultimatum, he'd dumped her.

"Exactly. I told her that I was helping a friend, and she said... Never mind the rest. The point is, we're done. So now you don't have to worry about hurting her feelings."

Sophia was flabbergasted. In a way, it was what she'd wanted, but now that the barrier had been removed between her and Drew, she felt scared, vulnerable. Suddenly, there was nothing standing in their way should their acting lead to something more. Nothing but fear.

Chapter 10

If there was ever a day that she wished she liked coffee, today was it! Sophia had slept fitfully the night before, and she might have cancelled her coffee date that morning if she'd had a way to contact Jake. She'd inadvertently left his business card on her desk at the library, and she'd feel horrible not showing up. Besides, she'd have to face him every Saturday morning when he brought Alissa in for story time. So, she'd put on her adult face and was now waiting for him at Starbucks while sipping her hot chocolate.

Glancing around the coffee shop, she noticed all the couples sitting with their heads bent over their steaming cups, deep in conversation or laughing over a private joke. There were plenty of singles there too, their heads buried in newspapers or books, or hunched over their laptops, looking for the most part like they didn't mind being alone. Sophia wondered if she was the only one feeling uncomfortable in such a warm, relaxed environment. And it was all thanks to Lexie!

If Lexie hadn't given Drew an ultimatum, they'd still be together, and Sophia wouldn't be feeling guilty for meeting Jake for coffee. Coffee, mind you! It wasn't even a real date! It was coffee! Which she didn't even drink! She took another sip of hot chocolate and sighed. *Where is Jake, anyway?*

"Sorry, I'm late," he said from behind her.

Funny, she hadn't even noticed him come in. "No problem. I was just sitting here enjoying my hot cocoa," she said, forcing a smile.

Jake shrugged off his jacket and hung it on the back of the chair across from her. "Mind if I grab a coffee, and then I'll join you?"

"Of course not. That's what we're here for!"

After he walked away, she noticed the logo on his jacket and stifled a laugh. It was the Rent-a-Husband logo that she'd seen on the white vans before. She forced herself to look away, hoping that she wouldn't break into hysterics and have to explain why. For some reason, she didn't think Jake would take too kindly to her laughing about his career choice. *This is all Lexie's fault*, she thought for the umpteenth time in the past twelve hours.

"So, I dropped Alissa off at my sister-in-law's house this morning, and she got to talking, and anyway, that's why I'm late," Jake said as he slid into the seat across from her.

"Sister-in-law? But I thought…"

"You thought right. I'm divorced, but I still maintain good relations with my sister-in-law. For Alissa and her cousins," he added.

"I see," Sophia said, although she didn't. Not really. She didn't have any friends who were divorced—at least, not yet.

"It's complicated, but for the most part, it works."

"Are you friendly with your ex-wife too?" The words slipped out before she could harness them, but Jake didn't flinch.

"I try to be. She's remarried now, and I only see her for drop-offs and pick-ups, but we're friendly."

Sophia took another sip of her drink. Could she handle dating a divorced dad? Would she even be questioning it if Drew hadn't suddenly become available?

"So, what about you? I know you're a librarian, but what else are you into?"

Acting? "Well, I obviously love reading, and I've recently discovered cross-stitching." *Ok, that sounded really lame!*

"Cross-stitching, huh? My grandmother does that too."

"Yes, well, it's very relaxing."

"What about your family? Do you have parents and siblings nearby?"

"Yes. My parents live on Lake Oakland, and I have a younger brother and sister who also live in the area."

"Are you close?"

"Sometimes."

Jake chuckled. "What do you mean?"

"Well, you know. Sometimes, we get on each other's nerves, but mostly, we love each other. Typical sibling stuff."

"I wouldn't know. I'm an only child, and so is Alissa."

And so is Drew. "Do you wish you'd had siblings?"

"I mostly wish that for Alissa. That's why I bring her to story time and to her cousin's house. I want her to interact with other kids as much as possible."

"What about school?"

"She'll be starting kindergarten in the fall."

Sophia was already to the bottom of her drink when she realized that the past twenty minutes or so had passed quickly. Jake might have a complicated life, but he was easy to talk to, and she admired his dedication to his daughter. He seemed like an upstanding guy, and he wasn't bad to look at. If only she could stop thinking about Drew...

"Can I buy you another hot chocolate?" Jake asked.

"Oh. No, thanks. But the muffins sure looked good!"

Jake stood immediately and reached for his wallet.

"I didn't mean for you to buy one. I was just saying..."

"Let me guess. Chocolate?"

She laughed. "That would be great."

"Be right back," he said, smiling as he walked away.

"Oh, so now you're two-timing Drew?"

Startled, Sophia whipped around to face her nemesis. "What are you talking about?"

"I saw you with that guy," Lexie sneered. "Does Drew know you're out having *coffee* with someone else this morning?"

Lexie might as well have accused Sophia of murder for the way she reacted. Shooting up from her chair, she leaned toward Lexie and hissed, "NOT that it's any of your business, but Drew and I are just friends, and so are Jake and I."

Lexie tossed her blonde hair off her shoulder and said, "You're a liar, and so is Drew. The only reason you asked him to that wedding was so you could get him away from me. It might have worked for now, but just wait. You won't be in his bed for long, and then he'll be on to the next woman." With that, she turned on her high-heeled boots and stomped off, her black poncho flying out behind her like the wicked witch that she was!

Visibly shaken, Sophia turned back around to find Jake eyeing her suspiciously. "Who's Drew?" he asked.

"I'm sorry," she said, brushing past him as she rushed out of the coffee shop.

She didn't know where she was headed until she pulled into Drew's driveway, and then she shut off the car and sat there for a few minutes, trying to regain her composure. Bending her head over the steering wheel, she repeated, "What am I doing here?" until the sound of someone knocking on her window caused her to jerk her head up. Drew.

He opened her door and asked her the same question.

It struck her that maybe Lexie had already called and told him. "How did you know I was here?"

"I heard a car pull up, and I came out to investigate."

"Oh," she said, visibly relieved.

"Do you want to come inside?"

She nodded and followed him into his warm, inviting house. Hanging up her coat and purse on the hall stand, she wondered how many times she'd been in this house. It was the same house he'd lived in when she'd first met him. The house where they'd played video games and watched movies as high schoolers. The house where she'd eaten countless meals at with their families and now just with him. It was like a second home to her. Somewhere safe, where she could truly be herself. No acting required.

Without speaking, Drew led her into the living room, where a large picture window overlooked the lake. It was an overcast spring day, and a blanket of dense clouds hovered over the water, which was in keeping with Sophia's mood. She inhaled deeply and then turned sideways to face Drew on the couch.

"I ran into Lexie this morning," she said.

Drew's eyes widened. "Where at?"

"At Starbucks."

"But you don't drink coffee."

"Would everyone please stop saying that?!" She sprang off the couch and paced over to the window, her back to him.

"Who's everyone?" Drew asked, coming up behind her.

"It doesn't matter. She said some horrible things to me—things about us."

Drew sighed. "Tell me."

"She accused us of lying about our...friendship. Accused me of trying to steal you away from her. And then..."

"What?" he asked, softly placing his hands on her arms and turning her around.

"She said that if I ended up in your bed, it wouldn't be for long. That you'd be on to the next woman in no time. Or something to that effect." Sophia looked down at the floor, which used to be carpeted but had been updated to rich wood planks.

Drew placed his index finger under her chin and tipped her head up. "She's just jealous, Soph. Don't believe a word she said."

But what if it's true? Thinking of the truth, she decided to come clean herself. Even though she hadn't done anything wrong, she didn't want to be thought of as a liar to anyone, least of all Drew.

"I was with someone at Starbucks. A guy. Jake."

He dropped his hands like she was on fire. "Jake? That jerk who dumped you? You've got to be kidding me!"

She shook her head vehemently. "No! Not that Jake. Jake Owen. A guy I met at the library."

Drew calmed down then, but he still didn't look happy. "Oh."

"I just met him. Well, not just. He's been coming to the library every Saturday, but not for me. For story time with his daughter."

Drew shoved his hands through his hair, which Sophia realized was damp, like he'd just taken a shower. "Oh," he repeated. "So, you're dating this guy?"

"Not exactly. I mean, it was just coffee for him and hot chocolate for me." *Why am I so nervous right now? Why do I feel like I cheated or something?*

"Do you like him? Are you going to see him again?"

Drew backed up a step with each sentence, and Sophia suddenly felt cold standing near the window without his heat to warm her. "He's nice, but I don't think so. No," she said decidedly.

A flicker of relief flashed across Drew's face, but it disappeared just as quickly. "You're not just saying that on my account, are you?"

She frowned. "No. Why?"

"Well, just because we're going to this wedding together doesn't mean you can't see someone else."

"But you're not seeing Lexie anymore."

"And now you can understand why. But if this Jake guy is nice, then what reason do you have not to see him again?"

She glanced around the living room like she'd never seen it before and then scowled at him. "Do you *want* me to see him again?"

"I didn't say that."

"Then what are you saying, Drew? Because, right now, I have no idea which way is up."

He'd backed away from her to where his legs now hit against the couch, and he sank down on it, clasped his hands together, and eyed her from across the room. "I don't have any claim on you, Soph. We're pretending to be a couple, but we're not one. So, if you decide to date someone, there's not a whole lot I can do about it."

"And vice versa, right? Is that what this is really about? Because I can give you a get-out-of-jail free card right now. I'll go to this wedding by myself, which is probably what I should have done in the first place!" When Drew didn't respond, she huffed and hurried out of the room. She'd grabbed her coat and purse off the hook and had her hand on the doorknob when Drew gripped her arm and spun her around.

"I don't want a get-out-of-jail free card," he said.

"Then what do you want?"

"This." And then he pulled her into his chest and kissed her. This time, it wasn't soft or gentle. It was firm and demanding, brooking no argument, and without apology. Her coat and purse fell to the floor, and her arms twined around his neck, pulling him down, pulling him closer. When their tongues met, her brain switched off, and all she could do was feel. His hard chest smashed against her breasts, his damp hair threaded through her fingers, and his erection jutted into her stomach. For a few glorious minutes, there was no wedding, no acting, no pretending. There was only her and Drew, the boy she'd once had a crush on and the man she still did.

Chapter 11

After he kissed her, Sophia left the house. She seemed stunned, just like he was. He hadn't meant to kiss her like that, but he hadn't been able to help himself. She'd looked so beautiful and passionate and vulnerable, and he'd been overcome with desire.

"Damn it, Drew!" he shouted. "Now you really screwed up!"

The last thing he wanted was for Sophia to believe what Lexie had said about him. That was exactly why he'd kept his feelings for Sophia in check over all these years: because he never wanted to hurt her. She was too good, too pure, too special. He'd placed her in a separate category from all the other women he'd dated—elevated her almost. He preferred fantasizing about her to this. In his fantasies, she couldn't get hurt. He could kiss her all he wanted to, and it wouldn't leave a mark. Wouldn't soil their friendship.

He'd thought about apologizing, but she'd run off so quickly that he hadn't had the chance. *I'll call her later. Give her some time to wind down. And me too.*

And then, just like clockwork, his phone rang.

"Hey, Mom," he said.

"Hey, sweetie. Just checking in. How's everything going?"

What a loaded question! "Not too bad." *I hope.*

"When are you going to come down and see us?"

Drew's mom called every Sunday, but for some reason, he hadn't told her that he and Sophia would be in Florida in May. It had been nice having something that was just between him and Sophia. But now that the wedding was only a few weeks away, he decided to come clean.

"Probably in a few weeks."

"What? Really?"

His mom's voice had risen a few octaves, and he held the phone away from his ear as he prepared to tell her the rest. "I'm coming down in May for a wedding on Sanibel Island, so I should be able to visit then."

As expected, the questions flew at him. "Whose wedding? When in May? Where are you staying? This is so exciting!"

"Mom. Settle," he said, chuckling.

"Sorry. It just feels like so long since we've seen you."

His parents had stayed with him for two weeks over Christmas, but that had been four months ago. *A lot can change in four months*, he thought as an image of him and Sophia kissing sprang to mind.

"Drew?"

"I'm here. I don't know the people who are getting married. I'm going there as a favor—to Sophia."

His mom was silent for a beat, and then she said, "That's so sweet of you. Are you going as friends or as dates?"

Good question! "I don't know. Both, maybe?"

"I'm so happy for you. You know how much we love Sophia. She's like part of the family."

Which is part of the problem! "I know how you feel about her, Mom. You've been singing her praises for years."

"It's just that she's so sweet. She's one of those rare women who are beautiful on the inside and the outside."

"Unlike some of the women I've dated. I know."

"I didn't say that, Drew. By the way, are you still dating that Lexie?"

He rolled his eyes, glad that she couldn't witness it. "No. We broke up a few days ago."

His mom might have tried to cover the phone, but he still heard her sigh of relief. "Well, then that leaves the door open for you and Sophia. Assuming that's what you want."

Drew sprawled out on the couch and shoved a hand in his hair. "It's not just about what I want, Mom. It's about what Sophia wants too." His friends used to tease him about how close he was to his parents. Growing up, he'd told them just about everything. He'd always thought it was because he didn't have any siblings to share things with, but now that he was older, he understood that it was more than that. He truly loved his parents. They were his biggest supporters and his best friends, aside from Sophia, that is. Even though he hadn't fully disclosed his feelings for her, he suspected that his mom (and probably his dad), already knew.

"I can't pretend to know what's in Sophia's heart, but I have a good feeling about this. You two have always been close, and maybe this wedding will bring you even closer."

If it doesn't tear us apart. "You could be right, but I'm taking it slow. I don't want anything to mess up our friendship."

"I doubt that will happen. Friendship is a solid foundation for love."

Love? "Anyway, we'll be down there the third weekend in May, so I'll try to squeeze you in."

"Gee, thanks," she said, laughing. "I'd love to see both of you, but I understand if Sophia's too busy with her friends."

He changed the subject then, feeling like he'd already given his mom enough to think about, and after a few more minutes, they hung up.

He continued to lay there for a while, turning his phone over and over in his hand and thinking about their kiss. He might have been a bit forceful, but Sophia hadn't backed away. On the contrary. She'd pressed her sweet body against his and had opened her mouth willingly. Afterwards, she'd just stood there, dazed, staring at him like she'd never seen him before. Then she'd made up some excuse about having a lot to do and practically run down the walkway to her car.

He'd stood there at the door, watching her leave, and right before she'd driven away, she'd turned and waved at him. It was a simple gesture, but he swore that she'd worn the same sappy smile that he had. At least he hoped so.

Chapter 12

"Swim trunks?"

"Check."

"Sunscreen?"

"Nope."

"Why not?"

"Because I never burn. I tan."

Sophia laughed. "That may be true in Michigan but not in Florida. You need to be prepared."

"Did you pack sunscreen?"

"Of course."

"Then I'm prepared. What's next?"

"Reading materials."

"*Sales Management for Dummies*?"

She giggled. "Or the *Wall Street Journal*."

"Neither, but I do have a brand-new copy of *Mastering the Kama Sutra*."

She was silent for a moment, and then Drew said, "Kidding, Soph."

Things had changed between them since the kiss. It was like they were trying to find their footing again, and they teetered between being friends or something more, although neither of them acknowledged it as such. They were being cautious, yet underneath it all sprang a new awareness, an undercurrent of desire that hadn't been there before. More accurately, it had been buried so deep for so long that it was just poking its head out, fearful yet optimistic, kind of like the spring blooms that were starting to pop up everywhere, bright and hopeful.

"How about pajamas?" she said, choosing to ignore his last comment.

"I don't wear pajamas."

"Don't you own a pair of sleep pants for colder weather?"

Drew chuckled. "We're not going to Alaska! Why would I need sleep pants in Florida?"

She cleared her throat loudly. "Hello? Because we're sharing a room together and it would be inappropriate to walk around in your underwear."

"Come on. How else will you find out if I still wear tighty-whities?"

"You're impossible!" But the idea of him walking around in his underwear wasn't unappealing.

"What about you? What kind of pajamas did you pack?"

She glanced down at her suitcase, which was lying open on her bed. There, on top, was her two-piece cotton pajama set in a black and white polka-dot pattern. It was short-sleeved with cropped bottoms, but it certainly wasn't sexy, unlike the silky red baby doll set that was buried at the bottom of her suitcase. She'd thrown it in at the last minute, but she was still debating about bringing it.

"I packed a respectable pair of pajamas that I wouldn't be embarrassed to be seen in," she stated firmly.

"Well, that's no fun!"

Rolling her eyes, she said, "Toiletries?"

"What about them?"

She sighed with mock exasperation. "Did you pack them?"

"Yes, although, if I've forgotten something, I can always buy it. It's not like we're going to a deserted island!"

Hmmm. Just me and Drew on a deserted island with nobody else around for miles...

"Soph?"

"Huh?"

"I've got everything, including my wedding attire. You don't have to worry."

Ha! Easy for you to say. It seemed like worrying was all she'd been doing lately, especially since the kiss. The Saturday after it had happened, she'd pulled Jake aside during story time. She'd explained everything about Lexie, Drew, and the wedding, leaving out the kissing part. She already felt rotten enough about walking out on the guy, envisioning him left standing in Starbucks holding a chocolate muffin. *I wonder if he ate it after I left?*

Surprisingly, Jake had been extremely understanding and gracious. Although maybe it was because she hadn't told him the whole story. She'd explained that she and Drew had been friends since high school and that he was accompanying her to the wedding as a favor. She hadn't said anything about having other feelings for him or vice versa. Not that she and Drew had admitted anything to each other. Since the incident, they'd skirted around the issue, choosing to focus on the wedding instead.

After her explanation, Jake had said, "You know where to find me. If you're interested in going out again, let me know."

And now, here it was, the night before her and Drew were departing for Florida, and they were going over their packing list instead of discussing what was really on their minds.

"I just thought of something else," she said.

"What is it?"

"Your mom's birthday gift."

"Got it."

"I'm excited to see your parents. It's been a long time."

"That's what my mom said too, but if it doesn't work out, they'll understand."

"I don't see why it wouldn't. We'll be there for four days, and the wedding will only take up one."

"But what about all the items on your 'things to do' list?"

"Those are just ideas. Nothing's written in stone."

"I'm looking forward to this weekend."

"Me too," she admitted.

"Is your alarm set?"

"Yep. Yours?"

"Six o'clock."

"I'll pick you up at six thirty." She'd insisted on driving to the airport, and after a brief argument, he'd agreed.

"Get some sleep," he said gruffly.

She glanced at the clock on her bedside table and realized it was already after ten. They'd been talking for an hour, and she hadn't even realized it. "You too," she said and was just about to disconnect when he spoke again.

"Don't forget your glasses."

The tortoiseshell frames were currently lying atop her book on the bedside table. "I won't," she said.

After they hung up, she stared at the phone quizzically. Had he reminded her about the glasses because he knew she needed them for reading, or was it because he liked the way she looked in them? And then she recalled his librarian fantasy, and her face flushed. "No. That can't be why," she said as she climbed into bed. She picked up the glasses and spun them around by one of the stems, deep in thought.

There was no sense trying to read tonight. She was too keyed up to concentrate. Instead, she set the glasses back down and switched off the lamp. Burrowing under the covers, she pulled them right under her chin and breathed deeply. Before long, she was asleep, dreaming about her and Drew. They were in the library after closing, and she had her glasses on...

"Ladies and gentlemen, welcome to sunny Fort Myers, Florida. Thanks for flying with us today, and enjoy your stay."

Drew glanced over at Sophia as they prepared to disembark the plane. "Look at your smile," he said.

"I can't help it. Florida always makes me smile!"

And it didn't hurt that Drew was there too. They'd been relatively quiet on the plane because of the early hour. Drew had even dozed off for a while, unknowingly leaning his head on her shoulder as he slept. Sophia had taken the opportunity to study his face, admiring the curve of his jaw, the slope of his nose, his thick eyebrows, and his long lashes. She'd wondered if he was dreaming like she had the night before, and what he would think if she told him her dream.

"They don't call it the Sunshine State for nothing," he said as they stepped out of the airport into a bright, beautiful seventy-eight-degree day.

When they'd left Michigan that morning, it had been a cool fifty degrees, and now, Sophia shucked off her hooded sweatshirt and tied it around her waist. She'd worn a short-sleeved t-shirt underneath in anticipation of the temperature change. Drew, on the other hand, had dressed in shorts and a t-shirt from the start, scoffing at the need for a jacket.

Soon, they were in the rental car, driving toward Sanibel Island. Sophia had booked the car in advance, but when they'd been checking in, the rental agent had offered them an upgrade from a four-door sedan to a sports car for fifty dollars more. She'd started to decline, but Drew had stepped in front of her.

"We'll take it," he'd said, reaching in his wallet for the extra fifty bucks.

So, now they were zipping along the highway in a current-model red Ford Mustang, and Drew was in his glory. "This thing is badass!" he said as he swiftly changed lanes.

Sophia gripped the door handle tightly. He was a good driver, but he was going a little too fast for her liking.

"You ok over there?" he asked, shooting her a grin.

"I'm good. Just keep your eyes on the road."

He laughed. "You're in good hands," he said, and she tried not to think of the double meaning.

Before long, they arrived at their destination. They were staying at the same place where the wedding would take place, a high-end luxury resort and spa just over the Sanibel Causeway. The location was perfect, set away from the string of hotels that lined the waterfront yet still close to everything.

"Showtime!" Drew said as he pulled into the circle drive, where a valet was waiting.

Her body flickered with nerves for the first time since they'd arrived in Florida. He was right about it being showtime. Her college friends could appear at any moment, and it was time for her and Drew to put their acting skills to the test.

She nodded at him as the valet approached the car. "Good morning, sir. Do you need help with your bags?"

"Certainly. Thank you," Drew said. He stepped out of the car and motioned for Sophia to stay seated. She wasn't sure what he was doing until he came around to open her door. He graciously offered his hand to her, and then she understood. Placing her hand in his, she unfolded herself from the car. Entwining their fingers together, he handed the valet some bills with his free hand and then led her into the hotel.

The lobby was breathtaking—open and airy and decorated in a soft cream color, with cherrywood accents and expansive windows overlooking the ocean. Drew stood by her side, one arm draped loosely around her waist as she checked in, the reservation having been placed under her name.

"As wedding guests of Cassie's and Greg's, you're invited to a reception this evening on the veranda," the hotel clerk said. "It starts at seven o'clock, and drinks and appetizers will be served."

"How nice. Thank you," Sophia said, accepting the keys from him.

"Enjoy your stay."

"Oh, we will!" Drew replied with a wink. He grabbed her hand again as they followed the porter to the elevator.

Her nerves kicked in again once they were alone in their hotel room, but Drew looked perfectly at ease as he walked around the room, commenting on the amenities and on the magnificent view. In need of a distraction, Sophia busied herself with organizational tasks. Opening her suitcase, she began removing her clothes, hanging some in the closet and placing others in drawers. Luckily, Drew's back was to her as she slipped the baby doll set in with her lingerie items. Next, she went into the large bathroom, and began putting her toiletries away. When she had finished, she found Drew standing outside on the balcony, peering down at the beach.

"You might want to hang up your wedding clothes so the wrinkles will come out," she suggested as she joined him.

"Look over there."

"Where?" she asked.

He pulled her in close and pointed.

"I see them!" she said. A pair of dolphins was swimming just offshore, and a crowd of beachgoers had gathered to watch them. They stood just like that for a few moments, enjoying the scene, until she realized his arm was still around her waist, and she pulled away. *No need to pretend when nobody can see us.*

"What were you saying before?" Drew asked, turning toward her.

"I said that you might want to hang up your suit."

When they reentered the room, he noticed her empty suitcase lying on the bed and chuckled. "You already put all your stuff away?"

"Yes, while you were watching the dolphins."

He shook his head. "You're amazing, Soph."

"Thank you."

"No. I mean, you're the only person I know who unpacks the minute they get to the hotel."

He was still chuckling as he went about unpacking his suitcase.

"No, no. Not that one. These drawers are yours," she said, pointing. *Whew! That was a close one!* Drew had been about to open her lingerie drawer.

"Gee. Thanks for leaving me *two* drawers!" he teased.

"Well, guys don't usually need as much space."

"True."

She perched on the edge of the bed and watched him unpack.

"You might want to turn your head," he said after a few minutes.

"Why?"

"I'm about to bring out my underwear."

She rolled her eyes, but she shifted sideways anyway.

"There! All set."

She turned back around and looked directly into his smiling eyes.

"Do you—?" she began.

"Want to—?" he said at the same time.

"You go first," Drew said.

"Do you want to go for a walk on the beach?"

"I was going to ask if you wanted to take a swim."

"Oh." *Bathing suit time—already?*

"We could do both," Drew suggested. "We can take a walk first and then hit the pool."

How could she say no? They were in Florida after all, and that's what people did in Florida! "Ok. Sure."

"You don't sound too thrilled about it," he said, cocking his head and eyeing her closely.

"No. It's just that..."

"Let me guess. This will be your first time in a bathing suit this year, and you're not feeling ready yet."

Her eyes bugged out. "How did you know?"

"You're not so different from other women, Soph. I've heard it all before."

She stiffened, not liking the reminder of how many other women he'd been with. Good thing his back was to her as he plucked out his swim trunks, and he missed her disgruntled expression.

"If you want to use the bathroom, I'll change out here," he offered.

She pulled out her two-piece tankini and hugged it to her chest. "Ok."

While she was changing, she heard Drew rustling around in the bedroom, and she squeezed her eyes shut to stop herself from picturing him naked. The closest she'd come to seeing him like that was when she'd seen him in his underwear years ago, and that image was still burned on her brain. She could only imagine what he looked like now—a grown man instead of a teenaged boy.

She took her time in the bathroom, tugging at her bathing suit to make sure that it covered as much skin as possible before slathering on the sunscreen. Remembering that Drew hadn't packed any, she decided to bring it out with her. When she stepped out of the bathroom, he was standing there waiting, and even though they'd seen each other in swimsuits dozens of times, she suddenly felt very exposed.

"Here you go," she said, holding out the bottle of sunscreen.

He took it from her while giving her an obvious perusal. "You look good. What were you worried about?"

She smiled, relieved. Not because of what he'd said, but how he made her feel. He'd always given her compliments, and they were the best kind—sincere, with no hidden agenda. "Thanks."

"Mind getting my back?" he asked, and then he turned around before she answered.

She stood still for a few beats, staring at the wide expanse of Drew's muscular back. "Sure." *I can do this.* Approaching the task methodically, as she did most things, she started at his shoulders and worked her way down, using broad sweeps to cover the entire area. It wasn't until she'd reached his lower back, where it narrowed at the waistband of his trunks, that Drew made a sound. It was somewhere between a moan and a sigh, and then he said, "Feels good."

Suddenly, she wasn't just applying sunscreen on her best friend. She was touching him like a woman touches a man—a man she was attracted to and had been since what felt like forever. She continued to rub in the sunscreen even though his back was thoroughly covered, enjoying the feel of his warm, smooth skin beneath her fingers and the flex of his muscles as he sighed again.

"You're really good at that," he said, his voice sounding a bit ragged.

Sophia took a step back. "I just don't want you to burn," she said, but her voice wavered.

Drew turned around to face her, his expression a mix of amusement and—desire? "Thank you."

"No problem," she replied, flapping her hand dismissively.

"All set to go?"

"Just one more thing." She opened a drawer and pulled out her cover-up, which was more like a short, sleeveless dress. She yanked it over her head, shook out her curls, and slipped on her flip-flops. "Now I'm ready."

Drew laughed. "Do you really need the cover-up?" he asked.

"Yes. I really do." And with that, she flounced past him and out the door as his laughter trailed behind her.

Chapter 13

They picked their way along the beach, which was layered with shells of all shapes and sizes. The island was known for its abundance of shells, and most of the people on the beach carried buckets for collecting them.

Drew had reached for her hand the minute they'd stepped off the elevator, and he was still clasping it tightly as they walked along. Sophia realized that she was already getting used to the feeling of his palm against hers, and she found it comforting and exhilarating at the same time. So far, she hadn't seen anyone she recognized, but she convinced herself that it was good practice, and she didn't let go.

After they'd walked quite a long way down the beach, they turned and headed back. Even though it was warm, the ocean breeze kept it from being stifling, although Drew's chest and forehead were glistening with sweat.

"I can't wait to dive in the pool," he said.

Sophia didn't return the sentiment. When they'd passed by the pool deck on their way down to the beach, it had already looked crowded. She wasn't thrilled about baring her body in private, let alone in a crowd. Here, she had Drew's undivided attention, but what was to stop him from ogling all the women at the pool?

"How about over there?" Drew asked when they had returned to the hotel. Two chairs had just been vacated at a prime location poolside, but Sophia was eyeing some empty chairs a few rows back, where they'd be less conspicuous.

"Nah. I like that spot better," she said, pointing to the back row.

Drew laughed. "I don't get it. You have a fabulous body, Soph. You should show it off more."

Luckily, her sunglasses covered her eyes so he couldn't see them bugging out. *Fabulous body? Really? He's never said anything like that to me before!*

Before she could respond, a woman's voice called out, "Sophia? Is that you?"

She turned in the direction of the voice to see her friend, Mia, heading toward them in a bright floral bikini, oversized sunglasses, and a floppy hat. If ever there was a woman who was comfortable in a bikini, Mia was it. What made it worse was that she used to be a cheerleader, so she had the bubbly personality to go along with it. Not to mention her wavy long brown hair, her big blue eyes, and her gorgeous smile. She was one of those women that other women envied, but you couldn't hate her, because she was just too damn nice!

"It is you!" she exclaimed, hugging Sophia tightly against her mostly bare body. "And who do we have here?"

Drew dropped Sophia's hand like a hot potato and immediately offered it to Mia. "Drew Kennedy. Pleasure to meet you."

I bet! Sophia thought jealously.

"Cassie told me you'd be bringing a date. Where have you been hiding him, Sophia?" Mia teased.

"Oh. Well..."

"We've known each other forever, but we've just recently started dating," Drew interjected.

Somehow, standing there in front of Mia, the words sounded flat. Sophia felt like an old, worn-in pair of blue jeans next to her perky, bikini-clad friend. But suddenly, she remembered something.

"Where's Joel?" Sophia asked.

"We broke up a few weeks ago. No biggie. There's plenty of other fish in the sea," Mia said cheerfully.

Sophia could have sworn that Mia gave Drew a sidelong glance when she said it. *Ok, that does it!* Rubbing her hand up and down Drew's arm, Sophia said, "That's too bad. I would have liked for Drew to meet him."

Drew looked between the two of them, and catching on, he looped his arm around Sophia's waist. "If you're with me, I'm happy," he said and then leaned over and kissed her cheek.

Good play!

Mia had been watching them closely, and now she said, "You two are adorable!" And then her phone rang in the beach bag that was slung over her shoulder. She fished it out, looked at the screen, and said, "Gotta go. See you at the reception!" Then she turned around and walked away, bottom swinging gaily as she chatted on the phone.

Sophia glanced up at Drew and saw him following Mia with his eyes, and she smacked him on the arm.

"Hey! What did I do?"

Ignoring him, she started walking toward the back row of chairs while he followed two steps behind. Flopping down in a chair, arms crossed over her chest, she glared at him until he repeated the question.

"You know what you did! You looked at Mia's butt when your focus should have been on me. What if she'd turned around and caught you? Our cover would have been blown!"

"Soph."

"Don't Soph me! I brought you here as my *date*, not so you could ogle other women!"

"No. You brought me here as your *pretend* date. If we were really dating, I wouldn't have looked twice at your friend."

She scowled at him, not finding his admission comforting in the least. But she could hardly argue. She had brought him here under false pretenses, and he didn't owe her anything. If he wanted to go out with Mia after this was over, she couldn't stop him.

"Are you attracted to her?" She couldn't help it. Her curiosity was killing her.

"I think she's attractive, but no. I'm not attracted to her."

"What's the difference?"

Drew narrowed his eyes at her. "You really don't know?"

"I want to hear your take on it."

Drew leaned over and lifted her sunglasses. Peering directly into her eyes, he said, "There's such a thing as chemistry. You either have it with someone or you don't. I didn't feel anything toward her." He let her sunglasses down and leaned back in his chair.

But Sophia wasn't done. "But I saw you look at her butt."

Drew threw up his hands, whipped off his sunglasses, and stood up. "I'm going in the pool!" he hissed and then stalked off.

She watched him dive into the water in a perfectly executed arc and then resurface, whipping his hair off his face. *Ugh! I swear the man is getting better looking every day. It's so not fair!* Drew proceeded to swim a few laps across the length of the pool, and she admired the strength of his body as it cut a graceful path through the water. She realized that he was probably cooling off from more than just the heat. He'd obviously been irritated by her accusation and had been anxious to get away from her.

Great! He's the one who was ogling another woman, and now I feel guilty! Drew was swimming laps underwater now, so she decided to make her move. Pulling the cover-up over her head, she laid it on the chair and then set her sunglasses on top of it. She kicked off her flip-flops and made her way to the pool's edge. If she'd been looking, she might have noticed a few of the men nearby glance her way, but she was oblivious as always. Right then, she was on a mission to get to Drew.

Carefully climbing down the ladder, she immersed herself in the cool water. Once she was neck-deep, she glanced around until she saw him leaning against the opposite edge of the pool, head tipped back, soaking up the sun. She slipped underwater, stealthily swam to where he was, and then popped up right in front of him.

"What the...?" Drew sputtered.

What happened next surprised them both. Sophia spotted Mia over Drew's shoulder, and she was watching them with a mixture of curiosity and envy. Sophia made a split-second decision, and sliding her hands up Drew's chest, she snaked them around his neck, pressed her chest against his, and kissed him.

It took a few seconds for Drew to respond, but oh, how he responded! His arms coiled around her waist, pulling her closer, and his lips parted, allowing her tongue to slip inside. Warm sun, the ocean breeze, cool water, and sizzling chemistry combined to make this their best kiss yet. Not a huge fan of public displays, Sophia forgot that people surrounded them—forgot everything except his strong arms around her, his full, wet lips claiming hers, his erection pressing into her belly.

A child's loud cry caused them to pull apart, but Drew didn't let go of her completely. Staring down at her, eyes brimming with desire, he smiled, their earlier argument obviously forgotten, or at least forgiven. "Wow."

She smiled back at him, because, yeah, wow! "I'm sorry," she said quietly.

"For the kiss? Don't be!"

"No. Not for that. For the thing with Mia. I was just..."

"Jealous?" Drew said, sounding hopeful.

"Don't push it!"

He chuckled. "I'll take another kiss instead."

"We're surrounded by people."

"Didn't seem to matter a minute ago."

He looked so adorable. Correction—adorable was for puppies and babies. He looked so *hot* standing there with his damp hair, bare chest, and sexy smirk that she couldn't resist. Coming up on her tiptoes, she kissed him again, but with a bit more restraint this time. When she stopped, he sighed.

"I love Florida!" he said, and for a minute there, she wondered if he loved her too.

Chapter 14

"You can open your eyes now."

Drew was perched on the edge of the bed with his eyes tightly closed, and now he opened them, blinking a few times as if to clear his vision.

"Well? Is it ok?"

"Wow, Soph. You look amazing."

And just like that, she released her breath. She'd bought a few new clothing items for the trip, and she'd decided on the red halter dress for the evening reception. It was feminine and flirty, and she liked how it swirled around her legs when she moved. She'd paired it with strappy sandals and long, dangle earrings that caught the light. Overall, she was pleased with her appearance, and Drew's reaction cinched it for her. With the way his eyes had raked over her, pausing at her full breasts and then on her bare legs, she couldn't help but feel sexy.

"Turn around," he said gruffly.

She did a slow turn in front of him, and there was no mistaking the catch in his throat when he saw the back. Other than the tie at the top, her back was bare, and that was another reason she liked the dress. From the front, it looked fairly conservative, but the back had a hint of sass.

"Jesus, Soph. You're breathtaking."

If only he weren't acting. "Stand up. Let me see you too."

He'd gone a step up from casual in dark rinse jeans, top-siders, and a light-blue button-down shirt with the sleeves rolled up. The man was gorgeous no matter what he wore, but tonight, there was an extra sparkle in his eye that made him even sexier.

"Did I do ok?" he asked, waiting for her to weigh in.

"Better than ok," she said, smiling at him. "Of course, you always look good." *Did I just say that aloud? The sun must have gotten to me today.*

"Thanks! Are you ready to do this?"

"Yes. No. I don't know."

He laughed. "It'll be fine. Just hold my hand and stick close. We can do this. We've been practicing for weeks."

And there it was: the reminder that that was all they were doing—pretending. She felt deflated, but she tried not to show it. They had a party to go to, and a lot of her friends would be there. Now was her chance to show off her new boyfriend, and she wanted to give an award-winning performance.

"You're right. I think we're ready. Let's go."

On the ride down in the elevator, Drew showed his first sign of nerves. "So, if I touch you or kiss you in front of your friends, you're not going to slap me, right?"

She turned to him and smoothed her hand down the front of his shirt. "Of course not. Are you sure you're ok with this?"

He nodded vehemently. "Just double-checking."

And then the elevator doors slid open, and they reached for each other's hand at the same time. For some reason, that broke the tension, and they were both smiling as they stepped into the lobby.

The reception was held outside on the long deck that stretched across the back of the hotel. Tiny white lights were strung on the railing, adding an intimate glow to the already beautiful setting. The sun was starting to descend, and the air was still balmy and smelling of salt from the light ocean breeze. Peering around, Sophia understood why Cassie wanted to get married there. It really was an idyllic romantic setting.

They'd just given a waiter their drink orders when Sophia heard her name being called.

"Sophia! I'm so happy you're here," Cassie said, throwing her arms around her.

"It's great to see you," Sophia said, and she meant it. She hadn't realized how much she'd missed her college friends until now. Life had become so busy since then, and everyone had scattered, so it had been difficult to stay in touch. And to think she'd almost declined the invitation.

Suddenly, Drew cleared his throat beside her.

"Cassie, this is my boyfriend, Drew Kennedy."

Cassie shook Drew's hand enthusiastically. "It's so good to meet you. I already heard that Sophia had a *hot* date from our friend Mia."

He smiled wide and said, "Well, that's quite a compliment!"

Compliment, my ass! Mia better watch out, Sophia thought, but she pasted on a smile and said, "Where's your fiancé?"

"He's around here somewhere. I'll introduce you later, but first, I have to greet some of the other guests."

"No problem," Sophia said. "We'll just mingle."

"Have fun!"

After Cassie scurried away, Drew leaned in and whispered, "Your friends are very…"

"Flirtatious?"

"I was going to say expressive, but yeah, that too."

"It's probably the alcohol. Everyone loosens up when they're drinking, don't you think?"

"You don't."

Sophia's mouth gaped open. "What do you mean?"

"I've never seen you lose control, not even when we were in high school at parties where everyone was getting drunk."

Shoving her hands on her hips, she cocked her head and said, "Are you calling me a goody two shoes?"

"Shhh. Lower your voice. We don't want your friends to think we're arguing." With that, he placed his hand on her lower back—her bare lower back—and led her further away from where the crowd was congregating.

"Just because I never got drunk, that doesn't make me a saint," she whispered.

Just then, the waiter approached with their drinks, and Sophia took a long swallow, still irritated at the implication that she was a prude.

"I didn't mean anything bad by it, Soph. I happen to like you just the way you are." And with that, he leaned in and kissed her softly on the lips.

"Geez. You two can't keep your hands off each other," Mia declared as she sidled up to them, drink in hand.

"Can you blame me? Look at the woman. She's gorgeous," Drew said, winking at Sophia like they shared a secret, which, of course, they did. Obviously, they'd convinced Mia that they were a couple.

"Aww. How sweet. He's a keeper, Sophia!"

"Yes. He definitely is," Sophia said and leaned her head on Drew's shoulder.

Soon, they were joined by a few other friends and their dates, and they stood in a tight circle, exchanging stories and pleasantries while sipping their cocktails. Drew stayed glued to her side, smiling at her friends, shaking hands with the guys, and fitting in seamlessly just like he always did. When the men got into a discussion about sports, he absently rubbed his hand up and down her back, and the feeling was exquisite. She broke out in goosebumps, and it wasn't because the sun had gone down. *I wonder if he feels them? He must, right? Does he realize that he's turning me on?*

She continued chatting and laughing with her girlfriends, barely noticing when Drew removed the empty drink from her hand and replaced it with a fresh one. After the conversation they'd had earlier, she wondered if he was trying to get her drunk, but then she dismissed the idea as foolish. Besides, she was already buzzing just from being with him. And to think that they would be crawling into the same bed together tonight! Instead of feeling nervous at the prospect, she tingled with anticipation. *Will we kiss again? Or is that only reserved for when we're around my friends?*

Usually, Sophia was one of the first people to leave a party, but tonight, she was in no hurry. Surrounded by her friends and with Drew by her side, she felt happy, giddy even. Add in the fact that she and Drew would be spending the next few days together, and she didn't think life could get much better.

It wasn't until a few hours later that the crowd began to disperse, starting with Cassie and Greg, who wanted to be well-rested for their "big day" tomorrow. Mia had disappeared awhile before with one of Greg's single cousins, which had been a relief, since maybe now she'd stop eyeing up Drew. When there were just a few of them left, Drew leaned in and whispered, "You ready to go?"

She nodded and said goodnight to her friends with the promise that they'd see each other tomorrow. She and Drew left the party hand in hand like it was the most natural thing in the world, and they didn't let go even when they stepped into the empty elevator.

"I don't know about you, but I'm starved!" he said after the doors had closed.

She giggled. "What about all the appetizers you ate?"

"Those weren't filling! That's why they're called appetizers. Bring on the main course!"

She giggled again and realized she might be a bit tipsy. Not drunk, mind you, but a bit looser in her limbs.

"I could eat something too," she admitted.

"Let's order a pizza when we get to the room."

"Sounds good."

The first thing she did when they got inside was kick off her shoes. She wasn't used to wearing high heels, choosing to wear more practical shoes at work and sneakers at home. Drew started unbuttoning his shirt while he perused the pile of menus next to the desk phone. His back was to her, and she stood there, staring, as he peeled the shirt off and tossed it on the bed, seemingly unaware that he was being watched.

Sophia's mouth watered, and she swallowed hard at the sight of him standing there in just his jeans, oblivious to the effect he was having on her.

"Yes, I'd like to order a large pepperoni pizza, a dozen breadsticks, and a two-liter of Coke please," he said into the phone. And then he unsnapped his jeans and started to peel down the zipper.

What the...?

"Great. Thanks," he said and set down the receiver. When he turned around, she was still standing beside the bed, staring at him.

"What's wrong?" he asked.

"You...your...your zipper," she stuttered.

"Oh, shit. I forgot. Sorry." He quickly zipped his pants back up. "I was feeling warm and..."

"No. It's ok. Why don't you change into shorts or something?" she suggested, feeling flustered.

"Ok. Be right out." Drew hurriedly plucked shorts and a t-shirt out of the drawer and disappeared into the bathroom.

Sophia used the reprieve to catch her breath as she waited for her turn to use the bathroom. *This is crazy. How is this going to work? What are we doing?*

Drew returned a few minutes later and said, "Your turn."

She took her time preparing for bed, changing, brushing her hair, and removing her makeup. She thought about leaving it on but decided to stick to her usual bedtime routine. It wasn't like she was trying to impress him. Besides, he'd seen her without makeup plenty of times before. The only thing she did differently was leave on her bra because she didn't want him to see her nipples through the thin material of her pajamas.

When she rejoined him, he was sitting cross-legged on the bed, flicking through channels on the television. "Anything you like to watch on Friday nights?" he asked politely.

She eyed the bed and then the chair that was across the room and decided it wouldn't make sense to sit way over there. "I don't usually watch TV this late. If I'm up at this time, I'm usually reading."

He chuckled and shut off the TV. "I should have guessed that."

"Well, you don't know *everything* about me," she pointed out as she climbed onto the bed and mirrored his cross-legged position.

"I know a lot of things though."

"True," she conceded.

"I didn't even get a chance to answer many questions about us at the party. I told you people wouldn't ask."

"But it was good to be prepared," she said.

Drew shifted to face her. "Tell me something about you that I don't know."

"Like what?"

"I don't know. Something private that you haven't shared before."

She plucked at the bedspread nervously. "It's not like I'm full of secrets."

"There must be something."

Just then, a knock came at the door, and a man's voice called, "Pizza delivery!"

Drew scrambled off the bed and answered the door. After the man left, Drew immediately began doling out pizza and breadsticks on the paper plates they'd been given. Other than the standard desk and chair, there wasn't a table in the room, so they decided to eat in bed. He poured them each some Coke in the plastic cups provided by the hotel and then rejoined her.

"Not exactly a gourmet meal, but it'll do," he said before taking a gigantic bite.

"Mmm. I didn't realize how hungry I was," she said, savoring the first bite of spicy pepperoni.

They ate in silence for several minutes, and Sophia thought she'd escaped his inquiry, but she was wrong.

"So, you haven't answered my question yet."

She gulped her Coke to buy extra time, but when she set the cup down, he was looking at her, waiting.

"Tell me one of your fantasies."

Her eyebrows shot up. "Like sexual fantasies?"

He shrugged. "Sure. We're all alone here, and I won't tell anyone. I promise." He made a cross over his chest and grinned at her.

She eyed him warily and then said, "Ok, but only if you tell me one of yours too."

"Deal."

She cleared her throat noisily. "Well, I've always had this thing about...being blindfolded. And it has nothing to do with reading a certain book or watching a certain movie. It's just something that I've wanted to try."

Drew had leaned forward a little, his hands clasped in his lap, listening intently. "So, you've never done that before, not even with Jake?"

She shook her head. "I never felt comfortable enough to tell him about it. I guess that should have been a sign that we weren't compatible, huh?"

"Maybe. It seems like when two people really love each other, they can tell each other anything."

Like we're doing right now? "So, there you have it. No big deal, right? It's not like some kinky fantasy or anything."

"What about being blindfolded appeals to you?"

She leaned back against the headboard and thought for a moment. "I guess I like the idea of relinquishing control. Of not knowing exactly what's going to happen because I can't see it coming. The element of surprise and all that."

"Hmm. Maybe it's because, in your daily life, you keep such a tight rein on things that it sounds good to let go."

"I never thought of it like that, but you might be right."

Drew nodded. "Ok, then. Thanks for sharing. Goodnight." He made a big show of turning his back to her and acting like he was going to sleep.

She swatted him on the arm and said, "Oh no, you don't! You promised to share one of your fantasies too."

"I did? Oh, right." He sat back up and leaned against the headboard too. "Ok, so, remember the librarian fantasy I told you about the other day?"

"Yes?"

"That one was kind of…well…mine."

"Oh," she replied, suddenly feeling self-conscious. "But you never finished telling it."

"Why don't we get under the covers and shut off the lights, and then I'll finish it?"

She eyed him skeptically. "This isn't a trick, is it?"

He chuckled. "No. I swear." With that, he switched off his bedside lamp and crawled under the covers.

Feeling like she had no choice, she followed suit. Once the room was plunged into darkness and the covers were tucked underneath her chin, Sophia said, "Continue."

Drew inhaled deeply like he was gathering courage, and then he spoke. "So, after the librarian retrieves the book I wanted and we kiss, she leads me into her private office."

"The library is closed now, right?"

"Right."

"Once we're inside the office, she locks the door and closes the blinds so it's pitch dark in the room."

"Kind of like now?"

"Um-hum."

"Anyway, I perch on the edge of her desk, and she comes to stand between my legs. She reaches up to pull the clips out of her hair…"

"Clips or bobby pins?"

"I don't know. Does it really matter?"

"I guess not. Continue."

"She starts to pull the bobby pins out of her hair, but I say, 'No. Let me.'"

"But how can you see them if it's dark?"

Drew chuckled. "Are you going to let me finish this?"

"Yes. Sorry!"

"So, I reach up and feel for the bobby pins and pull them out one by one until her hair tumbles down around her shoulders."

"Does she have blonde hair?"

"No. She's a brunette."

"Good. Continue."

"Next, I start to remove her glasses, but she puts her hands over mine to stop me."

"Why would she do that?"

"She says she wants to be able to see me up close."

"Hmm. Must be farsighted. Go ahead."

"So, she leaves her glasses on, which is fine by me because I think she looks hot in them."

You've said that about me. Interesting.

"What? No interruption?"

"Are you asking me or her?"

"I'm asking you!"

"No. What happens next?"

"I start to unbutton her blouse, slowly because I want to savor every moment."

"Um-hum."

"Once it's unbuttoned, I push it off her shoulders, and now she's standing there in her bra and skirt."

"What color is the bra?"

"Seriously?"

"I'm just curious."

"It's skin-toned."

"Oh, because she was wearing a white blouse, right?"

"Exactly."

"Makes perfect sense."

"Well, she is a sensible woman after all."

Sophia giggled. "Not really if she's willing to risk her job to have sex with a stranger in the library!"

"IT'S A FANTASY!"

"Geez. You don't have to yell!"

"Do you want me to finish or not?"

"Yes!"

"Where was I? Oh, right. So, before I can reach around and unhook her bra, she does it herself."

"Let me guess. She's large-breasted."

"She's well-endowed but not ridiculously so."

"Are they real?"

"Of course."

"That's a relief. Go on."

"I begin touching them, circling her nipples with my fingers until she tips her head back and moans. And then I bend my head down and suck one into my mouth."

Sophia squirmed under the covers, suddenly wishing she weren't wearing so many clothes.

"You ok?"

"Um-hum. Just getting comfortable."

"She tastes delicious, and I'm dying to get her naked, but she stops for a minute."

"Is she having second thoughts?"

"No way! She says she wants to undress me too."

"Oh."

"I'm wearing a t-shirt, so she yanks it over my head and tosses it to the side. And then she stares at me for a few seconds..."

"Because she's in awe of your body."

"Are you asking or telling?"

Telling! "Sorry. It's your fantasy. Continue."

"And then she starts to unbutton my jeans."

Drew was silent for a few beats, and she wondered if he'd fallen asleep, but then he shifted to his side, and she knew he was facing her in the dark.

"Drew?"

"Yeah?"

"Why did you stop talking?"

"I don't know if I should continue."

"Why not?"

"Because I'm getting turned on, and it's…uncomfortable."

"Oh." Her face was burning up thinking about Drew lying next to her with an erection. She wondered what he would do if she were to reach over and…

"Maybe we should go to sleep. It's already after one o'clock, and we have another performance tomorrow."

It was like he had just poured a bucket of cold water over her, and she clamped her arms across her chest. *You idiot! Just because it's a librarian fantasy doesn't mean it's about you!*

"Soph?"

"Yeah, you're right. We should get some sleep," she said tightly and then turned her back to him. *How am I supposed to sleep after all that?*

Drew must have misread the reason for her irritation because he said, "I'll finish the story tomorrow."

"Fine. Goodnight."

"Sweet dreams, Soph."

Yeah, right!

Chapter 15

Drew lay still for the longest time, waiting for Sophia to fall asleep, wondering if she was as worked up as he was. How he longed to reach over and touch her, to gather her in his arms and hold her close even if that was all that she'd allow to happen. God knows he wanted more though, so much more that it scared him. And it wasn't just a physical longing—that, he could handle himself, although not here in bed with her. He thought about sneaking off to the bathroom to relieve himself, but what if she woke up and heard him? No, he couldn't risk it. So, he lay there, alternating between staring at the ceiling and at the outline of her body beneath the covers.

Thinking back over the evening, he realized that he'd enjoyed it more than he thought he would. How could he not with someone as beautiful and dynamic as Sophia by his side? She'd glowed in her sexy red dress and heels, her naturally curly hair dancing on her shoulders as she talked and laughed with her friends. He'd loved seeing her like that, relaxed and loose, uninhibited. It was quite a departure from the persona she usually displayed to the world—the straitlaced librarian in her conservative clothes and glasses.

He smiled in the dark, recalling the fantasy she'd shared with him. What he would give to be the guy who made her fantasy come true. To have her lying beneath him, blindfolded, open to him in every way. If she'd trusted him enough to tell him her fantasy, maybe she'd trust him enough to try it out. They'd already kissed, and they'd touched each other more in the past few weeks than they had in the entire time they'd known each other.

She shifted in her sleep and mumbled something, but he couldn't make out the words. He sighed. *Does she realize how difficult this is for me?* Sleeping in the same bed together without touching, talking about their fantasies but not acting on them, kissing in public but not in private—it was an exquisite form of torture. *At least she asked me to be here instead of some other guy.*

Before they'd left for Florida, Sophia had told him that she didn't plan to go out with Jake again, but she didn't say why. *Could it be that she has feelings for me too?* The way she'd responded when they'd kissed, the jealousy she'd shown toward Mia, was that all part of the act? *I can't imagine that this will all be over in three days. How can we go back to the way it was before when we've become so close?*

"NO! NO!" Sophia yelled, startling him.

He quickly moved closer to her, and when he looked down, he saw that her eyes were still closed. She was having a nightmare.

"Don't go!" she said, her voice becoming a whimper.

"Soph? Soph? It's just a bad dream, sweetheart. You're ok," he said and gently brushed her hair off her face.

Her eyes flicked open, and she stared up at him for a moment, frozen, like she'd forgotten he was even there.

"It's ok, Soph. I'm here," he said.

"I was having a bad dream."

"I know. Come here. Let me hold you until you fall back asleep."

She hesitated for a moment, but then she snuggled against his side, and his arms instantly went around her.

"There. Better?"

She nodded against his chest, which was now bare. He'd peeled off his t-shirt after she'd fallen asleep in an attempt to cool off.

"What were you dreaming about?"

"I'm not really sure. It's all jumbled up in my mind."

He hugged her tight. "It's ok. Just relax and go back to sleep."

"What time is it?"

"Three in the morning."

"Did I wake you?"

"Not really."

Her hand was resting on his abdomen, and she said, "What happened to your shirt?"

"I was hot. Do you want me to put it back on?"

"No."

Can you feel my heart beating out of my chest right now?

"Drew?"

"Yeah?"

"Thank you."

"For what?"

"For taking such good care of me. For coming on this trip, for tolerating my lists, for…"

"Shhh. You don't have to keep thanking me. I like taking care of you." To seal the sentiment, he gently kissed her forehead.

They were quiet for a while after that, and Drew soaked up her closeness. He was hyperaware of her body where it pressed against his side—the curve of her breasts, her soft abdomen against his hip, her right leg slung over his. She was tracing some sort of pattern on his chest with her fingertips, and it felt incredible. Thank God it was dark and she couldn't see the rise in his shorts or the flush of his skin.

If it were any other woman, he would have already had her naked by now. But Sophia was different, special, and he wouldn't risk losing her friendship due to his selfish desire. He decided right then that if anything were to happen between them, she'd have to be the one to initiate it. He wouldn't make a move unless he was sure that it was what she wanted too. And if she didn't want him, well, then he'd just have to be content with her friendship. He'd rather have her in his life like this than not have her at all.

"Drew?"

"Yeah?"

"You're a good guy and the best friend I've ever had."

Her words were a harsh reminder of the truth. *She wants me to be her friend and nothing else.* "Thanks," he said, the word strangling him.

And then she nestled against him, and he held her tight until she fell back asleep.

Chapter 16

Sophia woke to the sound of seagulls squawking and to the hotel room awash with bright light. Once her eyes adjusted, she peered around for Drew and saw him sitting on the balcony with his feet propped up on the rail, sipping a cup of coffee. Shoving off the covers, she slipped out of bed and padded into the bathroom, where she studied herself in the mirror. She'd had a rough night, and it showed. Her hair had become a tangled mess, there were dark circles under her eyes, and she felt the beginnings of a headache. Not wanting to face Drew looking like she did, Sophia stripped out of her clothes and hung them on the back of the door. She was about to turn on the shower when she realized she hadn't brought any clothes to change into. Wrapping a towel tightly around herself, she opened the door just a crack and peeked out. Drew was still on the balcony, head tipped back in the chair, looking completely relaxed. Since he had gotten up with her in the middle of the night, she thought he might be dozing, so she tiptoed out of the bathroom and went to retrieve some clothes.

She was bent over an open drawer, intent on choosing an outfit, when Drew said, "Finally up, I see."

Startled, she quickly spun around, and the towel caught on the edge of the drawer. In horrifyingly slow motion, it fell to the floor, and there she stood, stark naked in front of her best friend. She made a loud sound between a squeal and a mortified gasp and covered her lady parts as best she could while Drew gaped at her, rooted to the spot. Considering her options, she turned and fled back into the bathroom, exposing her backside to his startled gaze.

Once inside, she locked the bathroom door and leaned heavily against it, trying to catch her breath. *Ohmigod, ohmigod, ohmigod*, she repeated in her head. *I can't believe that just happened!*

And then a soft knock came on the door, startling her again. "What?" she snapped.

"I'll be waiting for you downstairs in the restaurant," he said, cool as you please.

"Ok. Fine. Just go!" None of it was his fault, but her embarrassment made her snap.

"Soph?"

"Yes?" she replied, rolling her eyes.

"You have nothing to be ashamed of," he said.

Seconds later, she heard the door close, and she let out a loud sigh. As she washed up, she tried to calm down, but all she could think about was Drew seeing her naked. It had happened so fast that she couldn't be sure how long she'd stood there before covering herself up. She tried to convince herself that he hadn't seen *everything*, but there was a good chance that he had.

What a disaster! Sharing a room with him was proving to be more challenging than she thought. First, she'd had to listen to his sexy bedtime story that had made her want to jump on top of him. Then she'd woken up from a bad dream, and he'd offered to hold her when she'd rather he'd made mad, passionate love to her, and now he'd seen her naked and had left to go get breakfast!

Way to go, Soph! You really know how to reel 'em in!

Once she'd made herself presentable, she went downstairs to meet him, hoping that he'd ignore the incident and the day would go on as planned. When she walked into the restaurant, she was somewhat surprised to see Drew sitting at a round table with several of her friends, including Mia, who was leaned in close talking to him, her swingy hair up in a high pony tail and her pert breasts bubbling out of her tank top.

Sophia's heart sank as she saw Drew smile and laugh at something Mia had said. And then, as if he'd become aware of her presence, he turned and spotted her, waving her over. Drew stood up and gallantly pulled out the chair next to him, shooting Sophia a meaningful glance, his boyfriend mask already in place.

"There she is!" he said, giving her a quick peck on the cheek.

She didn't think she had it in her this morning, but she donned a smile, said hello to her friends, and sank into the chair beside him.

"Rough night, Soph?" Mia asked, giving her a look that was part smirk, part smile.

Has her voice always been this high-pitched and irritating? "Drew and I were up late, so I'm a little tired this morning," she replied, watching Mia's perky smile disappear.

A waitress came over to take their orders, so she was saved from having to explain further, and afterwards, talk turned to other things. The wedding wasn't until four o'clock, so everyone discussed their plans for the day. Some of the guys were going fishing, and they asked Drew if he'd like to join them.

"No thanks. Sophia and I already have plans," he said, slinging his arm around her shoulder.

We do? They hadn't discussed what they were going to do yet, although she did have a list of ideas...

Breakfast was delicious, but all throughout, Mia kept trying to get Drew's attention. She was an affectionate person by nature, but she seemed to be touching him every chance she got. Placing her pink manicured fingers on his bicep, she leaned over and said, "Would you mind passing the butter?" Another time, she put her hand atop his on the table and said, "Sophia's such a lucky lady," to which he replied, "I'm the lucky one."

Sophia shot him a smile and then laid her hand on his thigh and gave it a squeeze. She started to remove her hand, but he clamped his over it, and they finished their breakfast just like that.

It wasn't until they were in the Mustang, driving away from the hotel, that Drew brought up *the incident*.

"Sorry about what happened earlier, in the room."

Keeping her eyes straight ahead, she said, "It wasn't your fault. Let's just forget about it."

"Kind of hard to do," he said with a low chuckle.

She shot him a look. "How much did you see anyway?"

"Not enough," he said, his voice oozing sexiness.

"Well, good. You weren't supposed to see anything at all!"

"And here you were worried about me waltzing around in my underwear!"

A giggle bubbled up inside her, and at first, she tried to quell it, but then it erupted into full-out laughter, and Drew joined in.

After they piped down, she said, "I'm so embarrassed."

"But you don't need to be. You have a beautiful body. I've told you that before."

Yet you don't seem to have any trouble resisting it. She sighed.

This is the part where you say, "Why, thank you, Drew!"

She laughed again and then said what he wanted to hear.

"That's better. Now, where are we going?"

They were driving around the perimeter of the island, and Sophia had been admiring the scenery with no real destination in mind. "There's a wildlife refuge on the island. We could go there and walk around for a while. I read about it before we came here."

"Of course you did," he teased.

"Well, I didn't want us to get bored."

"I could never be bored with you," he said sweetly.

A short time later, they arrived at the wildlife refuge, and after stopping in at the visitor's center, they meandered down the paved trail. Sophia had bought a small guidebook, and she consulted it as they walked, reading certain sections aloud. After a while of that, Drew snatched the book out of her hand and slipped it into his pocket. Then he grabbed her hand, entwined their fingers together, and said, "I've got an idea. How about you stop reading and just be in the moment?"

"Ok," she said, glancing down at their hands. "But I doubt anyone we know is going to be here, so you don't have to do this."

"What if I want to?"

Her breath caught, and peering up at him, she tried to read his expression. He looked down at her as if he were waiting for something, but when she didn't reply, he just pulled her down the trail. They stopped at various lookout points along the way to admire the many coastal birds that had come to roost there, and soon, she forgot all about the morning debacle. Drew had been right. Instead of just reading about the wildlife, it was better to immerse herself in it, and for the next hour and a half, that's exactly what they did.

After they'd finished exploring the refuge, they still had some time to kill before they'd have to head back, so Sophia suggested they drive across the bridge to Sanibel's neighbor, Captiva Island. They drove with the windows down, enjoying the breeze that flowed through the car as they crossed over the bridge onto Captiva. Sophia had been there years ago with her family, but she hadn't appreciated the beauty of the islands until now. There were brilliant colors everywhere she looked—the teal-blue of the ocean, the faunas' varying shades of green, and the vibrant reds, pinks, and yellows of the flowers that bloomed everywhere.

She directed Drew to the shopping district, where she suggested they browse for a while and maybe have a light lunch.

"Whatever you want to do," he said, and she had to fight the urge to thank him again. Drew's "go with the flow" attitude was one she appreciated and admired, probably because it was the opposite of hers. There was no doubt in her mind that he would go along with whatever she asked him to do, and happily. Well, except for the one thing that she was beginning to want more with every passing second. But maybe tonight…

They were browsing inside a beachwear store, having drifted apart to look at different things, when suddenly Drew reappeared beside her holding something behind his back.

"What do you have there?" she asked, trying to peer around him.

"I have a favor to ask."

"Ok," she said hesitantly, wondering what he was up to.

"Try this on for me." With that, he revealed what was behind his back, and her mouth dropped open.

"What? Are you crazy? I'm not trying that on."

"Why not?"

"Because."

"That's not a valid reason."

"You sound like a parent."

"You don't have a good reason other than you're too self-conscious," he said, dangling the item before her.

Hands on her hips, she glared at him. "I'm not self-conscious. I'm tasteful, and there's nothing wrong with that."

"I'm not asking you to buy it and wear it in public. I'm asking you to try it on for me, your best friend. The guy who flew all the way here to escort you to a wedding. The guy who's pretending to be your boyfriend…"

"Alright, alright!" she said, throwing her hands up. "Give it to me." She snatched the hanger out of his hand and was walking toward the fitting room when she thought of something. "Give me your phone," she said.

"What for?"

"Just hand it over."

Drew extracted the phone from his pocket and reluctantly handed it to her.

"There. Now you can't snap a picture of me in this...this thing."

"Always thinking, aren't you?" he said, trailing after her toward the fitting rooms.

She ignored him and went into one of the curtained dressing cubicles at the back of the store. While she was changing, she heard a saleswoman ask if they needed any help, but Drew assured her that he had it covered.

Sophia glanced down at the tiny bikini and wished that she had it *covered* too! She did a pirouette in front of the mirror and frowned. The triangle top covered her nipples but not much else, and the bottoms were even worse. A patch of the leopard-print material covered her in front, and two strings on both sides connected it to the scrap of material in the back. The tag identified the bathing suit as "cheeky," which was a fitting name given that her butt cheeks were hanging out.

"Soph? Are you dressed yet?"

"If you could call it that. There's barely any material here!"

"Let me see."

"Is anyone else around?"

"No."

"Are you positive?"

"Yes!"

Sophia tried to tuck her breasts in but realized it was pointless. The swimsuit was obviously not designed for coverage. "Who would wear such a thing?" she muttered, and it took her a second to realize that Drew had poked his head in.

"Holy…"

"Yes. 'Holey' is exactly right! Who would pay a hundred dollars for this?"

Drew raised his hand, and it was then that she took a good look at his expression. Desire rolled off him in waves, and he wasn't even trying to hide it. He admired her unabashedly, his eyes roaming over her body like he'd never seen it before. And for the most part, he hadn't until today.

"Spin around," he said, his voice sounding gravelly.

Suddenly, she forgot to be shy. With the way he was eyeing her, she felt empowered, and she turned around slowly so he could look his fill. When she had turned back to face him, he was shaking his head.

"What are you thinking?" she asked.

"You don't want to know. I need to go outside and cool off." And then, just like that, he closed the curtain and left. She heard the bell ding on the front door, and she stood there for a minute, staring at her reflection in the mirror.

She was still young, and she took good care of herself. She was curvy but not overweight, and the only thing that kept her from wearing a bikini was fear. True, this one was skimpier than most, but if she were more confident, she could probably pull it off. She slipped it off, hung it back on the hanger, and redressed. When she stepped out of the fitting room, the saleslady was right there. "Should I ring this up for you?" she asked.

Sophia glanced around the store to make sure Drew hadn't come back inside. "Yes, please," she said and followed the lady to the counter.

When she stepped back outside into the warm sunshine, Drew was sitting on a bench, waiting. "What took you so long?"

"I was just looking around," she said and walked past him to the car. Her purse was large enough to hold the bag with the swimsuit inside, so Drew was none the wiser, and that was the way she wanted it. She didn't have it all planned out yet, but she wanted to surprise him with it. On the way back to Sanibel, they were quiet, each wrapped up in their own thoughts.

Sophia was busy thinking about all the things that had transpired between her and Drew over the past several weeks, wondering if she had misread the clues. *Is it all in my head? Is it because I want him so much that I'm imagining this? Has he become such a good actor that he's fooled me too?*

She prayed that she wasn't wrong about this, because what she was planning to do could backfire in the worst possible way. For the first time in her life, she was about to go with her gut instinct, but if she were wrong, she could lose the best friend she'd ever had.

Chapter 17

The wedding was held outdoors on the hotel grounds, and it was a beautiful affair; however, Sophia was distracted during the ceremony. Her date sat beside her, looking gorgeous in the suit and tie she'd helped pick out, and he smelled delicious. Sitting so close their thighs were touching, his arm was draped over the back of her chair, and knowingly or not, he was gently rubbing his fingertip along the base of her neck. She'd worn her hair up for the occasion—and for another reason too that she planned to reveal later.

Her nerves prickled with anticipation, and she kept looking over at Drew, wondering how he would react tonight. After she'd tried on the bathing suit earlier, he'd been uncharacteristically quiet. But when she'd come out of the bathroom dressed for the wedding, he'd whistled and complimented her like usual. She'd glimpsed them as they'd passed by a full-length mirror in the hotel lobby and thought that they made a good-looking couple, and then she'd had to remind herself that they weren't one. Not yet, anyway. Maybe tonight would change all that.

"Wasn't it a beautiful ceremony?" Mia gushed as they waited in the reception line.

Sophia nodded, although she'd hardly paid attention. She'd been too busy plotting and planning and sneaking peeks at Drew.

"I love the purple on you," Mia said, turning her attention to Drew. "Good choice."

"It was Sophia's idea. She gets all the credit," he said and gave Sophia a squeeze.

Mia wandered off after that, and Sophia saw her cozy up next to Greg's cousin. "Thank God," Sophia muttered after Mia had walked away.

Drew laughed. "I thought she was your friend."

"I think she's more interested in you than me."

"She's just being nice."

"Is that what you call it? If she knew that you were free, she'd be all over you."

"But I'm not free. I'm with you. Wait a minute, that didn't come out right."

"It's ok. I know what you meant."

"Soph?"

"Yeah?"

He leaned in close and whispered, "News flash: I'm not interested in her."

She peered into his slate-blue eyes and replied, "Ok, then."

After they went through the reception line, they were ushered into the hotel banquet room, where they found their assigned seats. Mia was seated at their table along with two other women Sophia had gone to college with and their dates.

"Can I get you ladies something to drink?" Drew asked, looking between Sophia and Mia.

"How sweet. I'll have Sex on the Beach!" Mia said with a wink.

Sophia turned away so Mia couldn't see her eyeroll as she gave Drew her drink order.

"Be right back," he said and sauntered off.

"He's awesome, Soph," Mia said, watching him walk away.

"So you've said. A thousand times," Sophia mumbled.

"Huh?"

"Yes, he's awesome," she said in a louder voice. The band had just started playing in the corner of the room, and between the music and the roomful of wedding guests, the noise level had risen considerably.

What's taking him so long? Sophia wondered, looking in the direction of the bar. There he was, leaning against the counter and talking to a woman that Sophia hadn't noticed before. She was tall—just a few inches shorter than him—with shiny blonde hair and a lithe body. *Just his type*, she thought, her heart deflating, yet she couldn't look away.

Leaning in close, the woman whispered something in Drew's ear before turning and walking away. Sophia was used to women noticing him, but something in the woman's demeanor seemed overly familiar, as if she already knew him. Sophia turned away so he wouldn't catch her looking and listened in on her friends' discussion about the boating excursion they had planned for tomorrow. But once again, she found it difficult to concentrate. Seeing Drew with that woman reminded her that she was the total opposite of anyone he'd dated before. She wasn't tall—not by a long shot—and she didn't consider herself sexy. Cute, maybe, but not sexy. She was a short, dark-haired librarian who preferred books to parties and felt more comfortable in sweatshirts and jeans than in the fancy dress she was wearing. How could she possibly expect to compete with the kind of women he preferred?

"Here we go," Drew said, setting the drinks down in front of her and Mia. "Sorry it took so long. It was busy at the bar."

Sophia narrowed her eyes at him, but he didn't flinch. He obviously wasn't planning on sharing whatever it was he'd been talking about with that woman. She took a long sip of her cosmopolitan, a drink she'd never tried before but liked the name of. After hearing Mia's drink order, she'd decided to come up with something more mature-sounding than a strawberry daiquiri!

"How is it?" he asked, smiling at her.

She smacked her lips together and said, "Great!"

"Just go easy. There's a lot of liquor in there."

"Don't worry about me. I'm a big girl now."

He laughed and took a slug of his beer.

Determined to make the most of the evening and to forget about the woman at the bar, she laid a hand on his leg beneath the table while swirling her cocktail around with the other.

Drew raised his eyebrows, but then, as if he remembered his role, he slung an arm around her shoulders.

"So, Drew. What do you do?" asked one of her friend's dates.

As he explained his job, Sophia slowly inched her hand further up his thigh. He continued to focus on the conversation, but she heard the slight hitch in his breath and smiled softly. *It's working.*

"Sounds like a pretty cool job," the guy said.

"I like it. I'm not the type to sit behind a desk. I'd rather be out interacting with people."

"I hear ya," the guy said.

She inched her hand up his leg again, and he shifted in his seat. And then the guy—Gary, if she recalled correctly—turned his attention to her.

"And what do you do, Sophia?"

"I'm a librarian," she said proudly. Drew removed his arm from around her shoulder, and she instantly missed the warmth. But then he slipped his hand under the table and placed it on her leg, just at the edge of her dress. *Uh-oh.*

"You don't hear much about that profession these days. What made you go into it?"

It was a common question, and she was prepared with a practiced answer; however, Drew was now inching his hand up her leg *under* her dress! "I've always loved books, and I wanted to share my love of reading with others, so becoming a librarian seemed like a good choice." *Did I say that right?* It was hard to know with Drew's hand creeping up her inner thigh.

"So many bookstores are going out of business. Good thing libraries are still around," Gary said.

She nodded and took another sip of her cosmopolitan. The conversation then turned to something else, and she and Drew listened politely, all the while taunting each other beneath the table. They caressed each other without crossing the boundary lines, but they were getting dangerously close. His hand was warm on her thigh, and if he inched it up any further, he'd feel how damp she was. She suspected that he had an erection and wondered what he'd do if she touched him there.

"Another drink, anyone?" Drew said suddenly, and he gently removed her hand from his thigh.

"Me!" Mia shouted.

"Soph?"

"Sure," she said, looking directly at him. There it was again, plain as day—desire brimming in his hooded eyes.

"I'll go with you," Gary said.

When Drew stood up, she noticed how he'd strategically placed his beer bottle in front of his zipper, and she congratulated herself. There was no doubt that he was trying to conceal his arousal as he walked away. She watched him cross the room to the bar and then realized that she wasn't the only one watching him. The tall blonde who he'd been talking to earlier was also tracking him from across the room, and her eyes were trained directly on his behind. *Bimbo!*

Sophia was halfway into her second drink when dinner was served, and it was good thing too because her limbs were starting to feel tingly. She and Drew were on their best behavior as they ate, keeping all four hands above the table. Never one to shy away from a good meal, she dug in with gusto.

"Enjoying it?" Drew asked.

Whether he was talking about the food or his teasing, her answer was the same. "Absolutely!"

"Me too." And his meaning was crystal clear.

She could hardly wait for the next segment of the reception to begin, and as soon as the plates had been cleared and the band struck up a slow song, she started to rise. Drew tugged on her hand and pulled her back down.

"Not yet," he whispered. "It's the bride and groom's turn first."

Embarrassed, she replied, "I knew that."

Everyone had shifted their chairs to watch the bridal dance, and Sophia ended up with her back toward Drew. Once again, he began tracing tantalizing circles on the back of her neck, and she had to suppress a moan. Between the dim lights and the soft music, the atmosphere was ripe for romance. It was the perfect lead-in to the rest of the evening.

"And now we'd like to invite the guests out to the dance floor," the lead band member said, and Sophia immediately stood.

"I guess the lady wants to dance," Drew said, and her friends laughed.

Several couples made their way to the dance floor, Sophia and Drew among them. He opened his arms to her, and she moved in—all the way in—not leaving so much as an inch of space between them. She entwined her arms around his neck and his encircled her waist, and they began to sway to the music just like they'd practiced in his living room.

But tonight, it felt different. The first time they'd danced together, there'd been no possibility of it leading anywhere. They had just been practicing, feeling their way with each other. Now the dance was full of intention, the air crackling around them and her heart swelling along with the music.

They were staring into each other's eyes without speaking, their bodies doing all the talking. There was no hiding his arousal this time as it pressed against her, hard and insistent. She was on fire for him—her nipples taut, her skin warm, her panties damp. The song was Ed Sheeran's, "Thinking Out Loud," which she thought was the perfect description for what was happening between them.

"Sophia?"

"Hmm?"

"Would it embarrass you if I kissed you right now?"

"No. I mean, please. Kiss me."

He chuckled, but then he dipped his head down and captured her lips, tugging the bottom one between his before releasing it.

"Why did you stop?" she asked breathlessly.

"I didn't want to, but in case you haven't noticed, we're on a crowded dance floor."

"That's why it's perfect. Nobody's paying attention to us." And then she realized what she'd just said. Before, it had been all about showing off in front of her friends, and now she'd just revealed her hand.

"Soph?"

"Never mind. Let's just finish the dance." As another slow song began, she felt a tap on her shoulder.

"Excuse me. Can I cut in?" Mia asked in her sugary-sweet voice.

Surprising herself and Drew, Sophia stepped back and said, "Sure." And then she turned and walked swiftly out of the banquet room. She'd needed a restroom break anyway, but that wasn't the real reason she'd left the dance floor. *I don't know if I can go through with it. What if he rejects me?* She took care of business, paralyzed with indecision and fear.

When she exited the stall, the blonde Amazon woman who'd spoken to Drew earlier was standing there in front of the mirror, reapplying her lipstick. She glanced up, met Sophia's eyes, and then turned to face her.

"So, you're Drew's latest, huh?"

Sophia stiffened, and a feeling of dread flooded her body. "Excuse me?"

"His flavor of the month. He rarely keeps anyone around for longer than that."

"Who are you?"

"Savannah. His flavor of the month from about six months ago."

Sophia's head spun, and she gripped the edge of the counter for support.

Savannah leaned her hip casually against the counter and smiled. "Don't worry. I'm here with a date. A friend of the groom's."

"I'm not...worried. We're not really together anyway." *Ok, why did I just share that? You idiot!*

"Could have fooled me. I saw you two dancing. At least *one* of you is in love."

Sophia cringed at the implication that it was her and only her.

Savannah pulled a powder compact out of her purse and turned back toward the mirror. "My advice is to enjoy it while it lasts because it won't be long. Believe me!"

Stunned, Sophia stared at Savannah's profile for a minute and then turned and hurried out of the bathroom. Frazzled, she stood in the middle of the hall, unsure of what to do. Suddenly, her plan for the rest of the evening flew out the window, and she didn't think she could pretend anymore. She had her purse and her phone, and she started toward the lobby, deciding that she'd text Drew and tell him she wasn't feeling well. She'd blame it on the cosmopolitans. And then she'd change into comfortable clothes and go somewhere— anywhere but here.

But no sooner had she reached the lobby, than Drew raced up to her, his tie slightly askew and a pink lipstick print on his cheek. *Figures!*

"Where are you going?" he asked.

"Out," she snapped, stabbing the elevator button with vehemence.

"Soph? What's wrong?" He placed his hand on her arm, but she smacked it away.

"Keep your hands off me," she growled, refusing to meet his eyes.

The elevator doors slid open, and she hurried inside, hoping that he wouldn't follow her. Naturally, she was wrong, as she had been about a lot of things when it came to him.

Once the doors had closed, he stepped in front of her and said, "What in the hell happened between the time we were dancing and now?"

Arms crossed defiantly over her chest, she glared at him. "Does the name Savannah ring a bell?"

Understanding flickered across his face, but he quickly donned a neutral mask. "What about her?"

"I saw you talking to her earlier at the bar. Funny, you forgot to mention it."

"I didn't think it was important."

"Why not? Because she was just another notch on your belt?"

Drew froze, his only movement an angry tick in his jaw. "What does she have to do with us?"

"What *us*? There is no us! There's only pretend us, and we're not even very good at that!"

"That's not what it felt like when we were dancing."

"Why, because you had a hard-on? That could have happened with anyone. It probably happened with Mia after I left."

"I already told you that she means nothing to me," he growled.

"Who, Mia? Or Savannah? Or Lexie? Oh, that's right. *None* of them mean anything. They were just more names to add to your list!"

"What list? I don't keep lists. You're the one who does that," he sneered.

Just then, the elevator doors slid open on their floor, and Sophia stalked out.

"Enjoy the rest of your evening—alone!" she shouted. This time, he didn't follow her, and the door slid shut just like the door to her heart.

Chapter 18

Sophia's heart was still pounding when she entered their hotel room, and after kicking off her high heels, she slumped down on the bed and dropped her head into her hands. Her emotions were all over the place, but mostly she was mad at herself for entertaining the idea that she and Drew could ever be a real couple. *Maybe it's just not meant to be. Maybe that's the reason we've never gotten together over these past years.*

Drew was meant to be with women like Savannah and Lexie, not a girl-next-door type like her. The irony didn't escape her that she had *literally* been the girl next door and that Drew probably still saw her that way. It also occurred to her that the only reason she was still in his life was because they'd never crossed the line. And yet here she was, trying to do just that. For someone who planned everything out to the tiniest detail and accounted for every contingency, she certainly hadn't been thinking straight when it came to seducing Drew.

"What a fool," she huffed as she pushed herself off the bed. "I won't ever make that mistake again."

Fishing her phone out of her purse, she pulled up Mia's number. She typed a quick text explaining that she wasn't feeling well, and asked Mia to give her apologies to Cassie. At least it wasn't a total lie. She felt fine physically, but emotionally she was a wreck!

Next, she stripped out of her purple dress and hung it neatly in the closet. She stared at it for a moment and ran her hands over the silky material. If the evening had gone the way she'd planned, Drew would have been the one to strip her out of the dress. Sighing, she removed her bra and pulled on her polka-dotted pajamas. She wasn't worried about Drew seeing her tonight, because she doubted he would even come back. She wondered where he'd gone and hoped he hadn't gone back to the reception. Even though she couldn't have him, she didn't want Mia getting her hooks into him, or, even worse, Savannah.

Leaving her hair up, Sophia removed her makeup and brushed her teeth before climbing into bed. She slipped on her glasses and picked up her book, doubtful that she'd be able to concentrate but unsure of what else to do. After telling Mia that she was sick, she couldn't risk getting caught walking through the hotel lobby. Besides, Drew had probably taken the car, and where else could she go at this time of night?

So, she cracked open her historical fiction novel about Alexander Hamilton. She'd considered bringing a romance novel, but she knew Drew would have teased her mercilessly, so she'd brought a *dry* novel instead. An hour later, she was still reading, her eyes popping out of her head. The life of Alexander Hamilton was anything but dry! On the contrary, he and his wife had been head over heels for each other, and their passion leapt off the pages. She knew that the story had a sad ending, but she was struck by Eliza's unfailing love and devotion to her husband, and vice versa.

If only it could be like that in real life, she thought as she flipped a page. Sophia was so enraptured, that at first, she didn't register the knock at the door. But when the sound came again, she set down her book. Thinking that it might be Mia, she padded to the door and asked, "Who is it?"

"It's me," Drew said.

Inhaling deeply, she opened the door. "Why didn't you use your key?"

Looking exhausted and slightly disheveled, he said, "Because I didn't know if you'd want me here. I was giving you the option of not opening the door."

"It's not a question about me wanting you here. You paid for half of the room, so you have every right to be here," she stated and turned away.

Drew gripped her by the elbow and swung her back around. "What's going on, Sophia? Why are you so upset with me?"

Much of her anger had dissipated by now, and she was left feeling resigned. Sighing heavily, she said, "Let's sit down."

He perched on the edge of the bed, and she sat a few feet away. "Do you want to change first? Are you uncomfortable?"

"I'm fine," he replied. "Actually, that's a lie. I'm not fine, but I want to hear what you have to say."

"This is all my fault. I shouldn't have asked you here, and I'm sorry for putting you in an uncomfortable position."

Eyebrows knit in confusion, he said, "Why do you keep apologizing? I've told you from the beginning that I wanted to do this. Why can't you accept that?"

Looking down at her hands, she continued. "I understand you were doing me a favor, but it's made things…awkward between us."

Crossing his arms over his chest, he said, "How so?"

He's certainly not making this easy. "We're friends. We're not meant to be kissing each other and pretending to be in love. It was wrong of me to ask you to do that."

"Do you really believe that?"

The intensity in his gaze made her breath catch, and she averted her eyes. "Yes."

"So, when we kissed, you felt nothing. Is that it?" He didn't wait for her reply. "And when we danced tonight, that was just two friends dancing, right?"

"Right," she said, clasping her hands tightly in her lap.

Drew shoved himself off the bed and started undoing his tie.

"What…what are you doing?"

"Getting ready for bed."

"But…out here?"

"Why not? If we're just friends, my being naked shouldn't affect you."

He undid the last button on his dress shirt and shoved it off his shoulders. Standing shirtless before her, he placed his hands on the button of his dress pants and started to undo it.

"Drew! Stop!" she said, bounding up from the bed.

"Why? Does this bother you?"

Just when she'd thought she'd regained control of the situation, he'd stolen it away from her. Chest heaving, hands on his hips, he stared at her, straight-faced and determined. *But determined to do what?*

"This is stupid," she said after a few seconds.

"You're right. It is." And then his expression softened, and the corners of his lips turned up. "You're wearing your glasses."

She adjusted them on her nose self-consciously. "I was reading."

"I see that," he said, peering around her at the book lying on the bed. "Alexander Hamilton?"

"I like to learn about our nation's history."

Drew chuckled. "He was a bit of a scoundrel, wasn't he?"

"That's a matter of opinion."

"Doesn't seem like your type of guy." He took a step closer.

"What's my type of guy?" she asked, hackles rising.

"Straitlaced. Bookish."

"If by that you mean intelligent, I won't deny it," she said indignantly.

"But what about passion?" He took another step forward.

"What about it?" she replied, her voice wavering.

"Isn't that important too?"

"According to this book, Hamilton was extremely passionate."

"I wasn't talking about Hamilton. I was asking about you."

"Why do you want to know?"

"Isn't it obvious?"

She shook her head, trying to rid herself of the confusion. Between their cryptic conversation and him standing so close to her, she couldn't focus.

"You still have your hair up," he said, reaching out and tugging on one of the bobby pins. "Mind if I take these out?"

"I...I guess not," she said, watching as he carefully and intently removed the pins. She caught the scent of his cologne and inhaled deeply. Once he'd removed the last pin, he set them on the bedside table and returned to stand before her.

"I like your hair down the best," he said softly, reaching out to finger a curl.

His eyes had become hooded, and she recognized that look. If she didn't put a stop to this right now...

"Drew?"

"Yeah?"

"What are we doing?"

"Nothing yet." He chuckled gruffly.

"You know what I mean."

He brushed a strand of hair away from her face. "What do you want, Soph?"

Oh God. Don't ask me that. You! I want you!

"Because if you don't want to do this, tell me, and I'll stop right now." He gazed down at her, not bothering to disguise his hopefulness.

"But we shouldn't," she said while reaching out to trace her fingernail down the middle of his bare chest.

"Why shouldn't we if it's something we both want?"

"Sometimes, the things we want are things that could cause us pain or regret."

"Do you honestly think that I would hurt you?" He placed his hands on her elbows, effectively locking her in place.

She forced herself to look into his eyes when she answered, "I don't know."

"What are you afraid of? Tell me."

Placing both hands on his warm, hard pecs, she said, "Do you want the list?"

He tipped his head back and laughed, and the sound of it filled the room. "You and your lists."

"Hey," she said, swatting his chest playfully.

"Tell me. I want to know."

She took a deep breath and plunged ahead. "I don't want to end up like Lexie and Savannah and all the others. I don't want to trade years of friendship for one night of passion. There, I said it." She took a step back and waited.

After what felt like an interminable amount of time, Drew sighed. "You're right. I got carried away. I'm sorry."

Brows raised, she said, "That's it?"

He shrugged. "What else do you want me to say? You made a very logical argument. If we don't cross the line, nobody will get hurt." Turning his back to her, he started to remove his pants again.

She was about to stop him but decided not to. If she couldn't have him in the flesh, she might as well enjoy the view. And oh, what a view it was. Instead of tighty-whities, he wore a pair of black boxer briefs, the kind that hugged his butt and thighs. She was still gawking when he turned around, and then she swallowed hard. The underwear was so snug that it didn't leave much to the imagination, and she zoned in on the outline of his...

"Uh-uh," Drew scolded, but his eyes lit up with pleasure. "No ogling the goods."

She quickly averted her eyes. "I wasn't *ogling*." *I was admiring.*

"No more pretending, Soph. Nobody's here but us. Do you want to use the bathroom first?" he asked, clearly enjoying her discomfort.

"I'm all set."

"Ok. Be right out."

Sophia placed her hand over her beating heart. Now that they'd agreed not to cross the line, she wanted him more than ever. How was she going to be able to sleep with him lying next to her tonight? While he was in the bathroom, she slid underneath the covers and picked up her book again. *Maybe if I ignore him and pretend to read...*

She'd just opened her book when he came back out, still wearing his underwear and nothing else. Instead of joining her, he slowly walked across the room and took out a bottle of water from the minifridge. "Want anything?" he asked, smiling wickedly.

He was purposely tempting her, but she wasn't going to fall for his charms. "I'll take a water," she said and then went back to her book. She felt him walk toward her, like a predator stalking its prey, but she didn't look up until he was right beside her.

"Here you go," he said. But instead of handing her the water, he held it in front of himself like he wanted her to reach for it.

Tipping her glasses down, she peered over the top of them. "Is this how you get women into bed?" she asked, sarcasm dripping from her voice.

"You're already in my bed," he teased.

"Give me that!" She reached for the water, but he snatched it out of her way.

Tilting her head to one side, she said, "Really?"

"If we aren't going to have sex, at least we can have a little fun!"

When she reached for the bottle again, he let her have it, and then he strutted around to the other side of the bed and hopped on top of the covers, crossing his legs at the ankles, casual as can be.

Sophia took a long drink of water and then tried to go back to her reading, but she was hyperaware of Drew's eyes boring into her. After a few minutes, she slammed her book down and said, "What?"

"I didn't say anything."

"But you're staring at me."

"I was just thinking how pretty you look tonight."

Is this what he says to all the girls before he pounces on them? "I believed you when you said it earlier because I was all dressed up. But now?"

He flipped to his side and rested his head in his hand, providing her with the full view of his magnificent body. "I mean it. You were gorgeous earlier, and you still are, but now you look more natural."

"Like a girl next door?" She hadn't meant to say it, but it had slipped out.

"Why do you say that like it's a bad thing?"

"Isn't it?"

"Not at all. In fact, a lot of guys have fantasies about the girl next door."

"Oh God. Not again. We're not going there, Drew."

"Suit yourself," he said and turned onto his back.

She picked up her book again and read two sentences before she slammed it back down.

"What's wrong?"

"I can't concentrate."

"It's the underwear, isn't it? Maybe I should just take it off."

"Drew!"

He chuckled and made a big show of crawling under the covers. "There. Better?"

"Yes." *No!*

She took another drink of water, laid her book on the bedside table, set her glasses on top of it, and switched off the lamp. They were quiet for several minutes before Drew broke the silence.

"Soph?"

"Yeah?"

"In all seriousness, I would never hurt you. You're my best friend, and I want you in my life. Always."

She smiled in the dark, and as if they were one, they reached for each other's hand across the bed. They entwined their fingers as if it were the most natural thing in the world, and Sophia felt an overwhelming sense of peace wash over her. "I feel the same way," she said softly.

They lay like that for some time, until Drew's breathing deepened, and then he turned away from her, breaking their connection.

She stared at his back for a while, watching the covers move up and down in time with his breathing, and she knew he was sleeping. If maintaining their friend status was supposed to protect her, why was there an ache in her chest and an empty space deep inside? And now that they'd stopped pretending to be a couple, how could she go on pretending that she no longer wanted to be?

Chapter 19

After he'd sucked on her breasts, making sure to give each one equal treatment, they made quick work of removing the rest of their clothes. Slivers of light filtered in through the cracks in the blinds, placing the voluptuous curves of her body in stark relief. She reached for him, but he placed a hand on her wrist to stop her.

"I just want to look at you for a minute," he said.

Her nipples were puckered, her lips moist, her gaze soft. He didn't have to touch her to know that she was ready for him. But oh, how he wanted to. She was leaning against her desk, clutching the edges, waiting for him to make his move.

"I've wanted you for so long," he said, stepping toward her.

"The feeling is mutual."

He reached out to finger her curly hair, and she sighed. He loved that she was so responsive to his touch. Moving his hand down, he slowly traced the curve of her neck, the rounded edge of her breast, the indention at her waist.

"Drew. Please."

"I'm getting there," he said, his erection so stiff it was painful. But he wanted to savor this. To savor her.

Continuing his assault, he ran his hand down the outside of her hip, and she shifted, parting her legs slightly in silent invitation. He found the gesture so pure, so honest, so erotic that he couldn't contain himself anymore. He ran his index finger along *the outer folds of her sex, feeling her arch into his hand, seeking his touch.*

Suddenly, she placed her hand atop his and moved it into position, looking down between them at their combined hands.

"Right here?"

"Yes. Please," she added.

He chuckled gruffly, burying his head in her neck and his finger deep inside her at the same time.

"Oh God. Drew." She clutched his shoulders so hard that he was sure to have marks, but he didn't care. Wanted them. Wanted her.

Her body tightened around his finger, and he knew she was close, but then she pulled back and said, "Condom. Now."

He fished out a condom from his pants pocket and hurriedly rolled it on while she watched. When he looked back up, he saw everything he'd wanted to see in her sparkling deep-brown eyes. Longing, attraction, friendship, love. He didn't take the time to question that last thought as he came back in front of her, hoisted her up on the desk, and lined himself up at her entrance.

He was careful at first, gliding in slowly, allowing her to stretch around him.

"Faster," she urged, and that was all it took. He plunged inside, giving her all of him at once in more ways than one. Their hips bucking wildly, he took her mouth in a scorching kiss, sending them even higher until they both cried out with pleasure, bursting with release.

It was everything I've dreamed of and more, *he thought as she clung to him afterwards, neither of them in a hurry to part.*

Wait a minute. What was that sound? Drew shifted in bed and patted the covers beside him. She'd been there a minute ago. What happened? And then he blinked his eyes open and squinted against the bright light. Hearing the sound again, he hoisted himself up on his elbows and realized it was coming from the bathroom. Sophia was taking a shower.

"Shit!" He'd already woken up hard, and now the image of Sophia all wet and soapy on the other side of the wall made him throb. First the dream and now this! Thank God this was their last day and night in Florida together. He wouldn't be able to take much more.

It didn't take much to picture her naked since he'd had a glimpse the other day. Slipping his hand beneath the covers, he took hold of his manhood, wishing that it was her hand instead. He closed his eyes and remembered how it felt to hold her in his arms on the dance floor, their bodies pressed together tighter than was completely necessary.

She could claim that it didn't mean anything, but he knew better. He'd seen the flicker of desire in her eyes when she'd looked up at him, felt her lips part when he'd bent to kiss her. The flush of heat on her neck and…

"Oh. You're up."

Drew froze, stilling his hand beneath the covers. "Yeah. Good morning."

She stood at the end of the bed, wearing two towels—one wrapped around her body, the other in a turban on her head. "I forgot my clothes," she explained.

"I see."

"How'd you sleep?"

"Great. You?"

"Ok. Mia sent me a text this morning asking if we wanted to meet everyone for breakfast. I thought I'd wait and ask you first. Are you up for it?"

Oh, I'm up! "Yeah, sure. If you want to."

"It will be the last time you have to pretend. I promise."

Right! Little does she know I've been pretending for years.

"Oh, and your phone beeped while you were sleeping. It was a text from your mom confirming that we're coming over today. I didn't mean to look, but I happened to be walking by..."

While they'd been talking, his erection had gone down, so now he pushed the covers off and stood up. "Don't worry about it. What time do we have to be down for breakfast?"

"Twenty minutes."

"Why didn't you wake me sooner?" he asked as he rummaged through the dresser drawers for some clothes.

"You looked so peaceful that I hated to disturb you."

"Hmm." *I hope I didn't talk in my sleep.*

"You were mumbling something, but I couldn't make out what you were saying."

Thank God. "I was having a dream."

Her eyes perked up. "Oh yeah? Anything interesting?"

Clothes in hand, he turned to look at her. They were standing close enough that he could smell the berry-scented body wash she'd used. From this angle, he could also see a peek of her cleavage where the towel wasn't quite covering it. "Do you really want to know?"

She swallowed nervously. "Maybe you can tell me later. We're running late."

He couldn't help but smirk at her, recognizing the shyness that came over her at times such as these. "I need to jump in the shower."

"Of course. I can finish getting ready out here. Let me just grab my cosmetics bag and the blow dryer."

He stepped aside so she could pass, and then leaned against the doorjamb, watching her as she gathered her toiletries. "Are you sure you want to do this again?"

"Do what?"

"Pretend in front of your friends. It didn't work out so well last night." Seeing the hurt look on her face, he could have kicked himself. "I mean…"

She waved her hand around dismissively. "It's fine. It'll only be for an hour. What could go wrong?" Averting her eyes, she scooted past him, a waft of her sweet scent floating up as she went.

Minutes later, while he was washing himself, he swore he could still smell her. He vigorously massaged shampoo into his hair and tried thinking about other things, but it was next to impossible. Soon, they'd be having breakfast with her friends, where they'd have to pretend that everything was wonderful between them.

To be believable, he'd have to show her affection, and she'd reciprocate even though nothing more would happen that day and maybe never again. Then they'd go back to being what they'd always been, friends and nothing more. If only he could come up with some way to convince her that he would never hurt her. And he'd have to act soon, or he'd be attending her wedding someday—to someone else.

Chapter 20

"What happened to you two last night?" Mia asked the minute they'd sat down.

Sophia had been hoping that Mia wouldn't bring it up, but she was prepared with her story. "I think the bartender made the drinks too strong. My stomach was upset, so I went back to the room."

"When I went to look for you, I saw Drew in the lobby, and I wanted to ask where you were, but he was busy talking to someone."

Sophia had a feeling she knew what was coming next, and she bristled. "Oh, well, that's Drew. I didn't want to make him stay in the room with me," she said, hoping that would be the end of it. At least Drew was away from the table, loading his plate with seconds at the buffet.

Mia leaned in conspiratorially and whispered, "He was talking to a tall, blonde woman. Savannah, I think her name is."

Jaw clenched, Sophia said, "They know each other."

"Who are you talking about?" Drew asked as he sat down beside her.

"You and Savannah. Mia saw you two talking last night after I went up to the room." She watched as a flicker of guilt passed over his face.

"Oh, right. I passed her on my way out. I went for a drive around the island since Soph wasn't feeling well," he added for Mia's benefit.

Mia studied them curiously and then went back to nibbling on her scrambled eggs. Sophia couldn't tell whether Mia had been looking out for her or if she were secretly pleased about the tension she'd created.

Throughout the rest of the meal, it was like a wall had been erected between Sophia and Drew, and she could barely look at him. If she'd had any doubts about staying in the friend zone, they had just been erased. She couldn't stand the thought of Drew being with Savannah, or any other woman for that matter. Not after they'd kissed, touched, and shared their secret fantasies. Once again, she cursed herself for allowing their game of make believe to get out of hand. What had started out as a simple request was becoming more complicated by the minute. If only she hadn't let herself get carried away.

After breakfast, she hugged her friends goodbye, and the men shook Drew's hand. She saw him exchange business cards with a few of the guys and heard them promising to look each other up when they were back in Michigan. She wouldn't be surprised if it happened. Drew was a man's man as well as a ladies' man. Sophia stood back and watched as Mia hugged him goodbye, pressing her lips against his cheek and leaving a lipstick print behind. *That was probably where he got the lipstick print last night*, she thought, hoping that it hadn't come from Savannah instead. As flirty as Mia was, Sophia didn't believe that she would do anything to hurt her.

The walk outside to the car was icy even though it was a hot, sunny Florida morning. They were leaving straight from breakfast to go to Drew's parents' house in Fort Myers, and up until now, Sophia had been looking forward to it. But once again, she'd have to don her pretend mask, because, inside, she was fraught with mixed emotions.

"Nothing happened with Savannah," he said after they'd pulled out of the parking lot.

"It's none of my business."

He sighed. "Then why are you upset?"

"I'm not."

"You could have fooled me."

"I just didn't like the idea of Mia seeing you with her when you and I are supposed to be..."

"Together?"

"Yes, but now that the wedding's over, we need to get back to being what we truly are—friends."

"Funny. It doesn't feel very *friendly* between us. In fact, it feels like we've just had a lover's quarrel."

Sophia shot him a look and saw his lips twitch like he was holding back a smile. *Damn it! Why can I never stay mad at him for long?* "Well, whatever it is, we need to get past it. I don't want your parents to notice our...tension."

"You mean sexual tension." He phrased it as a statement instead of a question.

"Nobody in this car is having sex!"

"Damn shame too because I bet it would be really good."

"Why do you keep doing that?"

"Doing what?"

"Making things more difficult."

Drew shifted in his seat and had the decency to look contrite. "You're right. Let's just set everything else aside and enjoy our last day together."

Something about the way he'd said, "last day," sounded ominous, but Sophia nodded. "I'm glad you agree."

A short time later, they arrived at Drew's parents' house, which was located in a sprawling community that boasted its own golf course, swimming pool, tennis courts, and event hall. Theirs was a neat Florida-style ranch with a beige stucco exterior and a red-tiled roof. Drew pulled into the circular drive lined with palm trees while Sophia admired the surroundings. Even though she was a proud Michigander, she appreciated southern living, especially the ever-prevalent sunshine, which was often lacking in Michigan. She completely understood why people flocked to warmer climates for the winter months, and she planned to do the same one day.

"This is it," Drew said.

"It's gorgeous."

"Wait until you see the inside."

They were walking up to the front door when Diane and Mark came outside to greet them, looking restful and happy, just like a retired couple should look.

"Oh, sweetheart. I'm so glad you're here," Diane said as she hugged Drew tight and smiled at Sophia over his shoulder.

"And you too," she said, opening her arms to Sophia.

Sophia hadn't realized how much she'd missed Diane and Mark until now. Over the years, they'd become like a second family to her, and when she was a teenager she'd spent just as much time at their house as she had at hers.

"You two look wonderful! Florida agrees with you," Sophia said.

Mark shook his son's hand and then gave Sophia a squeeze. "And you're looking prettier than ever," he said sweetly.

"Come on in. Let me show you around," Diane said excitedly.

Drew was right. The inside of the home was beautiful, filled with comfortable furniture in soft pastel colors and an abundance of windows to let in the light. After a tour of the inside, Diane led them out to the screened-in lanai that boasted a small pool, hot tub, and a cozy seating area with cushioned wicker furniture that would be perfect for reading in. It was completely different from the Kennedy's home in Michigan, but it still had a homey feel.

"Your home is beautiful," Sophia gushed. "I want one just like it some day!"

Diane beamed. "You're welcome to visit anytime, whether we're here or not."

Drew looked at his mother quizzically, which didn't escape Sophia.

"Are you two ready for lunch?" Diane asked.

"Not yet. We just finished breakfast a little while ago," Drew replied.

"How about something to drink? We can sit out here and talk," she suggested.

"Sure. Let me help you," Sophia said.

Diane motioned for the men to have a seat, and then Sophia followed her into the kitchen. "The glasses are in there," Diane said, pointing to one of the cupboards. Diane took a pitcher of lemonade out of the refrigerator and then began assembling a tray of cheese and crackers.

"So, tell me about this wedding that you and Drew went to," she said.

Glad for the reprieve, Sophia told her all about the wedding, minus the part about her and Drew pretending to be a couple.

"Well, it sounds like you two had fun. I know Drew was really looking forward to it."

"Really?" Sophia said. She knew how close he was to his parents and wondered what else he'd told them.

"Um-hum. He thinks the world of you, you know. We all do."

Diane was busy arranging the cheese and crackers and hadn't looked up when she'd said it. Sophia was glad because she felt a prickle of heat crawling up her neck, and she turned away to collect some napkins from the table. *He thinks the world of me? What does that mean exactly?*

"I'm so glad he stopped seeing that Lexie," Diane continued. "I met her once when I was talking to Drew on FaceTime, but I didn't get a good impression."

"She didn't like me very much," Sophia admitted.

"Well, I'm sure she was jealous. She could probably tell how much Drew cares for you."

This time, Diane glanced up, and Sophia met her eyes, bewildered.

"Did I say something wrong?" Diane asked.

Sophia shook her head. "No. It's just that Drew and I are friends. I don't know why someone like Lexie would be jealous of me."

Diane smiled warmly. "Have you looked in a mirror lately? You're a beautiful, intelligent woman with a lot to offer. Drew would be lucky to have you. And vice versa, of course," she added with a wink. "C'mon. Let's serve the men before they get suspicious."

Sophia followed her out to the lanai, carrying the pitcher of lemonade and trying not to spill it given her trembling hands. *Is Diane trying to play matchmaker? Has she done this with Drew too?*

She carefully set down the pitcher and looked around for a seat. Drew was sitting on the loveseat with his arm draped over the back of it, while his parents had taken chairs across from him. There was another empty chair, but Drew patted the cushion next to him like it was only natural that they would sit together. Not wanting to make a scene, she took the seat next to him, and he poured her a glass of lemonade before she even had a chance.

Why am I analyzing everything he does? As friends, he might have done the same thing, but now it felt different. *This is so confusing*, she thought as she accepted the glass from him.

For the next hour or so, the four of them talked, and Sophia relaxed in their familiar company. She got up again to help Diane serve lunch, but this time, Diane didn't make any comments about her and Drew. Sophia began to think that she'd mistaken Diane's intention until they were seated at the dining room table eating lunch.

"You know," Diane said, "the house will be empty for a week in September. Mark and I are going to visit my sister in Arizona. You and Drew are welcome to stay here while we're gone."

Sophia had just taken a bite of her tuna salad sandwich, and now it was stuck in her throat. She sputtered and hurriedly swallowed a drink of lemonade to wash it down while Drew looked on with amusement.

"You ok there, buddy?"

Buddy? Are we back to that? "I'm fine. Took too big of a bite is all," she said frostily.

"It would be a nice getaway for you two. And you can't beat free!" Mark chimed in.

"But we'd have to pay to fly down here," Sophia pointed out.

"We could always drive," Drew said.

Seriously? He's considering it? Just the two of us in this house all alone for an entire week? "I don't know if I can get the time off. September is usually a busy month at the library."

"Couldn't you get your friend Eve to cover for you?" Drew asked.

Sophia gaped at him but then quickly recovered. "I don't know. I'll think about it."

"Well, in any case, you're welcome here anytime," Diane repeated.

After lunch, Drew gave his mom the birthday gift he'd brought, giving Sophia some of the credit for helping him pick it out.

"I love it," she said, holding up the necklace for everyone to see. "Both of you have excellent taste," she added.

They stayed for a while longer, until Drew suggested they leave so they'd have time to do some more sightseeing before dark. Sophia was torn about leaving. She was enjoying the comfort of his parents' home and felt nervous about being alone with him again. But she couldn't stall forever, so after some tearful goodbye hugs from Diane and a few kind words from Mark, they headed back to Sanibel Island.

"What do you want to do tonight?" Drew asked as he sped down the expressway.

Sophia shot him a sideways glance, but his expression was neutral. Maybe he'd ceased flirting with her for the day. "We could take a walk on the beach or go for a swim. What sounds good to you?"

"I'm open," he said. "Whatever you want."

It was a familiar sentiment, but something about the way he said it gave her a rush. "I guess we'll see what happens, then."

"What? No list?"

"Not tonight," she said defiantly.

This time, when she peered over at him, his mouth had turned up in a broad grin. "I like the sound of that," he said.

Chapter 21

"Why do our parents insist on feeding us so much?" Sophia asked as they walked back into their hotel.

"Old habits, I suppose. Why, are you full?"

"I'm stuffed. Let's change and take a walk."

"Good idea."

Sophia went into the bathroom and changed from her skirt and sleeveless top into a pair of shorts and a tank top. When she came out, Drew stood there in his swim trunks and without a shirt, slathering sunscreen on his chest.

"I thought we were going for a walk?"

"We are, but afterwards, I might want to take a swim."

She hadn't wanted to wear her bathing suit until later, but she couldn't tell him why. "I'll just have to come back to the room and change after our walk," she said.

"Do my back?" he asked, holding out the sunscreen.

Oh no. Not this again. But she couldn't very well let him burn. It would ruin her plans for later. "Turn around," she said.

Once again, she reveled in the feel of his skin beneath her fingers as she applied the sunscreen. He bent his head down so she could access his neck and said, "Ahhh. You have magic fingers."

When she'd finished, he turned around and asked, "How about if I get your back too?"

Most of her skin was covered by the tank top and her hair, but she liked the idea of his hands on her. Turning around, she gathered her hair in her hands and exposed her neck and back to him. He took his time rubbing in the lotion, just as she had, and by the time he was done, she'd made up her mind.

I'm not ready for this to end. I'm not ready to give this up—whatever this is between us. As friends, they'd usually reserved their affection for celebrations like birthdays and Christmas, and even then, it was in the form of a chaste kiss on the cheek or a brief hug. But now that she knew what it was like to really kiss him—and to feel his body pressed against hers—she couldn't imagine going back to how it was before.

"There. All set," he said, setting down the sunscreen. Sophia went in search of her flip-flops to give herself a minute to catch her breath.

A few minutes later, they were strolling down the beach, but they weren't holding hands this time. To her knowledge, most of her friends had left for home except for the bride and groom, who were honeymooning on the island. While she enjoyed the sun and the sand and the sound of the waves lapping against the shore, she missed the feel of Drew's hand in hers, and she had to stop herself from reaching for it. *Game's over*, she reminded herself.

They walked along quietly, passing kids splashing in the water and people of all ages collecting shells. Boats bobbed on the water, and pelicans skimmed the surface, looking for their next meal. *What a romantic setting for couples. Too bad we're not one.*

"What did you think about my mom's offer to stay at their house?" Drew asked, breaking the silence.

"It was nice of her, but I don't know."

"Why not?"

They'd stopped, and she gazed up at him. "Do you really think it's a good idea? We've only been in Florida for three days, and look what almost happened."

"Are you afraid you wouldn't be able to resist me?" he teased.

She raised her eyebrows at him, but she had to smile. "That's being a bit cocky."

He reached out and brushed a wayward strand of hair away from her face. "But is it true?"

She didn't have time to respond, because, suddenly, Drew wrapped his arms around her waist and pulled her in. "Kiss me!" he demanded.

"What? Why?"

"Just do it. I'll explain after."

And then his lips descended on hers, full and inviting, parting to invite her tongue. Maybe the sun had addled her brain, or maybe it was his bare chest pressed enticingly against her breasts. Who cared? She looped her arms around his neck and sank into the kiss, oblivious to their surroundings. Too soon, he released her, and when she looked up, she saw the reason for his urgency.

Savannah was strolling toward them in a nude-colored bikini, her blonde hair arranged in a high ponytail, her long, tan legs glimmering in the sun. Drew grabbed Sophia's hand as she approached them.

"The lovebirds are still here, I see," she said in her silky-smooth voice.

"Where's your date?" Drew asked pointedly.

"He's at the bar. We're not attached at the hip like you two are."

Why is she goading us? What's she trying to prove?

"Since this is our last day on the island, we wanted to spend every minute together," Drew said, smiling down at Sophia.

Sophia wasn't prepared to play anymore games, so she just smiled back, deciding to let Drew handle it.

"Well, it was nice seeing you," Savannah said, looking directly at Drew. "You two take care." With that, she sashayed away, and Sophia stared in horror at the back of her.

Once Savannah was out of hearing distance, she said, "A thong? Seriously?"

Drew glanced at Savannah's backside but quickly looked back at Sophia. "She's obviously desperate for attention," he said dismissively.

Sophia stared after her for a few more seconds, amazed at the woman's confidence, and a little jealous if she were being truthful.

Drew finally pulled her away and headed in the opposite direction. "Forget about her. C'mon."

They walked for quite a while before Sophia worked up enough courage to ask him what was on her mind. "What is it about women like that that men find so appealing? Is it just their looks?"

He shrugged and kept his eyes focused straight ahead. "I think there's a certain challenge to it. When there's a woman around who's attracting a lot of attention, every guy in the room wants to be the one she chooses."

"And then after you're chosen, the game's over?"

"Maybe. All I know is that the thrill of the chase isn't quite as *thrilling* as it used to be."

"Hmm," she said, unconvinced.

"I haven't exactly been dating the kind of women I can take home to mom," he admitted.

She glanced up at him, realizing that she might be one of the few women who had actually met his parents and had spent any significant amount of time with them. For some reason, she was filled with a surge of pride. She didn't want to be one of the parade of women in Drew's life who never really meant anything to him.

"So, you're not attracted to Savannah anymore?" When he looked uncomfortable, she backed off. "Never mind. Forget I asked."

"No, it's ok. It's not that I don't find her attractive. It's that I'm learning to look closer. None of the women I've dated in the past have what it takes to go the distance. If you know what I mean."

"It's taken you quite a while to realize that," she said flippantly.

"Gotta grow up sometime, right?"

She was afraid to delve any further, so instead, she suggested they head back to the hotel. Since it was approaching the dinner hour, the pool area wasn't as crowded as it had been when they'd first started out. "You can wait here while I go up to the room and change," she said.

"Need any help?" he teased.

She gave him an eye roll and then walked away. Once she was in the elevator, she exhaled loudly. "Am I really going to do this?" Her heart was in her throat as she changed out of her shorts and tank top and into the leopard-print bikini. She refused to look at her reflection for too long for fear that she'd change her mind. Donning her cover-up, she tied the sash tightly around her waist and made sure that her bikini straps weren't showing.

As she rode the elevator back down, she breathed deeply, attempting to calm her nerves. She knew exactly what she was doing and what the outcome might be, but she couldn't deny what she wanted anymore. If her plan failed, she'd have to suck it up and return to the way things were, but if it succeeded... In either case, this was their last night together, and she wanted to take full advantage of it.

She spotted him immediately, leaned back in a lounge chair with one arm covering his eyes. She slid into the chair beside him, and he instantly removed his arm and cocked one eye open.

"Were you sleeping?" she asked.

"No, just resting."

"Ready to go for a swim?"

"Sure. You?"

"Um-hum," she said, glancing around and noting that there were even fewer people around the pool than before. *Thank God!*

Drew stood up and kicked off his flip-flops before noticing that she still had her cover-up on. "Um, Soph? You gonna take that thing off?"

Now that she had his full attention, she slowly untied the sash of the cover-up and began to take it off. At the first flash of the leopard-print material, Drew sucked in a breath, his eyes going wide. His reaction was better than she'd hoped for, and it gave her the courage to continue. Slipping the cover-up off her shoulders, she finished removing it and laid it on the lounge chair before meeting his eyes.

It felt like minutes had passed before Drew spoke. "Holy..."

"You said that the last time," she teased.

"Yes, but I never thought I'd see this on you again."

"Surprise!"

"How did you sneak it past me?"

"I bought it after you left the store, and the bag was small enough to fit in my purse."

"You amaze me. I never thought you'd buy it."

"Maybe you don't know me as well as you think you do."

"Got any other surprises in store?"

"Maybe," she said and started to walk toward the pool ladder. Drew put his hand out and gripped her wrist, swinging her back around.

"You know what you're doing, right? He glanced down at the front of his swim trunks, which were now bulging.

"I have an idea," she said, smiling sweetly. *Oh God. What am I doing?*

"This isn't about Savannah, is it?"

She shook her head vehemently. "It has nothing to do with her or anyone else but us."

They stared at each other for a few beats until she couldn't take it anymore. "C'mon. Let's go for a swim and cool off."

"Not likely," he muttered as he followed her to the pool ladder. Drew climbed down first and then gallantly offered her a hand. She shivered when the cool water hit her heated skin, or maybe it was because Drew hadn't let go of her yet. "Let's go over here where it's less crowded," he suggested, pulling her toward the deep end of the pool.

Other than a few families in the shallow end, there wasn't anyone else around, and she giggled. "There's hardly anyone here," she said.

"Good thing, because I wouldn't want all the other guys gawking at you."

He sounded possessive, and she liked it. In fact, she was feeling braver by the second. "So, you like my surprise?"

He was leaned back against the edge of the pool, his arms stretched wide, and she was nearby, but they weren't touching. "I believe you saw my reaction," he said drily.

She scooted a little closer. "I'm glad you like it."

"Soph?"

"Hmm?"

"If you're trying to get my attention, you've got it. But is that all you wanted?"

Ok, Soph. It's now or never. Twisting around to face him, she moved right in front of him and looped her arms around his neck. He automatically wrapped one arm around her waist to keep her in place. "I know what we said about not wanting to jeopardize our friendship, but..."

"But what?"

"But I want to be with you, at least for tonight."

He studied her carefully and then said, "If we do this, everything will change."

"But why does it have to change in a bad way? Sometimes, change is good."

"Are you trying to convince me or yourself?"

She looked down for a moment, starting to second-guess herself again.

Placing his index finger beneath her chin, he tipped her head back up. "Make no mistake that I want you, but you need to be sure. Once we cross the line, there's no going back."

"In case you haven't noticed, I'm all grown up, Drew. I know what I want." With that, she leaned forward and kissed him. It was brief, but her intention was clear.

"What happens after?"

"Have we switched roles here? I thought you were the one who likes to play things by ear and I'm the one that plans everything out." She could tell by his smile that she was breaking him down. And just to hammer her point home, she put her mouth by his ear and whispered, "Make love to me, Drew."

It was almost comical how quickly he dragged her out of the pool. They hastily dried off, and she slipped back into her cover-up before he grabbed her hand and led her back into the hotel. If there wouldn't have been a family of four on the elevator, they would have surely had their hands all over each other, but as it was, they were on their best behavior.

She laughed as he rushed her down the hall to their room, and they tumbled inside, Drew kicking the door shut behind him. And then it was just the two of them.

"What do you say we get out of these wet clothes?" he said, his voice husky.

Sophia nodded and started to loosen the tie on her cover up.

"Let me." Drew stepped forward and took over, removing the cover-up and hanging it over the desk chair.

He'd already seen her in the bikini, but here in the room, she felt even more exposed. She started to cross her arms over her midsection, but he gently pushed them away. "Don't cover yourself, Soph. You're beautiful."

There was nothing false about the way he said it, and so she loosened her arms. Then he reached up to untie the strings around her neck, standing so close that she could smell him. If there was ever a time to stop, now was it because, in two seconds, she'd be topless. He halted for a moment, searching her eyes, but she didn't flinch. In the next second, she felt the material fall away from her breasts, and her nipples puckered in the coolness of the air-conditioned room. Or maybe it was from the way he was gazing at them like he was burning the image on his brain. He leaned in and reached around to undo the strings at her back, and then he laid the top over her cover-up. His hands immediately cupped her bare breasts, carefully at first, as if they might break. Looking down at his hands on her, she sighed, and it seemed to break him out of his trance. He brushed his thumbs over her nipples until they were tight with need, and then he bent his head to them.

Sophia's hands threaded into his hair, and she massaged his scalp with her fingertips as he sucked one nipple deep into his mouth and then the other. She arched forward, silently begging him to continue, but he pulled back and trailed a hand down the middle of her stomach. Tracing the edge of her bikini bottoms, he asked, "We good?"

She nodded and gave him a full smile for reassurance.

Returning her smile, he tucked his fingers into the sides of her bottoms and began peeling them down. When he knelt to help her step out of them, she felt self-conscious again because now he was eye-level with her...

Oh God. And now he was licking a path up the inside of her thigh. "Drew. Wait," she said, shattering the quiet.

"What is it? What's wrong?"

Digging her fingers into his shoulders, she said, "I don't want to be the only one naked."

"Well, let's fix that." He came back to standing and started to untie the drawstring on his swim trunks. This was about to become another first—seeing her male best friend naked!

Unlike her, he seemed to have no qualms about ridding himself of his clothes, and the next thing she knew, he was standing there, hands on hips, penis jutting out proudly.

She recalled a conversation she'd had with her girlfriends where some of them had said penises were ugly. Staring at Drew, she begged to differ. Just like the rest of him, she found his penis to be smoking...

"Hot," she said without meaning to and then covered her mouth with her hands.

Drew peeled her hands away and said, "Too late. You already said it."

"I did, didn't I?"

"Uh-huh. You want to touch?"

God, yes. She reached out with both hands and clasped him tightly, liking the feel of his warm, hard shaft in her hands. A bead of arousal glistened at his tip, and she spread it around with her thumb.

"Soph?" he said, low and breathy.

"Yeah?"

"Why don't we get more comfortable?"

She nodded and backed up toward the bed without releasing him.

"I'm not going anywhere," he teased. "You can let go for a minute."

She was discovering that it was easier to feel embarrassed with her best friend than with anyone else. Because he knew her. He knew the *real* her, and she could truly be herself with him. No pretending.

"You just feel so good," she said as they lay back on the bed.

"So do you."

They lay on their sides, facing each other, and Drew had one hand in her hair while the other rested on her hip. "I don't want to rush this," he said.

"We have all night," she whispered.

He pulled her closer and kissed her then, and it was different than any kiss they'd shared before. This time, they weren't putting on a performance or holding back. They took their time, fully exploring each other's mouths, lips, and tongues. Tasting, licking, and nibbling until she was throbbing with need.

Drew had been caressing her back with one hand while his other hand was buried in her thick mane, but now he moved a hand around to her front and skimmed it over her belly.

She parted her legs slightly, anticipating what would happen next, but he continued to tease her, trailing his finger everywhere but where she wanted it. *If he can tease, then so can I*, she thought as she reached between them and wrapped her hand around his erection.

His lips parted as she rubbed her hand up and down his smooth skin while he watched. "Soph?"

"Hmm?"

"Not yet." With that, he rolled away from her and came up on all fours, his head over her midsection. "How do you feel about oral sex?"

Nothing like putting it right out there!

"Because I know that not everyone likes it, and I don't want to assume."

Smirking at him, she said, "Why don't you give it a try, and I'll let you know."

Eyebrows raised, he said, "Ok, then," and he dipped his head between her legs.

Truthfully, she'd never been a big fan, mostly because she was too self-conscious, but as she looked down at him pleasuring her, she changed her tune. Spreading her legs out wider, she arched her hips up, and when he flicked his tongue over her swollen nub, she moaned.

She tried not to think about why he was such an expert at this, and instead, she tilted her head back, buried her hands in his hair, and gave herself over to his masterful manipulations. After a few more minutes, her core tightened, and she ground out, "Drew! I'm going to…"

"Come, beautiful," he said.

And she did, riding out the orgasm that ripped through her until she was depleted, and then she sank back down in the sheets. Drew scrambled off the bed, rooted around in a drawer, and came up with a condom, which he quickly sheathed himself with.

While he knelt on the bed, she propped herself up on her elbows and asked, "How do you want me?"

Eyes blazing, he said, "You mean what position?"

She nodded. "Whatever you like the best, within reason," she added because there were some places she wasn't willing to go!

Chuckling, Drew rolled over on his back and motioned for her to straddle him. "I want to watch you ride me," he said.

Talking with him this way turned her on almost as much as touching him. It felt so intimate, so private, so new and exciting. Positioning herself over him, she rubbed his tip across her entrance a few times, and then, leaning up, she slowly began to lower herself down.

He watched, eyes hooded, and reached for her breasts at the same time. If there was one thing she was sure of, it was that she was a good student. She'd always done well in school, which she accredited partly to her good listening skills and partly to her powers of observation. Studying Drew right then, she adjusted her movements based on his reactions, and when she sensed him getting close, she clamped around him, increasing her rhythm until he shuddered inside her and then stilled.

Shortly after, she rolled off him and snuggled into his side, warm and sated. With her hand on his chest, she felt his heart pounding, and she smiled even though he couldn't see her. She wanted to get up and do a happy dance, but instead, she said, "We did it!"

Drew chuckled and gave her a squeeze. "Yes, we did."

And then he went quiet, and she wondered, *Now what?*

Chapter 22

"Are you hungry?" he asked.

"I could eat."

"What do you feel like?"

Drew à la mode! "I'm not sure. What sounds good to you?"

"You drizzled in chocolate."

Leaning up on her elbows, she looked down at him. It was dark now, although in their hurry to get naked, they'd left the curtains open, so some light filtered in. "I'd like that too."

He smirked. "My librarian has a wild side."

She shrugged. "Maybe a little."

"I have an idea, but I think we should eat first. We need to keep our energy up."

"Why don't we just grab something in the hotel restaurant so we don't have to drive anywhere?"

"Ms. Russo, are you anxious to get me back in bed?"

She pushed herself off the bed and padded naked to the dresser. Funny how just yesterday she'd made sure to keep covered up. She felt his eyes boring into her back as she took her time selecting a fresh set of clothes. Now that they'd been intimate, she felt like she had nothing to hide from him, and she liked the freedom of it.

"Perhaps," she teased, turning around.

Drew was sitting on the edge of the bed, watching her every move. Once she was dressed, she said, "Um, you might want to get dressed too."

"Oh. Right."

She giggled as he waltzed by her in all his handsome glory. They took turns using the bathroom, and Sophia attempted to smooth out her hair, but it didn't want to cooperate. Most of her makeup had come off during their romp in the sheets, but she didn't mind. Surveying herself in the mirror, she decided she looked deliciously rumpled—and a bit starry-eyed.

When they left the room a few minutes later, Drew reached for her hand and smiled sweetly at her as he entwined their fingers together.

Nobody was in the elevator on their way down, and he pulled her close and kissed her like they hadn't just been going at it a few minutes before. He released her right when the doors started opening, and they floated out into the lobby. Well, at least that was what it felt like to her. There seemed to be none of the after-sex awkwardness that she'd experienced before and that she'd worried might happen to them. Drew looked just as satisfied as she felt when they walked into the restaurant and requested a table.

Once they sat down, she realized how hungry she was, and apparently, he was too. They started out with an appetizer sampler platter and then ordered separate entrées and even split dessert—vanilla ice cream drizzled with chocolate sauce. Drew dug his spoon into the ice cream and reached across the table to give her the first bite. Eyes sparkling, she slowly licked it off the spoon and then ran her tongue over her moist lips. His gaze grew heated, and then they hurriedly finished the rest of the ice cream and asked for the check.

"I'm going to run to the restroom. Be right back," she said.

"Don't be long."

"I won't." She glanced over her shoulder as she walked away, and sure enough, he was watching her, his eyes trained on her behind. *Ha! Savannah isn't the only one who can catch a man's eye!*

Seconds later, her good mood deflated when she stepped into the restroom and saw the devil-woman herself standing there. *Not again.* "Hello, Savannah," she said, determined not to let the woman get to her this time.

"Hello. Sorry—what was your name again?"

Sophia wanted to wipe the smug look right off her face, but she clenched her fists by her side and answered, "Sophia."

"Oh, right. How are things going with Drew?" Savannah asked while giving Sophia a once-over.

Naturally, Savannah looked impeccable in her off-the-shoulder dress and heels, every hair on her head perfectly in place. Sophia didn't have to look in the mirror to know that she looked like a sorry mess in comparison since they'd just rolled out of bed and come downstairs. Strangely, the thought gave her a boost, and staring her competition directly in the eyes, she said, "Wonderful. Thanks for asking."

She started to go into a stall, but Savannah wasn't finished. "Of course it's wonderful now. It's brand new. Just wait a few weeks, and then he'll get tired of you just like he always does."

Shoving her hands on her hips, Sophia growled, "What makes you the expert on Drew's behavior?"

Savannah's mouth lifted in a sneer. "Because a couple of my friends had a ride on him too. None of us lasted more than a month."

Sophia's mouth dropped open. *A couple of her friends? Seriously?*

"It's true. Ask him. Well, I should get going. My date is waiting. Have a nice night, Sonia." With that, Savannah flounced out of the restroom, the door banging loudly behind her.

Never mind that Savannah had purposely called her by the wrong name, Sophia was flabbergasted. She knew that Drew had dated a lot of women, but to be confronted with it face to face just after they'd made love... Leaning over the sink, she stared at her reflection in the mirror. *Now my name is on his list of conquests too. Oh my God. What have I done?*

Realizing that she'd already been gone for a long time, Sophia quickly used the facilities, washed her hands, and left. When she walked out, Drew was standing there waiting for her, a concerned expression on his face.

"You ok?" he asked.

She nodded but averted her eyes. "Let's go back to the room. I think we need to talk."

Drew didn't look surprised. He simply placed his hand gently on the small of her back and led her to the elevator. This time, two other couples got on too, so Sophia was saved from having to talk to him. Instead, she used the reprieve to gather her thoughts and decide how to proceed.

They remained silent as they walked down the long hall to their room, but the minute they stepped inside, they both started talking at once.

"I saw Savannah—"

"Savannah said—"

"Let's sit down," Drew suggested. He started toward the bed, but Sophia stopped him.

"No. Let's sit on the balcony."

He nodded and followed her outside.

"What did she say to you this time?" he asked, sounding tired and frustrated.

"Only that she and a few of her friends had a go at you." She let the words sink in for a second as she sat with her hands tightly clasped together.

Drew hung his head. "That's a bit of an exaggeration. She was just trying to get your goat."

Her heart was pounding almost as hard as it had been when they'd been making love earlier, but now it was for an entirely different reason. "Drew. I don't know if I can do this."

His head snapped up. "Do what?"

"Do this—us. I don't want to end up like Savannah and Lexie, rejected and bitter, telling everyone my sob story of how you dumped me after a month."

He flung himself out of the chair and faced her. "You're nothing like them. They don't mean anything to me."

"But I do?"

"Yes, damn it! You've been in my life for years. Why do you think that is?"

"Because we were friends. Because we never crossed the line."

"No. There's more to it than that."

She shook her head sadly. "How can I believe you?"

"I've never lied to you, Sophia. Never."

"Why should I think it will be any different with me? Huh?"

Drew knelt before her, and placing his hands on her knees, he forced her to look at him. "Because you are different. You're special. I told you that I wouldn't hurt you, and I won't."

She went silent, warring with herself over whether to trust him. He searched her eyes, waiting patiently for her response. Part of her wanted to reach out and touch him, kiss him, lead him back to bed, but the other part, the sensible part, resisted. Finally, she said, "I can't think straight right now. I need some time."

Looking relieved, he sighed. "Thank you," he whispered.

She wasn't sure what he was thanking her for. In fact, she wasn't sure of anything just then. Her mind was whirling, and it was all too much. "Drew?"

"Yeah?"

"I think it's time to go to bed. To sleep."

"Ok." He stood up and offered his hand to her.

She took it, but it didn't comfort her as it had earlier. Before dinner. Before Savannah.

The air was stiff now. Awkward. He was polite yet distant, letting her use the bathroom first and changing out of sight. When she came back out in her polka-dot pajamas, he was already under the covers.

"Would you rather I sleep on the floor?" he asked as she climbed in on her side.

"No. That's ridiculous."

"Just checking."

They lay in the dark for a while, neither of them tired enough to sleep, each lost in their own thoughts.

"Sophia?"

"Yes?"

"I just want to say that no matter what you decide, I'll always be your friend. I don't ever want to lose that."

His voice was shaky, and her eyes welled with tears. Swallowing hard, she said, "Drew? Will you just hold me?"

"I'd love to," he said. Scooting together, they met in the middle, and she nestled against him, resting her head on his chest. She noticed he'd left his shirt on this time, and it made her feel even more conflicted. Just a short time ago, they'd been naked in each other's arms, exploring and loving each other.

Wait a minute. Love? Friendship? I'm so confused.

They lay like that for a long time, afraid to say anything more, aware of the tightrope between them, until finally, in the wee hours of the morning, they fell asleep.

The discomfort was still present the next morning as they sidestepped each other while they packed up and prepared to leave.

"We didn't leave enough time for breakfast," he said as he zipped up his suitcase.

"We can just grab something at the airport," she replied.

Walking out of the hotel with him felt bittersweet compared to when they'd first arrived there. She'd been looking forward to spending a weekend with him and had wondered if their make-believe relationship would turn into something real. Now they barely spoke unless they had to, and as they drove away, Sophia stared forlornly out the window.

It was a short drive to the airport, and then there was the usual chaos as they checked in and walked down to their gate. They stopped at a bagel shop to get something for breakfast and ate in silence. When Drew's cell phone rang, he glanced down at it and said, "I need to take this. Work." He walked away from the table, and she watched him standing among the throngs of people hustling around him to get where they needed to be.

Sighing, she finished her bagel and juice and continued the debate that had been swirling around in her brain since last night. On one hand, what they'd shared had been wonderful, and she'd never felt closer to him. But then when she'd been faced with reality, she'd realized that she might have just made the biggest mistake of her life. It was like the adage: "Be careful what you wish for." She'd wanted to make love with Drew, had dreamed about it repeatedly over the years, and as she'd expected, he'd been the perfect lover bent on treating her right. But what about outside of the bedroom? What did she think would happen next? That he'd profess his undying love for her and carry her off into the sunset. Hardly! She'd been a romantic fool, and she was angrier at herself than at him. Besides, it was hardly fair to chastise him for his past. He was an eligible bachelor with no commitments. His love life was none of her concern, or at least it didn't used to be. Now she felt differently, and she hated the thought of him having been with so many women. Hated the idea of ending up just like the rest of them.

"Sorry about that," Drew said when he returned to their table.

"No problem," she said, flapping her hand dismissively.

"Vacation's over. It's back to business as usual."

Don't I know it!

Once they were seated on the plane, she immediately pulled out her book on Hamilton and let herself get swept up in the story. According to the author's description, Alexander had been a handsome, charismatic man who'd commanded attention whenever he'd walked into a room, from women and men alike. *Just like Drew.* But of all the women who wanted him, Eliza was the one who'd captured his heart and held it. *Could I be Drew's Eliza?*

Beside her, Drew flipped through a sports magazine, but every so often, he'd glance over and catch her eye. She was dying to know what was going on inside his head, but she didn't dare bring it up there on a crowded airplane. It seemed like he was waiting for her to say something, following her lead. But where did she want them to go? Back to being friends? Was that even possible?

One of the things she liked best about visiting Florida was how short the flight was to and from Detroit. After reading for most of the flight and partaking of the complimentary drinks and snacks, the pilot announced their descent into Metro Airport. And then came the scurry through the airport to retrieve their luggage, followed by the shuttle bus ride to the parking area. Before long, they were on the expressway, heading for home.

Sophia put on the radio to fill the empty space and concentrated on driving while Drew bent over his phone and returned some work calls. What a difference from when they'd driven down to the airport a few days ago. Then she'd been filled with excitement and anticipation. Now she was filled with dread.

When she pulled into his driveway, she popped open the trunk, expecting him to hurry and get out of the car. But instead, he turned toward her, and with a serious expression, he said, "I'd still like to meet you for our weekly dinner if you want to."

He looked so sweet and sad that she almost jumped over the console and into his lap. "Ok," she replied because she couldn't stomach the thought of not seeing him anymore.

"Good. Whose turn is it to pick the restaurant?"

"I'm not sure."

"I'll let you pick. Just let me know which day works best for you."

"Ok," she repeated.

"Soph?"

"Yeah?"

"I had a really good time this weekend, and I'm sorry about the way it ended."

"Me too," she said.

"Well. I guess I should go. Thanks for everything."

Before she knew it, he'd leaned forward and swiftly kissed her cheek before opening the car door and hopping out. She watched him walk up to the door with his suitcase and dig his keys out of his jeans pocket. Once he had the door open, he turned around and waved, shooting her a hopeful smile. She returned the wave but not the smile and backed out of the drive.

Originally, she'd planned to go straight home, but suddenly, she realized that she didn't want to be alone. Spotting her mom's car in the driveway two doors down, she pulled in and got out. Her mom, Lynda, didn't work and hadn't ever since she'd had kids. She'd embraced her role as wife and mother and prided herself on keeping a smooth-running household. Now she filled her time with quilting club, book club, golf, and volunteering at the senior center, and she seemed just as happy. There were very few people who knew Sophia as well as her mom did, and right then, Sophia really wanted her advice.

She gave a brief knock and then stepped inside. "Mom?"

"In the kitchen," Lynda called.

"Hey," Sophia said, setting down her purse and giving her mom a hug.

"Hi, honey. I didn't expect to see you today. How was your trip?"

And the floodgates opened.

"Oh no. What happened?" Lynda rubbed Sophia's back just like she used to do years ago when she'd had her feelings hurt on the playground.

Sniffling, Sophia replied, "It's Drew. Well, not just Drew. It's me and Drew."

"Come and sit down," Lynda said, leading Sophia to the kitchen table.

Sophia took a napkin out of the napkin holder that read *Home Sweet Home* and blew her nose loudly. And then she proceeded to give her mom a synopsis of what had happened, substituting the word "intimate" for "sex."

Her mom listened closely and patted Sophia's hand where it rested on the table. "I always hoped that you and Drew would get together."

"Really?"

Lynda nodded. "Diane and I used to talk about it all the time when you were growing up. With how close we all are, we thought it'd be neat if you two ended up together. Why do you look so surprised?"

"I guess I never knew that. You never said anything."

"Because I didn't want to meddle. I wanted to let you kids make your own decisions. I figured if it was meant to be, it would happen."

"But now what? Why do I feel so miserable?"

Lynda chuckled. "Love is a tricky business. It doesn't always feel good even when it's right."

"Love?"

Lynda raised her eyebrows. "You've loved that boy ever since high school. You just never called it that."

"Loved him as a friend maybe..."

"Sophia. Do you remember the night of Drew's senior prom? You sat and watched him and his date out the window while they had their pictures taken in the front yard."

"Yeah. So?"

"You were heartbroken, wishing that he had asked you instead. You moped around here the rest of the night, and even your favorite meal couldn't make you happy."

Sophia had to laugh because it was well-documented that she liked to eat! "I remember," she said.

"And then, through the college years, when you and Drew were home visiting and we'd all get together. Sometimes, he'd have a date with him, and you walked around like you'd just sucked on a lemon."

"Ok, ok. I get it!" Sophia said, throwing her hands in the air.

"Sometimes, it's hard to see what's right in front of you," Lynda said. "And in Drew's case, sometimes, it takes a while to grow up."

"But what do I do now?"

"You trust your heart."

But can I trust his?

Chapter 23

The week after they returned from Florida felt like the longest week of Drew's life. Even though he had plenty of work to do, his thoughts kept drifting to Sophia and everything that had happened between them. He checked his phone dozens of times each day, hoping that she'd text or call to set up their next dinner date.

Date? Really? He used to think of them as friendly get-togethers, but now he thought of them as dates because that's what he wanted them to be. It was getting easier and easier to admit that to himself, and it confounded and exhilarated him at the same time. He'd never been so excited to have dinner with a woman before. And that was probably all it would be—dinner. After the way they'd left things, it might never be anything more.

"Damn it!" he shouted, thankful that the walls of his house were so thick. *There must be some way to prove that she can trust me. That she can take a chance on me.*

He understood her concerns, but he didn't want to be that guy anymore. He wanted to be worthy of Sophia's time and affection. He wanted to be a man that she could be proud of. Someone she could count on. Someone who wouldn't fail her. But if she wouldn't let him get close to her, how could he convince her?

On Thursday night, he sat on a barstool at his kitchen counter with a pen and a notepad. He'd had to scrounge around for the paper because he'd never been one to write lists. "I keep lists in my head," he'd explained to Sophia more than once. The queen of lists. It was just one of the quirks that he found endearing about her.

"Ok, let's see." He tapped the pen on the blank notepad a few times and then started to write. At the top of the page, he wrote: *HOW TO WIN HER BACK*. It took a while, but in the end, he had a list of ten ideas to get her back in his good graces. There was no guarantee that they'd work, but he'd give it his best effort because the bottom line was that he wanted her in his life for more than just an occasional dinner. Before Florida, they hadn't spent that many consecutive hours together since they'd been in high school.

His thoughts drifted to one summer a long time ago when their parents had decided to take a trip together to Mackinac Island. They'd loaded up two cars (since Sophia's was a family of five) and headed Up North for a few days. Sophia hadn't wanted to sit in the cramped backseat with her brother and sister, so she'd ridden with him instead. They'd laughed, talked, and eaten snacks during the four-hour drive, and the time had passed quickly.

Drew had been between girlfriends at the time, and Sophia had also been free, although, for the life of him, he couldn't understand why. She was so pretty, and smart, and sweet. He'd expected her to be fighting off the guys in school. All he could figure was that her shyness held her back, yet she seemed completely relaxed around him. At the time, he remembered thinking, *Lucky for me*, even though he'd had no intention of making a move on her.

It wasn't that he saw her as a sister. It was more that he thought she was too good for him. He'd put her on a pedestal of sorts, and he didn't want to soil her. He'd wanted to keep her up there where he could admire her without hurting her. It was kind of like guys who were into classic cars. They took good care of them, washing and waxing them on a regular basis, but they hardly ever drove them. They strove to keep the cars in pristine condition rather than expose them to the hazards of the road. But whenever they wanted to, they could open the garage door and admire the beauty before them. He'd felt the same about Sophia at the time, and he'd accepted it for what it was—a crush on the girl next door.

That weekend in Mackinac Island, they'd had a blast together, doing the things that teenagers do (within reason since their parents were there). One day, they'd rented bikes and ridden them around the perimeter of the island. He and Sophia had ridden ahead on a bicycle built for two, and they'd laughed hysterically as they'd attempted to keep the bike upright. Another time, they'd gone swimming at the beach and had swum out a little too far, where the water was over Sophia's head. Drew had given her a piggy-back ride back to shore, and he remembered the feel of her sweet curves pressed against his back.

Thinking about her sweet curves made him squirm because now he knew what it felt like to caress them, kiss them, lick them. He closed his eyes and remembered the way she'd responded to his touch, so warm and open, trusting. Popping his eyes open, he realized how much he wanted that again. And it wasn't just the sex. It was the way she'd looked up at him with adoring eyes and a sweet smile. How she'd shared her fantasies with him, let him into her secret world. How she'd clung to him on the dance floor in her silky purple dress, easily the most beautiful woman in the room. And don't even get him started about the way she'd looked in the leopard-print bikini. It made him sweat just thinking about it.

Savannah and Lexie didn't hold a candle to his Sophia. *My Sophia? Not really. But I'd like her to be.* Tapping his pen against the list again, he read it over. "This better work. It has to."

And then, as if he'd willed it to happen, his phone rang. Glancing down at the screen, his heart skipped a beat, and he quickly answered. "Hey," he said, hoping he sounded casual enough.

"Hey."

"How's it going?" *Real original, dumbass!*

"Ok. I was calling about dinner."

Thank God. "What did you decide?"

"I'm kind of booked up this weekend."

"Oh," he said, not bothering to hide his disappointment.

"My boss is on vacation, and one of the other librarians had to have emergency surgery, so we're short-handed. I'm going to be working until closing time all weekend."

"Well, what about next week? My schedule is pretty open." *And if it's not, I'll clear it.*

"Sure."

He glanced down at his list and read what he'd written next to number one. "How about if I cook for us?"

"Really?"

"Why do you sound so surprised? I've cooked for us before."

"Sure, if you count heating up water for noodles." She giggled, and to him, it was the sweetest sound.

"Laugh all you want, but I'm a good cook when I put my mind to it. Let me do this for you."

"Ok. If you insist."

"I do. What night is good?"

"How about Monday?"

"That works."

"Ok. I'll see you then."

"Looking forward to it," he said, and when they hung up, he didn't have to look in the mirror to know that he had the sappiest smile on his face.

"Man, you are so screwed!" *Now, to find a recipe guaranteed to win her heart…*

Chapter 24

"Wow! This is delicious," Sophia exclaimed.

"Thanks, but some of the credit belongs to my mom. It's her recipe."

"Well, I'll have to let her know the next time I see her."

Drew had made them chicken parmesan and a tossed salad, and he'd even served an expensive brand of red wine. When she'd arrived for dinner, he'd had it all prepared, with the table set and everything. With June approaching, it had been nice enough to eat outside on the deck overlooking the lake. It wasn't quite boating season yet, so the lake had been quiet, just the way Sophia liked it—calm and peaceful. Too bad her emotions didn't match the setting.

While she was impressed that Drew had gone to all this trouble, she'd questioned his motives. If he thought that food would get her back into his bed, he was going to be sorely disappointed. Although this meal was particularly scrumptious...

"So, how was your work week?" Drew asked as he dished them each another helping of salad.

"Chaotic for the library. In addition to being short-handed, we got a large shipment of new books that had to be catalogued and shelved. And we're putting together the summer schedule for book club meetings and story time."

"Sounds hectic."

"It was, but I don't mind being busy. How about you? What was your week like?"

"Same, although it was hard getting back in the groove after being in Florida."

Her head shot up just as she had been transferring a forkful of lettuce to her mouth. One of the lettuce leaves fell right on the front of her blouse, leaving an oily streak of Italian dressing behind. Drew jumped up to get her a wet cloth, but she knew it wouldn't help.

"I'll throw it in the washer as soon as I get home," she said.

"Or you could wash it here."

Her eyebrows lifted suspiciously, but he quickly covered his tracks.

"Obviously, I would loan you one of my shirts until yours is dry."

"Thanks, but..." She didn't bother finishing her sentence because Drew had already gone inside. A minute later, he returned with a t-shirt that she recognized from long ago.

"Here. You can go change while I clean up."

She took the shirt from him because it would have seemed ridiculous not to, but she sat and stared at it for a few seconds.

"What's wrong? Don't like the color?" he teased.

She shook her head. "It's not that. I was just wondering if this is the t-shirt you bought when we were on Mackinac Island. Our families, that is."

He nodded. "Yep. It still fits, so I kept it."

"That was a fun trip, wasn't it?"

"Um-hum. One of my favorites."

"Really? Out of all the places you've been, you'd rank Mackinac Island as one of the best?"

He smiled wide and started stacking their plates. "Of course."

"Why?"

"Because I was there with one of my favorite people." He glanced up from gathering the dishes and made eye contact with her, and she felt her blood heat.

"I better get this in the wash," she said. She quickly stood up and went into the house before he noticed her flushed cheeks. Using the first-floor bathroom, she changed out of her soiled blouse and into the soft blue t-shirt he'd given her. It was too long on her, but she liked the feel of it against her skin, and she could smell him on the fabric. Noticing her red cheeks in the mirror, she turned on the faucet and splashed some cold water on her face to cool off.

How stupid! It's just a shirt! Being familiar with the house, she went into the laundry room, treated the stain, and put her blouse in the washer. When she came back out, Drew was standing in the kitchen, waiting for her. The way he perused her in his shirt, you have thought she'd been wearing the leopard print bikini again.

"It's a little big on me," she said, stating the obvious.

"I think it looks great on you."

Ok, first dinner, now compliments. What's next?

"What would you like to do now?" he asked.

It sounded innocent enough but for the slight smirk at the corners of his lips.

She shrugged. "We could watch TV, but just until my shirt's dry, and then I'll have to leave."

Nodding, he led them into the living room and plopped down on the couch. After he'd bought the house from his parents, he'd swapped out most of the furniture. Oversized brown suede furniture had replaced the floral print couches and chairs, and chunky oak pieces had taken the place of the more delicate furniture his parents had owned. The only feminine touch in the room came from a colorful crocheted blanket that his mom had obviously made. Still, Sophia found the place warm and inviting, just as she always had.

Not wanting to make things more awkward than they already were, she decided to sit on the couch too, though she kept a respectable distance between them.

"Ok, let's see what's on," he said as he fired up the big screen. After flicking through the channels, he paused on a rerun of *Friends*. "Remember when we used to love this show?"

"I still do," she said. "Let's watch it."

It happened to be the episode where Ross and Rachel make love for the first time, and while it was sweet and funny, it hit a little too close to home. Sophia kept peeking over at Drew to gauge his reaction, but he seemed intent on the screen, and if he noticed her looking, he didn't acknowledge it. Right when the characters were sharing a deep kiss, the buzzer rang on the washing machine, and Sophia jumped up.

"Just wait until this is over. It'll only be a few more minutes," he said, motioning for her to sit back down.

Watching the scene made her think about the first real kiss she'd shared with him and how magical it felt. Which led her to back to the night they'd made love and how it had exceeded all her expectations. She crossed her legs tightly and waited for the episode to end so she'd have a good excuse to leave the room. Being alone with him and watching a show that brought back all the feels made the air feel charged and a bit dangerous.

It would be so easy to tumble back into bed with him, but she wanted more than that. She wouldn't be so willing this time!

The minute the show ended, she stood up and left the room to put her shirt in the dryer. When she returned, Drew had turned off the television and was just sitting there, arms casually draped across the back of the couch, waiting. An image of a long-limbed spider sitting patiently in the middle of its web sprang to mind, and she shook her head to clear it.

"Something wrong?" he asked, eyeing her closely.

"No. Everything's fine. Good. Everything's good." She always repeated herself whenever she was nervous.

"I have a favor to ask you," he said.

Curious, she replied, "What kind of favor?"

"Well, it's kind of like the favor I just did for you."

Chest constricting, she said, "You mean pretending to be a couple?"

"Not exactly. My boss invited all the salespeople in my group to his house for dinner next Saturday night. The thing is, everyone will be bringing dates except for me. I thought, or hoped, maybe…"

But she was already shaking her head. "I don't think so, Drew."

"Why not?"

Clenching her hands in her lap, she said, "If we're trying to go back to being friends, I don't think it's a good idea to go out on a formal date."

"But it's not a formal date. It'll just be a group of us sitting around drinking, eating, and talking. We wouldn't even have to stay that long."

Tilting her head, she studied him for a few seconds while she considered it.

"I promise not to treat you as my date. I'll even introduce you as my friend if that's what you want."

Is that what I want? Honestly? "Why me? You've never had trouble getting a date before." After she'd said it, she realized how snide she'd sounded and wished she could take it back.

"But I don't want to go with just anyone. I'd rather go with someone I...care about."

This would be another first for them—she'd never met any of his co-workers. "Drew..."

"Ok. Never mind. Just thought I'd ask."

"I was going to say ok."

He perked up instantly. "Ok?"

"Ok."

"Great! Just out of curiosity, what made you change your mind?"

"After everything you did for me, it's only fair that I return the favor."

He nodded, although he looked somewhat disappointed with her answer. And then she realized that not only had he attended the wedding with her, but he'd made a real effort to get to know her friends. He'd not only shown up, but he'd enjoyed himself, and as his friend, she could certainly try to do the same.

"I'd like to meet your co-workers. It'll be fun," she added.

He smiled then, the first genuine smile he'd given her all evening, and it warmed her insides.

"Thanks, Soph. I really appreciate it."

And then the buzzer rang on the dryer, marking the end to their evening.

"I'll just change back into my blouse, and then I'll take off," she said as she stood up.

Drew stood too and took a step closer. "Just wear my shirt home. You can give it back the next time I see you."

"Are you sure?"

He laughed. "I know where you live. If I want it back, I'll come over and get it."

You can say that again! Staring up into his gorgeous blue-gray eyes, she fought the urge to reach out and touch him. He was so close that she smelled his body wash, the same manly scent he'd used in Florida.

"Ok, thanks. I'll give it to you next weekend."

Only when he smiled so big that all his teeth showed did she realize how that had sounded.

"Your shirt! I'll give you back your shirt next weekend!"

"No worries, Soph. Whenever you're ready."

At this rate, she'd be ready long before next weekend! She hurried out of the room to take her blouse out of the dryer, and when she returned, he was standing there with her purse in hand.

"I'll walk you out."

"You don't have to."

"What if I want to?"

She was too flustered to argue. "Ok."

He walked her out to the car and opened the door for her. *Has he ever done this before? Is he playing the part of the perfect gentleman for my benefit?*

She slid inside and laid her purse and blouse on the passenger seat. "Thanks a lot for dinner. It really was delicious."

"You're not just saying that to make me feel good, right?"

Why did their conversations suddenly feel so loaded? She shook her head. "I mean it."

"Drive carefully," he said, gently shutting the door. He stood in the driveway and watched her leave, and it wasn't until she was safely out of sight that she exhaled loudly.

Was it going to be like this from now on? Every time they got together, was she going to have to fight the urge to kiss him, touch him? "That's what you get for crossing the line," she said. Instead of satisfying her curiosity, being with him had only made her want him more. And if she wasn't mistaken, the feeling was mutual.

"Let me get this straight. You had sex with him, and then you decided to go back to being friends, and now you're going on a date with him next weekend, where you may or may not have to pretend to be his girlfriend." Eve stared at her across the desk and shook her head incredulously. "This is getting more messed up by the minute! I don't know how you can keep it all straight."

They were eating deli sandwiches on their lunch break in Sophia's office, and Sophia had just brought her friend up to speed on the latest happening in the "Drew drama," as Eve had labelled it.

"He said he would introduce me as his friend so we won't have to pretend this time."

"Well, that makes it all better!" Eve said before taking a gigantic bite out of her tuna on rye. Sophia was amazed that her friend could stay so trim with the way she ate. She tackled every meal like it was her last, yet she wore a size two! "Fast metabolism," Eve had claimed. Sophia was somewhat envious, as it seemed like every morsel of food she ate went straight to her hips, adding to her curvy figure. Although Drew hadn't seemed to mind...

"Yoo-hoo, Sophia? Where'd you go?" Eve said, waving her hand in front of Sophia's face.

"Sorry. Just thinking."

"Well, do that on your own time. Right now, we need to discuss when you're going to have sex with Drew again."

"What? I'm not going to have sex with Drew again."

"Repeat that with a little more conviction this time," Eve teased.

"This is ridiculous."

"You're right. It is ridiculous that you went from pretending to be a couple to actually being a couple to pretending to be friends again. Why don't you go back to what you really want to be? Drew's girlfriend. His main squeeze. His one and only."

"That's just it. Drew doesn't have girlfriends. He has women who have sex with him until he gets tired of them and moves on to the next one."

"So what? You're going to keep meeting him for dinner once a week, attending social functions with him, and pretending that you don't want to see him naked again?"

Sophia nodded. "Essentially. Yes."

Eve glanced down at her watch and stood up to leave, shoving her empty sandwich wrapper in the bag. "If only I had the problems that you do!" she said before turning and walking out.

Chapter 25

"Question."

"Answer."

"What should I wear tonight?" Sophia had been standing in front of her closet for a half an hour, perusing her wardrobe options and trying things on, until she'd gotten so exasperated that she'd decided to call Drew for advice. Standing there in her bra and underwear while talking to him on the phone might have been a bad choice. The minute she'd heard his voice, her nipples had risen to attention.

He chuckled, which caused another of her lady parts to twitch. "It's just dinner, Soph. Wear whatever's comfortable."

She glanced at the preponderance of jeans and sweatshirts in her closet and shook her head. "I can't do that."

"Why not?"

"Because I'll look like I'm going to a football game instead of to your boss's house for dinner."

He laughed again, and this time, she squeezed her legs together. "What about a casual dress?"

"Is there really such a thing? Because, if there is, I've yet to find one that feels as comfortable as my boyfriend jeans."

"Boyfriend jeans?"

"Yeah. Haven't you heard the phrase?"

"Can't say that I have. What are they?"

"They're jeans that have plenty of stretch for curvy girls like me who don't like the term 'skinny jeans.'"

Drew sounded like he was truly enjoying this, while she was standing there frustrated and cold. "Why don't you wear your boyfriend jeans with a nicer top and a pair of heels?"

Eyes wide, she said, "Have you been reading *Glamour* magazine recently?"

"I might have flipped through it at the dentist's office last week."

This time, she laughed—a full-out, loud guffaw (she'd always liked the word guffaw even though it was difficult to work it into sentences).

After she'd calmed down, she said, "You know what? That's not bad advice. I'll see what I can scrounge up."

"I'm sure whatever you choose, you'll look stunning."

"Smooth operator."

"I mean it, Soph. I've always thought you were beautiful."

Ok, then. Now what do I say?

"Anyway, I'll be over in a half an hour to pick you up, so make sure you're ready."

"All I have left to do is get dressed. My hair and makeup are already done."

Drew cleared his throat loudly. "You mean you're naked right now?"

Looking down at her bra and underwear, she replied, "Not exactly."

"You're in a towel?"

"No."

"How many more guesses do I get?"

She giggled and decided to put him out of his misery. "I'm in my bra and panties." Why did that sound so provocative compared to the word underwear?

He was quiet for a few beats. "What color?"

"Does it matter?"

"Just curious."

"Black."

"Practical yet sexy."

"That's me. I mean...wait a minute..."

Drew laughed. "Just hurry up and get dressed. I'll see you in a few." With that, he hung up, and she was left staring at the phone. She didn't have long to feel embarrassed, as she wanted to be fully clothed when he arrived. Talking about being in her underwear was one thing, but actually being in it would be asking for trouble!

She pulled on her favorite pair of boyfriend jeans and a short-sleeved red sweater. Next, she added a rose gold heart necklace and matching earrings for a touch of shimmer. Then she rummaged through the shoeboxes on the closet floor until she found the red heels that her sister, Gina, had loaned her six months ago and that she'd never returned.

As she slipped them on, she made a mental note to add "return Gina's shoes" to her to-do list. If it wasn't on her list, it wasn't going to get done. That was why she was so diligent about keeping lists. People often commented about how organized she was, but if it weren't for a notepad and a pen, she'd be a mess!

She went into the bathroom and checked her appearance once more, making sure that there wasn't anything stuck in her teeth from her afternoon snack and that her hair was still cooperating. She'd inherited her

Italian father's thick, wavy, and often unruly hair, which was both a blessing and a curse. If it was behaving, it looked full and lustrous. If not, it was like she'd just been through a tornado, or at least a very bad storm.

Minutes later, the doorbell rang, and she rushed to answer it. Sophia owned a small two-bedroom house a few miles north of where Drew lived. It wasn't much, but it was hers, and she was proud of it. She'd eventually like to upgrade, but until then, at least she had a roof over her head. She swung open the door to find Drew standing there holding a bouquet of flowers in front of him and looking as handsome as ever in his black polo shirt and jeans.

"Are those for me?"

"No. I thought I'd give them to your neighbor. Of course they're for you!"

She was too flabbergasted to be embarrassed. "But why?"

Raising his eyebrows, he said, "Just because. Is that ok?"

No. Not really. Not if I have any hope of resisting you. "Well, yes. I guess so. It's just that you've never given me flowers before."

Lowering the flowers down by his side, he said, "And now I know why. You're not making this very easy."

She snapped out of it then and decided to view the flowers as a friendly gesture. "You're right. Sorry. Come on in while I get a vase."

Drew had been inside her house many times, although she preferred to hang out at his house instead, mainly because of the lake. She'd never cared before that her furniture was mostly hand-me-downs from her relatives, that the carpet was worn, or that the walls needed repainting. She'd simply been grateful to be out on her own and paying her own way, even though the house needed updating. But suddenly, she saw the house through Drew's eyes, and she wondered what he thought of her living situation. He had to know that librarians didn't make nearly the amount of money that he did, not that it had ever mattered before. So, why should it matter now?

"There," she said after she'd arranged the flowers in a vase and set it on the kitchen table, a hand-me-down from her grandmother.

"Beautiful. Just like you," he said from behind her.

Turning around slowly, she narrowed her eyes at him.

"What?"

"You've been giving me a lot of compliments lately."

He tipped his head back and laughed, and there went her nipples again, tightening under her sweater. "Do you make it this hard on all your dates?"

"You're not my date. You're my friend."

"So you say."

"I do say. Shouldn't we get going? We don't want to be late to your boss's party."

"After you," he said, waving his arm out in front of him.

They stepped outside, and as she was locking the door, he said, "Good call on the boyfriend jeans."

A wave of heat rushed into her cheeks, and she double-checked the door to buy herself some time. When she turned around, Drew's eyes were focused right on her behind, and he slowly raised them, taking his sweet time before meeting her eyes.

He shrugged. "I might be your friend, but I'm still a guy. I won't apologize for noticing."

"Noticing is fine. Gawking is something else!" she said and gave him a little shove in the direction of his car.

This time, she was walking behind him, and she couldn't help but look too. She'd always admired Drew's athletic physique, and even though they weren't teenagers anymore, he was still in excellent shape. In the summertime, his exercise consisted of swimming and biking, and in the winter months, he ran on a treadmill in his basement. Sophia exercised too, mostly to workout DVDs in her living room, but she'd never been as consistent as he was.

To distract herself from his body and his heavenly scent, she asked, "So, what can you tell me about your boss and your co-workers?"

"What can I say? They're salespeople. They basically blow sunshine up people's ass's so they can make a sale."

"That's a bit crude."

"But it's true."

"Is that what you do too?"

"At work, yes."

"But not in your personal life?" She wasn't sure why she'd said it, but she quickly realized that it had been a mistake.

"Not with you, Soph. Never with you."

Nodding, she looked down at her hands. "Sorry. I didn't mean to imply…"

"I know what you meant, and I've been guilty of playing games with women, but I've never done that with you until you asked me to."

He was right. If she hadn't asked him to pretend to be her boyfriend, they wouldn't have been in the predicament they were in right now. She decided to cut him some slack, at least for the rest of the night.

"Does your boss know that you're bringing me?"

He nodded. "I told him I was bringing a friend, so just be yourself. No pretending tonight."

"Ok," she said and shot him a smile, hoping to make up for her earlier comment.

He smiled back, which she took as a good sign, and before long, they'd pulled up in front of his boss's house in a beautiful newer subdivision in Grand Blanc.

"Wow!" she said as Drew parked the car.

"I know. He had it custom built by DeMarco & Sons Building Company."

"I've heard of them."

"They build homes all over Oakland County. If I ever have a home built, I'd use them."

"You'd move off the lake?" She wasn't sure why that surprised her, but it did.

"I like lake living, but I wouldn't mind having a bigger piece of property someday."

"Would you want a bigger house too?"

"Depends."

"On what?"

He shrugged. "Just depends. C'mon. We should go in before they wonder what we're doing out here."

They didn't hold hands as they walked up to the front door, and she missed it even though this wasn't a date. They were just two friends going to a party together. That was all. But when her heel got caught in a crack in the pavement, she stumbled, and he was right there with a hand at her elbow to keep her from falling.

"I'm not used to these heels," she said, but when she started to pull away from him, he gripped her around the waist.

"Just until you're safely on the porch," he said when she eyeballed him.

There went her emotions again. They were all over the place these days. As promised, when they stepped onto the porch, Drew let go of her, and she immediately missed his warm hand on her hip. He rang the doorbell, and seconds later, his boss, Jared, opened the door.

"Hey, Kennedy! C'mon in," Jared said, opening the door wide and motioning them inside.

"Jared, this is my friend, Sophia," Drew said.

"Hello, Sophia. Welcome, welcome. Everyone's in the kitchen. Come on back."

As they followed him to the kitchen, Sophia glanced around. The home looked like it could have been featured in *House Beautiful*. It wasn't really her taste—more modern than homey—but it was impressive nonetheless.

Once they were in the kitchen, Jared introduced Sophia to the rest of the guests, who numbered about fourteen people including Drew's co-workers and their dates. Everyone seemed friendly enough, and she was glad to see that she wasn't underdressed. Most of the women wore casual clothes too, other than Jared's wife, Renee, who wore a flowery dress.

"What can I get you two to drink?" Renee asked, playing the perfect hostess.

"Whatever beer you have is fine with me," Drew said.

"I'll have a beer too. A light one if you have it," Sophia said.

"Of course," Renee replied and walked away to get their drinks.

Sophia heard snippets of conversation floating around her, but her brain was a million miles away. For some reason, she was envisioning her and Drew in a situation like this: married, with a large house on a sprawling piece of property, entertaining his co-workers on a Saturday night. Although something about the scenario didn't feel right. Whenever she'd thought about being with Drew, she'd thought about the two of them in his cozy house on the lake, curled up on the couch, watching movies and munching on popcorn. Simplicity. That was what she liked. Of course, Drew could slip into any situation with ease, and now was no different. She wondered if she were one of the few people who knew the real him.

Later, after a dinner made up of fancy dishes that she couldn't even pronounce, they all moved into the spacious living room, and the guests split off into separate groups. Observing the interactions throughout the evening, Sophia noticed that Jared seemed particularly fond of Drew, insisting that he and Sophia sit next to him and Renee at dinner and bragging about what a great salesman he was. In the living room, she and Drew took a seat on the plush wrap around couch, and Jared came over and sat beside them.

Placing a hand on Drew's shoulder, he said, "Has Kennedy told you that he's up for a promotion?"

"No, he hasn't," she replied somewhat surprised. In the past, they'd told each other practically everything, yet Drew hadn't said a word.

Looking slightly uncomfortable, Drew said, "I must have forgotten."

"You're too humble, Kennedy! My boy here has an opportunity to expand his sales territory, and of course, there'd be a hefty raise to go along with it."

The part about the larger territory struck her more than the raise. "That's great. Where would your territory extend to?"

Twirling his beer around in his hand, Drew looked up and said, "Tennessee."

She didn't bother hiding her shock. While it was great news for him, she wondered what it meant for them. But wait a minute, there was no "them."

"Wow. Does that mean you'll have to travel a lot?"

"Some. Yes."

"And he'd be managing some of the other sales reps. This boy is going places, I'll tell ya!" Jared said, slapping Drew on the back. Then, glancing past them to his wife, he said, "Duty calls. You two enjoy yourselves."

After he'd walked away, Sophia turned to Drew and whispered, "Why didn't you tell me about your promotion?"

He shrugged. "I haven't accepted it yet. Besides, it won't affect us since we only see each other once a week."

Does he really believe that, or is he pretending again? She searched his eyes for the answer, but he seemed guarded, like a wall had gone up.

"Well, I guess I should just say congratulations, then. It sounds like a big step up for you."

"*If* I take it," he repeated.

Studying him as he took a long slug of beer, she wondered why he didn't seem happier. And then, suddenly, he stood and said, "Are you ready to get out of here?"

"Sure, if you are."

Drew led her around the room to say his goodbyes, and a few minutes later, they were outside in the cool night air. With a hand on her elbow again, he walked her to the car and opened the passenger door for her. Aware of his mood shift, she didn't bother arguing. Besides, she was enjoying his gallant gestures.

After riding in silence for a few minutes, Sophia decided to press a little further. "I'm still surprised that you didn't tell me about your promotion. We usually tell each other everything."

"Not *everything*, Soph."

"Well, we should be able to. That's what friends…"

"Stop saying that, ok. Just stop!"

It was one of the few times he'd ever raised his voice to her, and she was stunned. Unsure of the reason for his outburst, and afraid to say anything else that might set him off, she kept silent for the rest of the drive home, which thankfully, wasn't very long. When he pulled into her driveway, he shut off the car, and started to get out.

"What are you doing?" she asked, trying to keep her voice steady.

"Walking you to the door."

She started to say that he didn't have to, but then thought better of it. As she was fishing her keys out of her purse, he put his hands on her shoulders and gently turned her around to face him.

"I'm sorry," he said, and it was almost a whisper. "I didn't mean to snap like that."

"Just tell me what's wrong, Drew," she said, looking up at him, pleading with her eyes.

"How are you doing this?"

"Doing what?"

"Pretending that we're just friends after everything that happened. Did it mean that little to you?"

It meant *everything*, and that was the problem. But she couldn't find the words. Not yet.

"Because I can't stop thinking about it. About you. About us. About how good it was."

She inhaled sharply, her arms itching to go around him. It took every fiber of her being not to invite him inside, but she knew that wasn't the answer. "Drew…"

"Tell me that you didn't enjoy making love with me. Tell me that you haven't thought about it, dreamed about it. If you can do that, I'll walk away right now, and I won't ever bring it up again."

His hands were still on her shoulders, and then he slid them down her arms and entwined their fingers together.

Shaking her head, she said, "I can't tell you that because it would be a lie."

It was the first time he'd smiled in the past hour, and it lit up her whole world. "But…" she continued.

"But what?" he asked, taking a step forward.

"I want to go slowly this time."

"I can do slow."

"Do you know what I mean by slow?" she asked, cocking her head skeptically.

"Enlighten me."

"It means we don't jump back into bed together right away. We build up to it—slowly."

"So, you want me to seduce you?"

"What I mean is that maybe we need to date each other for a while to make sure this is what we both want."

"So, you want to go backwards?"

She sighed. "You're not cooperating."

He chuckled. "Ok, ok. I think I get it. You want me to court you the old-fashioned way."

She smiled. "Something like that. Yes."

"And then we get to have sex, right?"

"Drew!"

"Ok, fine. We'll do things your way, but if we're starting over, this counts as our first date."

"Okayyyy…"

"And as part of the courting process, I would like to kiss you goodnight."

"Are you…asking?"

"Um-hum."

"Since we're dating now, the answer is yes."

"About time," he said, and without wasting another second, he bent his head down and kissed her. Softly, but with conviction.

Sophia came up on her tiptoes and looped her arms around his neck, pressing her body tightly against his. And when it was over, her head was spinning, her heart was pounding, and her smile matched his.

"Thanks for coming with me tonight and for the kiss," he said sweetly, his arms still wrapped around her waist.

"You're welcome." *Now what?*

Drew stepped back and shoved his hands into his front pockets. "Goodnight, Soph." He was halfway to his car when she called out to him.

"Wait a minute. Don't we need to plan our next date?"

He laughed loudly, guffawed really. "There you go with your to-do list again. Don't worry. I'll call you." And with that, he got into his car and drove away.

A little while later, as she was climbing into bed, she laughed aloud. *Wait until Eve hears this!*

Chapter 26

Drew was too keyed up to sleep. Instead, he sat at his kitchen counter and reviewed the list he'd made. Now that he and Sophia were officially dating, the list took on a whole different meaning. He wanted to prove to her that he was serious about this, about her. He wasn't just playing a game or trying to get her back into his bed. But if it was courtship she wanted, then courtship she would have.

Glancing at the list, he drew a line through three of the items: make her dinner, give her flowers for no reason, and introduce her to his co-workers. There were still seven more ideas on the list, and his eyes lingered on "buy her a gift." And then he pulled up the calendar on his phone. Perfect! He had a few weeks to come up with something special for her birthday.

In the past, they'd exchanged token gifts such as a book or DVD, but this time, he wanted to give her something more personal, romantic even. "Ha! Since when have I become a romantic?" And then he realized that he'd never given a woman a romantic gift before. This whole courting business was a first for him, and he decided that he kind of liked it.

Having come up with a game plan, he went off to bed, although he still wasn't tired. Instead, he lay there replaying the evening, starting with the image of her in her boyfriend jeans and heels and ending with the kiss. It had been years since he'd settled for a kiss at the door and not been invited inside. Instead of damaging his ego, it humbled him, and the situation seemed appropriate given that it was Sophia and not some woman he'd just met and had no intention of ever seeing again.

Yes. This felt right. This felt real. *This feels frustrating in the absolute best way*, he thought, glancing down at the tent in his underwear. But if everything went according to plan, soon he'd be with the woman of his dreams. Honestly, he'd never believed it would happen. He'd figured she'd have been snatched up by now, and he'd worried she'd end up with Jake. He could tell that she'd been serious about him, but Drew had never liked the guy. He'd questioned Jake's sincerity from day one, and it hadn't surprised him when they'd broken up.

She was too good for the asshole anyway, and it wasn't that long ago that Drew had felt the same about himself. But now he was buoyed by the fact that she'd said yes to dating him, and given the way she'd kissed him, well, that had boosted his confidence too. "Just don't screw it up."

He glanced over at this clock and saw that it was past midnight. Probably too late to call her even though he would have loved to hear her sweet voice. He could send her a text, let her know he was thinking of her, even though she wouldn't see it until the morning. *Too cheesy?* He decided not to press his luck. If he came on too strong, she might back away, and that was the last thing he wanted. No. He'd have to play it cool. *She said slowly, remember?*

He chuckled, recalling the stricken look on her pretty face when he'd left without scheduling their next date. He was typically the spontaneous type who didn't need everything planned out to the letter. But maybe he'd need to adjust his way of thinking when it came to Sophia. She was a planner, a list-maker, an organizer, a details girl. He'd told her that was one of the things he loved about her, and he did...

Drew bolted upright in bed and shook his head rapidly while the word sank in. "Wait a minute. Did I really say that, or did I just think it?" But he already knew the answer. He loved her. Wow! He loved Sophia Russo, his best friend since high school. The girl he'd kept at arm's length and the woman he'd done the same thing to for far too long. The revelation should have scared the shit out of him, but it didn't. It just gave him more incentive and made him more determined than ever to make this work.

He sat there for a while longer, leaning against the headboard, shaking his head. He felt exhilarated, energized, exuberant, but too bad he didn't have anyone to share it with. Glancing at the clock again, he saw it was after twelve thirty. There was no way Sophia was still up, and even if she were, he couldn't ring her up and casually drop the L-bomb on her. One, she might not believe him or think it was too soon, and two, she might not feel the same. The thought of that gave him pause.

There was no way he was going to tell her that he loved her without feeling certain that she'd reciprocate. He recalled the *Friends* episode where Ross told Emily that he loved her and she said, "Thank you." He never wanted to be in that awkward position—ever! He would tell her when he was sure she'd say it back, and no sooner.

In the meantime, he'd concentrate on the list and make sure that he courted Sophia so that she felt loved, cared for, and respected. He could do this. He was up for it. He was ready. *I hope she is too!*

Chapter 27

      Luckily, Sophia had to work the next day, because, otherwise, she'd have sat at home wondering what Drew was doing and whether she should call him. Since they were officially dating, that meant she could ask him out too, right? She'd pondered it over breakfast as she'd stared at the flowers he'd given her and as she'd driven to the library. If he was so anxious to be with her, why hadn't he made another date? She'd checked her phone first thing upon awakening, hoping there might be a text from him, but nothing. Could it be that dating Drew would be just as complicated as dating...?

      "Jake?"

      "Hello, Sophia. I hoped you'd be working today."

      "What...what are you doing here?"

      "Not the greeting I was hoping for."

      She stared at him like she was seeing a ghost. This was the same guy who'd broken up with her yet he'd expected a nice greeting? Since she was sitting at the reference desk, she felt trapped. She couldn't just get up and walk away in case a library patron needed help. Luckily, it wasn't very busy, and nobody was nearby to eavesdrop.

      "I'm sorry, Jake, but what did you expect? You broke up with me, remember? I never expected to see you again, let alone here at my place of business, which you always scoffed at."

"I didn't scoff at it."

"Do the words 'Libraries are so antiquated' ring a bell?"

"I don't recall saying that, but to change the subject, how have you been?"

Was he always this cocky? Why didn't I ever notice it before? "Fine. Actually, better than fine."

"Good to hear."

A mother and her two children approached the reference desk then, and Sophia was glad for the distraction. "Can I help you?" she asked pointedly, turning her back on Jake.

"Yes. We were wondering if you had any book recommendations for a fourth grader," the woman said, and then leaning over the counter, she added, "a fourth grader who doesn't particularly enjoy reading."

Sophia heard similar comments all the time, and it always made her sad. She couldn't fathom it. To her, reading was one of the greatest joys in life. It ranked right up there with eating and kissing Drew! She reached into a drawer and came up with a list that she handed the mother (a list that she had composed herself). "Here's a list of recommendations for kids his age. I would suggest the starred titles as they're the most requested books for his age group."

"Thank you so much," the woman said, sounding relieved.

"You're welcome," Sophia said, smiling as they walked away.

Her smile disappeared when she looked back at Jake, who was leaning against the counter like he owned the place. Deciding to get right to the point, she said,

"Why are you here, Jake? And I know it's not to check out books, because the only reading I've seen you do was on your phone in the middle of our dates."

He sighed and had the decency to look contrite. "I'm sorry for the way I treated you, Soph. I was a jerk."

"No argument here."

"I came to apologize."

"Why now? We broke up months ago."

"I know, and I miss you."

Her mouth gaped open, but no words came out. She studied his face carefully and couldn't find any indication that he was being insincere. Not that she'd ever known him to lie to her before, but she hadn't seen their breakup coming. It seemed to have come out of nowhere, but he had to have been thinking about it for a while, right? So, he must have been keeping his list of grievances to himself. She'd been too trusting, too naïve to notice that something was wrong, and she'd vowed never to make that mistake again. From here on out, she wanted full disclosure and open communication, whether it was good or bad. Thankfully, she didn't see that being an issue with Drew. Drew. Oh God. Good thing he wasn't here to see this. He never liked Jake, though he'd tried to hide it for her sake. He'd been politely sympathetic after she and Jake had broken up, but once she'd gotten over it, he'd admitted his true feelings.

"It took you six months to realize that?" she said, not bothering to hide her sarcasm.

"I didn't think you'd take me back right away, but I was hoping, now that some time has passed…"

"Did you ever consider that I might be dating someone else?"

"Are you?"

"Yes, as a matter of fact, she is! Hello, Jake," Drew said, coming up from behind and roughly clamping his hand down on Jake's shoulder.

Jake jerked his head around, obviously surprised to see Drew standing there, and so was she. She'd been so engrossed in their conversation that she hadn't seen Drew approach. She doubted that there'd ever been a time she was happier to see him.

"Hey," she said softly.

"Hey," he replied and smiled warmly at her.

"Wait a minute. Is it him? Are you dating *Drew*?" Jake asked, his voice rising with every word.

"Shhh!" Sophia and Drew said at the same time, and it was almost comical. Almost.

"You're in a library," she scolded Jake.

"Well? Is it true?" he asked again, lowering his voice.

"Yes," she replied proudly, and Drew grinned at her over Jake's shoulder, which was still tightly clamped in his grip.

"Huh. I always wondered about you two."

"What do you mean? I never gave you any reason to doubt me," Sophia said, her hackles up again.

"I know, but it's not natural for two people of the opposite sex to be so close without..."

"Don't even say it," Drew said menacingly. "Now, I would suggest that you let Sophia get back to work. You've wasted enough of her time."

If she could have, she'd have jumped over the counter and straight into Drew's arms. For him to stick up for her like that—it was like she had her very own romantic hero straight out of a romance novel!

Jake ignored Drew, and, looking straight at her, he said, "Fine, but don't come crying to me when this guy dumps you for one of his bimbos." With that, he twisted out of Drew's grip and stalked out of the library.

She must have looked visibly upset, because Drew said, "Can you take a quick break?"

She nodded and used the pager to call another staff member to the reference desk. After her replacement arrived, she motioned for Drew to follow her and led him into her office, where he closed the door behind them.

"I always knew that guy was an asshole, but for him to come here and harass you... Soph? Are you ok?"

She was still in shock, and she went to lean against her desk, but Drew pulled her into his arms. "Lean on me instead," he said.

Laying her head against his chest, she took a few deep breaths before speaking. "Thank you."

Cupping her chin, he tilted her face up and said, "Anytime, sweetheart."

Later, she decided it was because emotions were running high, but right then, she felt an overwhelming need to be close to him. Closer than they already were. She knew it wasn't smart, knew that they only had a few minutes, but her need trumped all logical thought.

Backing up to her desk, she pulled him with her, and then she boosted herself up to perch on the edge of it. Threading her fingers in his hair, she whispered, "Kiss me, Drew. Kiss me like you mean it."

It was spontaneous combustion—mouths clashing, tongues tangling, bodies struggling to get closer. Drew's hands caressed her back, and then he moved one hand around to the front, where he cupped her left breast. She was wearing a thin top given the warm weather, and she felt his touch all the way down to her toes. Her body was on fire for him, and she surely would have let him have her right on the desk if she thought they could get away with it.

He continued to fondle her breast through her shirt as he broke their kiss to dip his head into the crook of her neck. He sucked on the sensitive skin there, and she felt a surge of wetness between her legs. And then she remembered his librarian fantasy, although in his fantasy, the library had been closed, and they'd been all alone.

"Drew?"

"Hmm?" he mumbled against her neck.

"We have to stop."

"Can't," he mumbled again, dipping his head further down into the vee of her shirt.

"We have to!" she repeated, although she was half-laughing when she said it.

Finally, he popped his head up and moved his hand back down to her waist. They were both breathing hard, and his hair looked rumpled where she'd been playing with it. They beamed at each other, unwilling to tear their eyes away.

"I wish we didn't have to stop," she admitted as she straightened her top, "but you know we do."

Drew took a step back and ran his hands over his hair. "Just answer me one question. If we were alone…?"

She hopped down off the desk and stepped closer, placing her palm over his beating chest. "I couldn't have stopped if I tried," she replied.

Looking satisfied, he leaned down and brushed his lips over hers. "Ok, then. My work here is done." He turned to leave, but she stopped him.

"Wait. You never said why you came here."

"I just wanted to stop by and see you, and I had an errand nearby, so it worked out."

"I'm glad you did."

"Me too, and not just because of the kiss. Although it was pretty spectacular."

"Agreed. But now I have to get back to work."

"Can I see you later?"

"Sure."

"Maybe we could go get some ice cream or something."

"Sounds great."

"I'll call you."

"Not if I call you first," she answered, enjoying flirting with him.

She walked out of the office with him and waved goodbye as he left. Funny how she'd known him for years, yet everything felt brand new. The flirting, the kissing, him stopping by to see her just because. It was awesome, and she couldn't wait to experience more of it.

She went through the rest of the workday in a bit of a fog, anxious to get home and be with Drew again. She loved how he'd come to her rescue with Jake, loved that he'd popped in to see her unexpectedly, and especially loved what had almost happened in her office. And then, glancing down at the notepad on her desk, she realized she'd been doodling the word "love" across the entire page. Smiling, she stared long and hard at the word and decided it fit. She'd loved Drew as a friend since they were teenagers, and now she loved him as a woman loves a man.

But she couldn't tell him that. Not yet. It was too soon. Things were still new, and she didn't want to scare him off. Just as she'd kept her crush on him a secret in high school and college, she'd have to keep this a secret too—for now. She'd know when the time was right to tell him. In the meantime, she looked forward to their next encounter and whatever it might bring.

Ice cream. That's all you're having. Ice cream, she reminded herself. Unless ice cream was a code word for something else…

"So, your birthday's coming up soon," Drew said between licks of his rocky road ice cream cone.

They'd taken a short drive north of Waterford to a local dairy farm that was known for serving mammoth scoops of ice cream. The place was doing great business, especially during the summer months, when people from the neighboring communities flocked there to partake of the dairy delights.

"Yes, but I'm not excited about it."

"What? Why not?"

"Because I'm just that much closer to the big three-oh."

He chuckled. "The big three-oh isn't old, Soph."

"Sometimes, it feels like it. All my friends are settling down and having babies."

Drew paused mid-lick and studied her thoughtfully. "Is that what you want too?"

"Someday," she replied.

"Well, anyway, the reason I brought up your birthday was not to remind you that you're becoming a spinster."

She laughed. "What was the reason?"

"I wondered if you could get away for that weekend."

"I might be able to. Why?"

"Because I'd like to whisk you away somewhere."

She'd opted for ice cream in a cup instead of on a cone because of her spilling habit, and until then, she'd been doing a good job of keeping her clothes stain-free. But while she'd been listening to him, she'd forgotten about the large spoonful of ice cream poised to go into her mouth—until Drew made a strangled sound between a laugh and a grunt and pointed at her top. Sure enough, there was a lovely glob of chocolate running down the middle of her chest. "Crap!" she said as he handed her a pile of napkins.

"Guess you'll have to borrow another one of my shirts again," he teased.

"I haven't even given you back the last one." She omitted the part about wearing it to bed every night since he'd given it to her.

"It's no big deal. What's mine is yours," he said and winked at her.

"So, are you going to tell me where you're whisking me off to?"

"Nope. You'll just have to trust me that it will be somewhere good."

"But how will I know what to pack if I don't know where we're going?"

Drew took another lick of his cone and smirked at her. "Can't stand it, can you? The not knowing."

"I like to know things so that I'm prepared. For example, I need to know the weather so I know what kind of clothes to bring."

"It's pretty much summer everywhere right now, Soph. Pack light clothes."

"Will I need a bathing suit?"

"God, I hope so."

She frowned at him. "I'm not always going to wear the leopard-print bikini, you know."

"Whatever bathing suit you bring will be fine with me."

"What other activities are we going to do while we're there—wherever there is?"

"Outdoor activities, so pack casual, comfortable clothes."

"Ok."

"So, you'll go with me?"

His expression was so hopeful that she leaned over the table and kissed his cheek. "Yes, as long as I can get the weekend off."

"Great! Now, let's get you home and out of that shirt."

Good thing she already had the spoon in her mouth that time; otherwise, she might have bobbled it again. Suddenly, the idea of Drew taking her shirt off sounded very appealing, and if she were lucky, maybe he'd take his shirt off too.

By the time they returned to Drew's house, her body was thrumming with anticipation. Ever since their mini make-out session in her office earlier that day, she hadn't stopped thinking about how good it felt to have his hands on her again. How much she'd missed it and longed for it since they'd returned from Florida. While she had some concerns about hopping back into bed with him, she was willing to have a little fun, as couples who were dating tended to do. Somehow, it was still stuck in her head that Drew was the forbidden fruit that she could look at but not touch. She had to remind herself that it was ok to touch him now. One thing was certain: she wasn't going to settle for a chaste kiss goodnight.

Once they were inside, he started walking down the hall toward his bedroom, and he motioned for her to follow him.

There went that flutter of nerves again. "Where are we going?" *As if I don't know!*

"To my bedroom so you can pick out which shirt you want to borrow this time."

Sophia hadn't been in Drew's bedroom since he'd taken over the house. When they were teenagers, they used to hang out in his room, which his parents allowed if they kept the door open. It had never been an issue before because there'd been no danger of anything physical happening between them. But now...

She stepped into what used to be his parents' room and glanced around, noticing all the changes he'd made. Gone was Diane's feminine touch, and now the room had a distinctly masculine vibe. He'd repainted the pale-yellow walls a smoky blue with gray trim, and he'd bought all new furniture made of rich cherrywood. The room was relatively neat other than the unmade bed, which she'd always used to tease him about. "Why should I make it when I'm just going to mess it up again?" he'd said.

Following her eyes, he chuckled. "I know what you're thinking, and no, I still don't make my bed." He pulled open one of the dresser drawers and said, "Here you go. Take your pick."

Standing beside him, she tried to ignore his fresh scent while she rifled through the drawer of t-shirts. When she found one with the green and gold emblem of Wayne State University on it, she pulled it out of the drawer. "Didn't I buy you this?"

"Um-hum. You gave it to me for Christmas during your freshman year."

"And you still have it?"

"I've kept everything you've ever given me, Soph."

She didn't know why that surprised her, but it did. "Well, I guess I'll go change, then," she said and turned to leave the room.

"Or I could help you," he said, his eyes hopeful.

Swallowing hard, she nodded and slowly lifted her arms overhead. Taking a step forward, he placed his hands on the hem of her shirt and gently lifted it up and off, leaving her standing there in her plain white bra. Since she'd come to his house straight from work, she hadn't had a chance to change into something more provocative, and now she wished she had. At least he wouldn't see her matching white granny panties, since she intended to keep her pants on!

"So pretty," he said, chest heaving. "Can I...?"

"Yes." She didn't need to hear the rest of the sentence to understand what he meant.

He reached out and ran his index finger along the edge of her bra where the fleshy parts of her breasts were sticking out, leaving a trail of goosebumps in his wake. "More?" he asked, raising his eyes to hers.

She nodded, entranced by his slow, seductive movements and the heat that was rolling off him in waves. Slipping his fingers underneath her bra straps, he gently pulled them down until her breasts were fully exposed to his hungry gaze. Cupping them in his hands, he brushed his thumbs over her taut nipples, and the tingling sensation made a beeline to her core.

"Earlier today, in your office—I wanted you so bad. I wanted to strip you naked and kiss every part of you."

"Drew..."

"Did you want me too?"

"Yes. I still do."

He took that as permission, and he dipped his head down and drew a nipple deep into his mouth. She dropped the t-shirt she'd been holding and shoved her hands in his hair, pulling him closer, desperate for more contact. His erection brushed against her thigh, and she shifted her hips to rub against it. Drew released her nipple and kissed a path across her chest to the other one, sucking and licking until she was a bundle of raw nerves.

Suddenly, he popped his head up, and eyes ablaze, he said, "You're in charge here. Tell me what you want to do."

At that moment, she was tempted to push him down on the bed and have her way with him, but something held her back. She was still stuck on the idea of progressing slowly, although it was difficult to think clearly under the circumstances.

Drew must have sensed her hesitation, and he started to pull back, but she grabbed his hand and placed it on the button of her pants. "I want you to keep touching me," she said, realizing that her voice sounded like a croak.

He smiled and then turned his attention to unfastening her pants.

Suddenly, she experienced a moment of clarity and slapped her hand over his wrist. "Wait. Stop."

"What is it?" he asked, looking concerned.

"For the record, I didn't know we'd be doing...this, so I'm not exactly...prepared."

Staring at her quizzically, he said, "Prepared how?"

"I'm wearing granny panties," she blurted.

Eyes dancing with merriment, Drew repeated her. "Granny panties?"

"Yeah. You know, the kind that come up to your belly button and cover everything. The kind a grandma would wear!"

He chuckled then, but he kept his hands poised on her zipper. "Does that mean you want me to stop? Because it's your call."

Eyebrows raised, she said, "So you don't mind granny panties?"

"I don't expect they'll be on you for very long."

"Oh. Ok, then."

"You sure?"

"Yes. Please continue."

Smiling, he unzipped her pants, and to his credit, he didn't even flinch when he saw her stark-white granny panties. Instead, he slipped his hand inside them and cupped her soft, damp center.

"Ohhhh."

"Good?"

"Yes," she said, her head automatically tipping back.

Supporting her with one arm around her back, he continued to tease her with his fingers, alternating between caressing her swollen folds and inserting a finger deep inside. All thoughts of granny panties slipped away as she writhed against his hand. When Drew's mouth closed over a nipple, she moaned, and clutching his shoulders tightly, she ground against him, coming more undone with each swirl of his finger, each kiss of her breast. All the pent-up frustration, all the longing, the craving, burst inside her and came pouring out as she clenched around him, riding out her orgasm until her limbs went numb.

Drew continued to hold her as she drifted back down—nibbling on her neck, along her jaw, and finally capturing her lips in a silky-sweet caress. She hadn't even realized her eyes were still closed, and now they fluttered open to find him staring at her with as much pleasure as he'd shown earlier when he'd been licking the ice cream cone. Maybe more. Hopefully more.

"Good?"

"Good doesn't cover it," she replied, smiling back at him.

He was still standing close, and when she felt his erection nudge up against her, she reached between them and wrapped her hand around it through his shorts. He was wearing nylon athletic shorts, so she felt every ridge of his skin as she moved her hand up and down and watched his eyes become hooded.

"Soph?"

"Yeah?"

"You don't have to…"

"Shh. I want to."

With that, she slipped her hand under the waistband of his shorts and into his underwear, where she encased his silken shaft. And then, in a move that surprised them both, she dropped to her knees in front of him.

She was just about to remove his shorts when he questioned her again. "Are you sure? I don't want you to have any regrets."

Shaking her head vehemently, she said, "I won't. I want this. I want you."

Nodding, he helped her out by tugging down his shorts and underwear at once, his manhood springing forward to greet her. It felt like forever since she'd seen him like this. Naked, aroused, pulsing with desire and need. A bead of wetness glistened at his tip, and she rubbed it around in a slow, enticing circle, watching him watching her.

Scooting closer, she closed her mouth around him, encasing his hard length, reveling in the sounds he made as he thrust his hips forward. She felt feminine, powerful, confident as she used her lips and tongue to bring him pleasure, gripping his strong thighs for support as she loved on him.

"Keep going?" he asked, but it was almost a plea, and there was no way she'd stop now. Besides, she wanted to do this for him and with him.

She nodded, and seconds later, he climaxed, head tipped back, hands threaded in her hair, body pulsating until he was completely drained.

When she stood back up on wobbly legs, she glanced between them and giggled. They looked hilarious with his shorts wrapped around his ankles and her granny panties sticking out of the top of her unzipped pants.

Thankfully, he recognized the humor in it too and laughed along with her. "Maybe we'll make it to the bed next time," he said, grinning.

Next time. She loved the sound of that. She started to say so but then clamped her mouth shut. There was still that twinge of fear that things were moving too fast, so she swallowed her words. Instead, she looped her arms around his neck and kissed him, and for now, that would have to do.

Chapter 28

"So, what's the latest installment in the Drew drama?" Eve asked the next day.

They were on their lunch break at the same diner that she'd eaten at with Drew the day she'd helped him pick out his mom's present. She couldn't believe how much had changed between them since then.

After Sophia relayed the story about her ex coming into the library and Drew coming to her rescue, Eve shook her head with wonder and maybe a touch of envy.

"So, you dragged him back to your office and had your wicked way with him?"

Sophia almost choked on her fries. "NO!"

"But you wanted to. I can tell," Eve said, popping another fry into her mouth.

Sophia had purposely downplayed what had happened in her office, and she'd also omitted the details of what had happened later. There were some things that were too personal to share, and now that she and Drew were being intimate, she wanted to keep a few things to herself.

"Let's just say he's hard to resist," she said, smiling broadly.

"Evidently…" Eve said, her voice trailing off as she became distracted by something out the window.

"What is it?" Sophia asked.

"Don't..."

But it was too late. Sophia had already looked in the same direction, and her eyes widened with shock. Drew and Lexie were standing on the sidewalk across the street, in front of the jewelry store. But they weren't just standing there. They were locked in a tight embrace.

"Oh no," Eve said.

Sophia's heart sunk like a stone, but she couldn't tear her eyes away. It was like driving by the scene of an accident where you know you shouldn't look but you can't help it. It was human nature—the need to know. Only, she didn't need to know this—didn't want to believe what she was seeing.

The hug seemed to go on forever, and then Lexie kissed him on the cheek, turned, and sashayed away. If that weren't bad enough, Drew stood there and watched her until she'd turned the corner and was out of sight. Then he glanced down at his watch and, looking like he needed to be somewhere, turned and walked in the opposite direction. Sophia kept her eyes on him until he disappeared, and then she just sat there, staring down at her plate in a state of shock.

Tears threatened, but anger was the predominant emotion, and she considered chasing him down and calling him out on what she'd just seen. She warred with herself as Eve rubbed her arm soothingly from across the table.

"Maybe it's not what you think," Eve said, not sounding completely convinced.

"What I think is that Drew is *not* a one-woman man. He never has been, but I wanted to believe that he'd changed. I wanted to believe that I'd be enough..." Her throat caught, and then the tears came.

"Oh, sweetie. I'm so sorry," Eve said and then slid into the seat beside Sophia. Slinging an arm over her shoulder, she held Sophia tight until her tears subsided, waving the waitress away when she came to check on them.

Sniffling, Sophia wiped her face with a napkin and said, "I'm ok now. I'll be ok." Maybe if she kept saying it, she'd actually believe it.

"You should go home. Take the rest of the day off. I'll cover for you."

Shaking her head vehemently, Sophia said, "No. I have to face this, Eve. Besides, if I go home, I'll just sit there and wallow. I need to be distracted."

When they returned to the library ten minutes later, one of their co-workers approached and said, "Sophia, someone stopped by to see you. Some hot guy named Drew Kennedy," she added with a smile.

"Thanks, Cheryl," Eve said and whisked Sophia away.

Drew was here? He came here after being with Lexie? The idea irritated her even further, and she found it almost impossible to concentrate for the rest of the afternoon. At the end of the day, she checked her phone and saw a text from Drew that read: *Stopped by to see you today. Plans tonight?*

Staring down at the phone, her hands trembled as she replied: *Going out with Eve.* Eve had asked her to come over after work, so she wouldn't have to be alone, but Sophia had declined. Drew didn't need to know that though.

Seconds later, he wrote back: *I'm jealous. Tomorrow then.*

You're jealous? You've got some nerve, Drew Kennedy. Instead of replying, she shut off her phone so she wouldn't be tempted to write back and tell him what an asshole he was.

On the drive home, she kept replaying the image of him hugging Lexie. It drove her crazy wondering whether they'd planned to meet there and, if so, why so close to the library? Hadn't he been the least bit worried that he could have been caught? Obviously not, since he'd been hugging her in the middle of a busy sidewalk at lunchtime. And why Lexie? He'd sworn she hadn't meant anything to him, that she was just another fling. Sophia recalled how mad Drew had been when he'd heard about Lexie confronting her at the coffee shop. *And now he's seeing her again? Behind my back?*

Maybe it was because Lexie was a sure thing. She wouldn't make Drew court her to sleep with her again. "Damn it! I'm such a fool!"

Once she got home, she went through the motions of making dinner, cleaning up, and preparing for bed, but she couldn't stop thinking about Drew and Lexie. None of this would have mattered if she and Drew hadn't crossed the line. If only she would have kept her fantasies to herself and not asked him to pretend to be her boyfriend, then she wouldn't be feeling so miserable right now.

She turned her phone back on right before bed and saw that she had a few text messages from Eve asking if she was ok and a missed call from Drew. She quickly fired a response to Eve and then listened to his voice mail.

"Hey, Soph. I know you're out with your friend, but I just wanted to call and say that I'm missing you. I know that might sound stupid because I just saw you yesterday, but there you have it. Anyway, if you're up to stopping by on your way home, my door is always open.

Or if you just want to give me a call, that's fine too. Talk to you soon."

She replayed the message at least five times until she finally shut the phone off again and lay there, staring at the ceiling, mind whirling. *Is he really that deceptive? Is he so used to lying to women that it's as natural as breathing? Maybe I don't really know him at all.* Throwing off the covers, she got up and paced the room. Back and forth and back again.

Realizing that there was no way she was ever going to sleep without knowing the truth, she left the bedroom still in her pajamas, shoved on her shoes and a jacket, grabbed her purse, and went out the door.

If he wanted her to stop by, then she was going to stop by all right. But it wouldn't be for a booty call! He was in for a rude awakening, literally! But if she couldn't sleep tonight, then neither should he. Not until he explained what kind of game he was playing.

When she pulled into his driveway a few minutes later, she noticed the inside lights were off but the porchlight was on. He was sleeping, then. Perfect! It was probably better to catch him off guard before he had a chance to generate more lies! Glancing in the direction of her parents' house, she noticed their lights were off too. No surprise there. They'd be sleeping at this late hour, and with her dad's snoring, she doubted they'd hear her yelling at Drew. Even if they did, once she explained why, they'd probably support her on it.

Standing on the porch in her pajamas, she rang the doorbell, waited a minute or two, and then rang it again. Suddenly, a light came on in the foyer, and Drew was at the door, yanking it open. When he saw her standing there, his eyes lit up, but in the next second, his face fell as she pushed her way inside and slammed the door behind her.

"You complete and utter asshole!"

"Huh?" He backed up a step, looking at her like she was deranged.

"You heard me. You thought you could get away with it, didn't you?"

He narrowed his eyes at her, his voice rising slightly as he replied, "What on earth are you talking about? Get away with what?"

Hands on her hips, eyes wild, she said, "You came to see me earlier today, right?"

"Yes…"

"But I wasn't at the library."

"I know. They said you were out to lunch with Eve."

"And do you want to know where?"

He shrugged, obviously not understanding why it mattered.

"I was at the diner across the street from the jewelry store. You know, the store where you bought your mom the initial necklace."

Suddenly, dawning struck, and she watched his expression carefully as he replied, "So, you saw me there."

"Yes. You thought you could get away with it, didn't you? Right in the middle of the day in the center of town, not a mile away from the library!"

And then his eyes flickered with greater understanding, and he said, "Ahh. So, you saw me with Lexie."

She couldn't believe how casually he said it, as if it shouldn't bother her. Bewildered, she yelled, "YES!"

"Calm down," he said, reaching out to take a hold of her arms.

She twisted away. "Calm down? Really? After what I saw?"

Shaking his head, he punched his hands on his hips, and it was then that she noticed what he was wearing, or, more accurately, what he wasn't. Shirtless, he stood there in a pair of gray boxer briefs that clung to his body like a second skin. She glanced down and then quickly glanced away, angry at herself for looking. The corners of his lips tipped up, and she wanted to smack the cocky smirk right of his face, but wisely, he backed up another step.

"You mean what you *think* you saw," he corrected.

"I know what I saw, Drew. I'm not stupid."

"No, you're not, but sometimes, you don't give yourself enough credit."

"What are you talking about?"

"Come and sit down."

"Hell no. If you're trying to lure me into your love den, it's not going to work. Not this time."

"Love den?" He chuckled, but then, realizing that she wasn't going to budge, he sighed and said, "Ok. You saw me with Lexie, but you didn't hear what she was saying."

"Well, of course not. But I didn't need to hear her to know what she was after."

Shaking his head, he said, "Well, you're wrong this time. Hear me out."

Impatient, she nodded, curious as to what kind of story he was about to come up with.

"I was coming out of the jewelry store when I ran into Lexie. She asked me what I was up to, and I told her the truth."

"Which is?"

"That I was shopping for a birthday present for my *girlfriend*."

"Your...girlfriend?"

"Um-hum. Anyway, she asked who my girlfriend was, and I said you."

"Me?"

"Um-hum. At first, she looked upset, but then she said she always knew I had a thing for you and that she was happy for me."

Suddenly, Sophia felt dizzy, and she started to sway. Drew quickly grabbed her hands and pulled her into the living room, forcing her to sit down on the couch.

"Are you ok?"

"Yes...I think I just got overheated." Shrugging out of her coat, she tossed it aside and said, "Continue."

Glancing down at her pajama top, he smiled, a full, no-holds-barred grin. Her shirt read: *If it involves books and pajamas, count me in!*

Clearing her throat loudly to regain his attention, he moved his eyes back up to meet hers. And then she remembered that she was still wearing her glasses. When she'd first gotten into bed that evening, she'd thought she'd be able to read, but she'd been wrong. Then she'd been in such a hurry to yell at him that she'd flown out the door with her glasses still on.

"So, I'm supposed to believe that Lexie *accidentally* ran into you on Main Street while you were buying a present for me, your *girlfriend*."

He nodded, continuing to smile at her in that cocky, charming way of his. *Damn him!*

"It's the truth, but you're welcome to call Lexie and ask her yourself."

Blinking her eyes rapidly, she said, "Well, why the hug, then? The extremely lengthy hug, I might add!"

"After she said she was happy for me, she hugged me, and her last words were, 'Goodbye, Drew, and good luck.'"

"But you hugged her back."

"What should I have done, Sophia? The woman had just apologized, a rarity for her, I'm sure. I was just being polite. Besides, if I were being sneaky, why would I have stood in the middle of Main Street with her, like you said? The minute she left, I went to the library to see you, but you weren't there. Even if you had been, I might not have told you the whole story, because I didn't want you to know that I was at the jewelry store buying something for you."

"Were you going to tell me about Lexie?"

"Yes, because I didn't want you to run into her somewhere and have her tell you before I could."

She had to admit that it all sounded very logical. But still...

"Sophia?" He pulled her hands onto his lap and clasped them tightly. "Look at me."

She looked deep into those eyes, the eyes that she'd always admired, and said, "I'm looking."

"Don't just look. *See.* See me. See how much I...care about you. How much I want to be with you, how important you are to me."

And she did see, but she was still skeptical. Uncertain.

"So, now you've ruined your birthday surprise," he teased, attempting to lighten the mood.

"I still don't know what you bought."

"And you're not going to know. Not until you go away with me."

Her heart skipped a beat, and she thought, *Traitor!*

Sighing, he said, "I don't want to have to beg you to believe me, but I will if that's what it takes. I told you before that I don't care about Lexie, and I don't. You're the only woman I see, Soph. The only woman I want."

It was starting to sink in, and she wanted so badly to believe him that she felt herself softening.

"I was so mad, so jealous when I saw you with her. I wanted to race out into the street right then, but I couldn't. And then I lied to you about going out with Eve. I went home instead, but I couldn't sleep, and then…"

"You came over here to call me an asshole," he finished for her. But he was laughing this time, and it made her laugh too.

"I hope I didn't wake up the neighbors."

"Including your parents!"

"Are you kidding? Dad sleeps through everything, and Mom wouldn't be able to hear over his snoring!"

"True."

He reached over and brushed her cheek with the back of his hand. "Are we ok now?"

"I think so."

"What else can I do?"

She thought for a few seconds and then said, "You could hold me."

"Gladly." He held his arms out to her, but she stood up instead.

"Not here."

He looked confused until she started down the hall, and he said, "Oh."

She stepped into his dark bedroom and slipped underneath the covers. She might have been impulsive earlier, but now she knew exactly what she was doing.

Drew went around the bed and crawled in on the other side, and then he immediately pulled her into his arms. She nestled against him, placing her hand on his bare chest.

"Ahhh. This is much better than being called an asshole," he said, giving her a squeeze.

Leaning up on her elbow, she gazed down at him and said, "I'm sorry about that."

He shrugged. "I've been called worse."

"But I should have waited to talk to you. That's what Eve told me to do."

"I like Eve," he said, smiling.

"I'm not telling her you said that."

"Why not?"

"Because she thinks you're hot, and you don't need another woman boosting your ego."

Drew leaned up on his side and brushed her hair away from her face. "All I care about is what you think of me, Soph."

Suddenly, she realized that she was lying in bed with him with very few clothes on in the dark, and the scene felt very intimate. Her anger had morphed into an aching need, and there was little she could do to stop it. Laying her hand on his stubbled cheek, she said, "I think you're hot too. I always have."

Smiling wide, he said, "Again. So much better than being called an asshole."

She laughed, feeling the sparks sizzle in the air between them.

"Sophia?"

"Yeah?"

"I'd really like to kiss you right now."

"I'd really like that too," she whispered.

Chapter 29

Gazing down at her, he couldn't believe she was in his bed. Soft. Warm. Hair curling around her perfect face. And the glasses. The glasses did it for him every time. He almost didn't want to take them off, but he didn't want to break them.

"Can I?" he asked as he placed his hands on the stems.

She nodded and he slipped the glasses off and laid them gently on his nightstand.

"I've always wanted to do that," he admitted.

"Part of your librarian fantasy?"

"Part of my Sophia fantasy."

"Oh…"

And then he cut her off with a kiss. Leaning over her yet taking care not to crush her, he sank into her full, plush lips, and they instantly parted, inviting his tongue. She wrapped her arms around his neck, pulled him even closer, and arched her beautiful curvy body up to his.

He could hardly believe that just moments ago, she'd been furious with him, her eyes shooting daggers as she'd stood there, anger rolling off her in waves. He popped open his eyes and saw that hers were open too, but the daggers had been replaced with—desire, warmth, *love*? And then he kicked the last option out of his head because he had no proof. Desire, yes. Affection, sure. Friendship, absolutely. But love?

"Drew?"

"Hmmm?"

"Take my clothes off. Please."

Words that every man loved to hear, yet he hesitated.

"Drew?"

Shaking himself, he said, "Are you sure?"

Sitting up, she narrowed her eyes at him. "If you won't do it, I'll do it myself." And with that, she whipped off her pajama top and flung it off to the side.

Frozen, he stared at her breasts like he'd never seen them before. Her nipples rosy and taut, her chest heaving, she stared back at him and then started to remove her bottoms. Suddenly, he broke out of his trance and said, "Let me."

Lifting her hips to assist, he began to tug her pajama bottoms down, and once he'd passed her belly button, he realized that she wasn't wearing any underwear.

"No granny panties this time?" he teased.

"I threw them out."

He chuckled as he slid off the bottoms and tossed them aside with her top. And then, sitting back on his haunches, he perused her naked body from head to toe and back again. This was the stuff his fantasies were made of. Sophia, warm, wet, and willing in his bed. Yet it meant so much more in reality than it had in his dreams. Knowing her, he understood that this wasn't a casual thing. She'd never been the type of woman to give herself to a man without being in a serious relationship. For her to want him, to trust him like this, was the biggest compliment she could ever pay him.

He didn't know everything about her past sex life, but he knew enough. She'd confided that it took her a long time to feel comfortable enough with a man to be intimate with him, like with that ass, Jake. And look how he had hurt her, taken her for granted, and then expected her to rush back into his arms. Jerk! There was no way that Drew would ever treat her like that. He wanted to take his time with her, cherish her, treat her like a queen. But right now, his fantasy woman seemed a bit...impatient.

She reached out and tugged on the waistband of his boxers. "Off," she said.

He quickly removed his underwear and came back over her, where she instantly clasped his erection in her hands. It felt so good. Too good, really, and after a few strokes, he pulled her hands away and raised them up over her head.

She smiled at him as he lowered his head to her breast and pulled a nipple deep into his mouth. Twirling his tongue around it, he held her wrists captive with one hand while he lowered the other hand to her center.

Feeling her wetness on his fingers ramped up his own arousal, but he reminded himself to go slow. Kissing a path across to her other breast, he dipped a finger inside her, swirling it around as her hips arched off the bed. They'd only been together like this a few times, yet it was amazing how comfortable it felt. How real. Having known her for so long and now knowing her intimately was like two halves becoming a whole.

In his excitement, he'd let go of her wrists, and now she plunged her fingers into his hair, massaging his scalp and urging him on. He released her breast and glanced up at her, thinking how gorgeous she looked with no makeup or accessories other than her sexy smile.

"Get a condom," she said, brooking no argument.

Moving off to the side, he reached into his drawer and quickly rolled on a condom. When he turned back around to reach for her, she motioned for him to lay down, and then she straddled him. In this position, she took control, and he watched with reverence as she slowly lowered herself down on him.

Gripping her hips, they began to move, rocking against each other in the quest for the ultimate friction. Watching her gliding up and down along his hard length, he thought he'd lose it at any second, and when he reached up to cup her bountiful breasts, she moaned loudly and unabashedly.

He loved seeing her this way, free and uninhibited, open and loving. That was what she was— loving. And that was what it felt like they were doing— loving each other.

"Drew..."

"Let go, sweetheart," he said.

And in the next second, she came in a series of pulses and breathy gasps, and then he joined her— pouring out everything he had, all that he was, all that he wanted to be with the woman he now knew he could never live without.

Chapter 30

While Drew was in the bathroom, Sophia pulled the sheet up over her and nestled deeper into the mattress. Drew's bed, a place she'd once considered the forbidden zone (or the danger zone was more like it), was now someplace that she felt comfortable, wanted, loved. She felt like she belonged there, and she was in no hurry to leave, although she probably should since they both had to work the next day.

She'd just sat up to retrieve her pajamas when Drew waltzed back into the room buck naked.

"Where are you going?" he asked, sliding under the sheet and drawing her near.

"We have to work tomorrow."

"So."

"So, it's late, and if we don't go to bed right now, we'll get less than the recommended night's sleep."

He laughed. "I'm willing to risk it," he said, dipping his head into the crook of her neck and placing a warm, moist kiss there.

She silently asked him to do it again by tipping her head to the side. "I guess I can stay for a few more minutes."

Drew treated her neck, jaw, and cheeks to soft, fluttery kisses that were meant to be sweet but were having a different effect on her body. She couldn't be close to this man without wanting him to touch her. Rubbing her palm over his stubbly jaw, she said, "I like the scruff."

His head popped up. "You do?"

She nodded. "It feels prickly but in a good way, if you know what I mean."

"I was afraid it was hurting you," he said, tracing her nipple with his fingertip. "I left some red marks."

Sucking in a breath, she said, "I don't mind."

"Good to know," he said and then traced his finger around the other nipple. "Do you know how long I've wanted to do this?"

She shook her head.

"Only since I first met you."

Eyes wide, she said, "Really? Back when I was a scrawny teenager with no boobs and too much hair?"

"Um-hum," he replied, leaving her breasts to trail his hand down to the curve of her hip. "I always liked your body, what little of it I got to see."

This was news to her. She used to think that Drew never noticed her that way. She certainly didn't look anything like the girls he'd dated even as recently as Lexie. Ugh. She really didn't want to be thinking about him and Lexie while she was lying in his bed.

Seeming to sense her discomfort, he asked, "Everything ok?"

"Yeah. I'm just not used to hearing you say these things. I have to admit it's a little strange."

"But it's a good strange, right? I mean..."

Smiling at him, she traced the outline of his lips with her finger. "Yes. It's very good."

"What about you? What did you think of me back then?"

Full disclosure. Wasn't that what she wanted? Here was her chance to tell him how she felt, not just when they were teens, but right now. But her heart and her head were having a tug-o-war, and once again, her head won.

"I had a crush on you just like all the other girls at school, but..."

"Yes?"

"But we were friends, and I didn't want anything to ruin that." At least it was a partial truth. The part she couldn't admit to was how insecure she'd felt back then. How she didn't think she could possibly compete with the other girls for his affection, which was why she'd settled for being his friend. It had been easier that way, and there'd been less chance for getting hurt. Some of those old feelings had resurfaced when she'd seen him with Lexie and Savannah, and she hated herself for it. Especially when she was lying naked in his bed, his arms around her, his eyes beaming at her like she was the love of his life.

Wait a minute? Was that even possible? *You're getting carried away, Soph. You're naked, not engaged!*

"I felt the same way. I denied my real feelings for so long that I assumed eventually they'd disappear."

Real feelings? "Yet here we are—together," she said. She'd been tracing random patterns on his chest, and now she felt his erection brush against her thigh.

"I'm glad we don't have to pretend anymore," he said.

"Me too." But weren't they? She was still holding back, and she had a sense that maybe he was too. It was all so confusing, yet there was no place else she'd rather be than right there in his arms.

"Soph?"

"Yeah?"

"Stay with me tonight. And before you recite a list of reasons why you shouldn't..."

"I'll stay," she said, stopping him in his tracks.

"You will?"

Maybe she wasn't the only insecure one here. "Yes, but only on one condition."

"I promise to set the alarm."

"It's not that."

"What then?"

"I want you to make love to me one more time."

Drew's smile lit up the room and the dark corners of her mind. "Only once?"

"We have to sleep eventually."

"Eventually is kind of vague, Russo," he teased. But before she could respond, he scooted down beneath the sheet until his head was lined up at the apex of her thighs.

Her body seemed to have a mind of its own when it came to him, and she automatically opened her legs. The first swipe of his tongue caused her hips to buck off the bed, and a few minutes later, her fears and worries melted away. He seemed intent on lavishing her with his full attention, feasting on her with his lips and tongue while she writhed beneath him. She waited for him to get a condom again, but he didn't stop, and soon, neither could she.

Afterwards, he gathered in his arms, pulled the covers up over them, and whispered, "Good night, sweet Sophia."

Staring up at him in the dark, she argued, "But what about you?"

"I got to have you twice in one night, and you're staying over. I'm good."

"Seriously?"

"Um-hum. We're not keeping score here, Soph. I'm just happy I pleased you."

She was overcome with the urge to shout, "I love you!" But once again, she hesitated. These were still early days. There'd be plenty of time to shower him with words of love down the road. So, for now, she snuggled in close, shut her eyes, and breathed in his manly scent. Cradled in the warmth of his body and lulled by his rhythmic breathing, she was soon asleep.

"Soph. Time to wake up. Soph?"

She felt a nudge on her shoulder, and she peeked one eye open. Drew must have opened the blinds, as the early morning sunshine was already filtering in.

"What time is it?" she mumbled, still trying to shake the cobwebs.

"Six thirty. I have to leave, but I made you some breakfast," he said.

Her other eye popped open then, and she sat up straighter. "Breakfast?"

He chuckled. "I figured that would do it!" Playing the role of waiter, he procured a tray from the bedside table and set it on her lap. "Breakfast is served. I did the best I could on short notice," he added.

Sophia looked down at the tray, which contained a bowl of Cheerios in milk, two slices of wheat toast, a can of Coke, and a yellow daffodil. When she looked back up, Drew was eyeing her expectantly.

She was so touched that it took her a minute, and then she said, "This is the sweetest thing ever. I love it." *And I love you too.*

He smiled. "I'm glad. Now, as much as I'd like to crawl back in bed with you, I really need to get to work. Stay as long as you want, ok?"

She nodded, feeling like a queen who's just been served breakfast in bed after having been served in other ways the night before. "I'll lock up when I leave. Have a good day."

"You too. I'll call you later, ok?"

She nodded and puckered her lips at him, inviting a goodbye kiss.

He leaned over, being careful not to bump the tray, and kissed her deeply before reluctantly parting. "I really have to go now," he said, but he hadn't budged.

"You already said that." She giggled, loving that he wasn't in a hurry to leave.

"Can I see you later?"

"Yes! Now go, or you're going to be late."

Laughing, Drew pushed himself off the bed and left the room. Or at least she thought he had until he jogged back in, leaned down, and gave her another kiss. "One more for the road," he said before truly leaving.

She waited until she heard the garage door close and his car drive away before digging into her breakfast. Afterwards, she'd have sworn that Cheerios never tasted so good! Setting the tray down, she got out of bed and padded into the connected bathroom to use the facilities. While she was in there, she glanced around, pleased to see that Drew was relatively neat. His products were lined up on the counter, towels were neatly folded over the towel bar, and the floor and sink looked clean. It might not have mattered to some, but after having dated Jake, who was a bit of a slob, it was a refreshing change. She'd often thought that if she and Jake had ended up married, she'd be forever cleaning up after him, and she hadn't relished the task. Now, if only she could get Drew to make his bed!

At the risk of sounding like a nag, she decided to make it for him. Besides, she'd slept in it too, and since he'd made her breakfast, it was the least she could do. When she had finished, she stood back to admire her work, but she ended up drifting off to memories of the night before. Of Drew's expert hands and mouth bringing her greater pleasure than she'd ever experienced. Of his warm, hard body beneath hers as she took him deep inside her. Of his gorgeous blue-gray eyes gazing up at her, looking deeply into hers and really seeing her—not just as a friend, but as a woman, a lover.

She was filled with such happiness, such peace and satisfaction, that she made her decision right then and there. Tonight, when she saw him, she would tell him that she loved him. She wanted to give voice to the feelings that bubbled up inside her even if he wasn't ready to say it back. Why waste another moment when you never knew what life might throw at you? Besides, it's not like they'd just met. They'd been building up to this moment, and it finally felt like the right time.

She felt a twinge of nervousness, wondering what Drew's reaction would be. Hopefully, she'd been reading him right, and he reciprocated her feelings. If not, she hoped it wouldn't derail their relationship. She couldn't stand the thought of not being with him anymore. Not now, after all they'd shared.

Tingling with anticipation, she left the bedroom, taking the breakfast tray with her. She rinsed the dishes, placed them in the dishwasher, and then wiped off the tray with a damp paper towel. Moving around the kitchen with ease, she began opening drawers and cabinets, looking for a place to store the tray. In the process, her pajama top got caught on the edge of one of the drawers and nudged it open. Glancing down, she saw a notepad with Drew's writing on it, and something about it caught her attention.

Setting the tray down, she pulled the drawer all the way open and realized it was a junk drawer filled with the usual assortment of odds and ends. Since Drew had bought the house from his parents, she hadn't seen notepads lying around, and she'd never seen him write a list. In fact, she'd often teased him about it, which was why she was surprised to see one in the drawer. Lifting it out, she scanned the list, and her eyes grew wide.

At the top in large block letters, he'd written: *HOW TO WIN HER BACK*. Swallowing hard, she felt a twinge of guilt and made her own internal list of reasons why she shouldn't be reading this. One, Drew probably hadn't wanted anyone to see it; otherwise, it wouldn't have been tucked in a drawer. Two, what if the list wasn't about her? What if it was something he'd written about another woman? Three... *Ok, that's enough. Either read it or put it back in the drawer!*

But her mind was already made up, and she leaned against the kitchen counter and began to read. The first item read: *Feed her.* She laughed at that one, deciding the list must be about her. Who else in Drew's life liked to eat as much as she did and admitted it? The only other woman she could think of was Eve, and it couldn't be her. The second item read: *Give her flowers for no reason.* She smiled, remembering when Drew had done that and how she'd questioned him. Silly girl! The third item read: *Buy her something shiny (birthday gift?).* Thus, his recent trip to the jewelry store. And to think she'd accused him of cheating on her with Lexie. She felt another twinge of guilt as she recalled how many times she'd called him an asshole for no good reason!

Skimming over the next several items, which included surprising her at work (check), introducing her to his friends (check), and giving her a massage (*ooh, looking forward to that one!*), she froze when she came to the last item on the list. And then she took off her glasses and wiped them off with her pajama top, thinking they might be smudged and she wasn't seeing clearly. Putting them back on, she held the notepad closer and stared at it until the words finally sank in.

There, in Drew's neat handwriting, was item number ten: *Tell her that you love her.* Sophia clasped the list to her chest, looked up at the ceiling, and said, "Thank, God!" She suppressed the urge to dance around the kitchen in celebration, and instead, she carefully placed the notepad back in the drawer and closed it.

Drew. Loved. Her. Everything she'd needed to know had been right there in black ink, and now his words were engraved on her heart, making it pound with joy and excitement. Later, she'd barely remembered leaving his house, driving home, and getting ready for work. She was still in a state of euphoria as she drove to the library, running through various scenarios in her head. Now that she knew how he felt, she was anxious to tell him that she felt the same. She wondered what he'd think about her reading his list, but then decided that it really shouldn't matter. They loved each other! What could possibly go wrong?

Eve spotted Sophia the minute she walked into the library and followed her into her office, closing the door behind them.

"Wait a minute. You don't look like a woman scorned," Eve said.

Plopping down in her chair, Sophia shot her a wide smile. "That's because I'm not! I'm a woman in love."

Leaning on her desk, Eve said, "Well, I could have told you that a long time ago!"

"But now I know for sure, and I know that Drew loves me too."

"He told you?"

"Not exactly." And there went the twinge of guilt again.

Eve narrowed her eyes. "How *exactly* did you find out, then?"

"A love note."

"Back up a minute. I must be missing something here. Last I knew, he was having a clandestine affair with his ex in the middle of downtown Rochester. How about if you start from there?"

Sighing, Sophia shook her head. "You were right. There was more to the story. Apparently, Lexie ran into him on her lunch hour while he was shopping for jewelry for me!"

"An engagement ring?" Eve asked excitedly.

Sophia's heart raced. "No. I mean, I don't think so. I guess I don't know for sure..."

"Well, what then?"

"Something for my birthday, but he's making me wait until then."

"So, how did you find all this out?"

Fiddling with a pen on her desk, Sophia replied, "I went over to his house last night. I couldn't sleep, so I decided to confront him."

"Oh boy. I would have liked to see that! Hell hath no fury..."

"Like a woman scorned. Yes, it's well documented. I might have called him an asshole a dozen times or so!" She could laugh about it now, and so did Eve.

"And after that?" Eve said, motioning impatiently for Sophia to continue.

"I stayed the night." Sophia felt a surge of heat crawl up her neck as the memories came flooding back.

Eve smiled knowingly and said, "So, you kissed and made up."

"Among other things."

"I get it. Now, what about the 'I love you'?"

Sophia leaned forward and told her about the list she'd found, and specifically about item number ten.

"Wow! How romantic," Eve said wistfully.

Sophia had often wished that her friend would find someone special. Eve hadn't had much luck with men, although she kept a positive attitude about it. She'd taken the stance of "when it happens, it happens" and hadn't let it get her down. If only Sophia knew someone she could set Eve up with...

"Ok, so, now what? When are you going to tell Drew that you love him too?"

"I've been thinking about that. We're planning on seeing each other tonight, so I want to come up with something good."

"Hmmm...let me think. Skywriting might be too expensive..."

Sophia laughed, and stood up. "We need to get to work. Let's talk more later."

As they walked back into the library, there was Jake Owen, standing by the information desk, anxiously glancing around. Sophia had seen him on Saturdays, when he brought his daughter to story time, but they hadn't talked much since the coffee shop debacle. He had remained friendly though, waving and saying hello to her, but he hadn't made any attempt to ask her out again. She wondered if he was looking for her now when Eve placed a hand on Sophia's arm.

"I think he's here for me," Eve said, looking up at Sophia with an unreadable expression. "I'll tell you about it later." And with that, she walked off toward Jake, who gave her a warm smile as she approached.

This was the second time in one day that Sophia wanted to break out in a happy dance. Why hadn't she thought of it before? Jake was the perfect choice for Eve. Kind, intelligent, warm, and handsome in an unassuming way. His daughter was adorable, and Eve loved kids whether she wanted to admit it or not. Sophia was dying to know when this had happened. Had she been so caught up in the "Drew drama" that she hadn't seen it? Or maybe Eve had felt uncomfortable telling her because she'd dated Jake. Although, it could hardly be called a date. One, she didn't even drink coffee. Two, Lexie had ruined the entire outing, and three… *Oh God, here I go with my lists again!*

None of it mattered anyway. If Eve was happy, that was all Sophia cared about. Picking up a stack of mail from the checkout desk, she slipped back into her office to give Eve and Jake some privacy. For the next two hours, she delved into her work, responding to emails, making phone calls, and reviewing the schedule for the next couple of weeks.

Drew had asked her to go away with him for her birthday, and she could hardly wait. She was curious about where he planned to take her, and she began weaving all kinds of fantasies around it. And to think that by then, she would have already told him she loved him.

The sound of her cell phone ringing in her purse broke her out of her reverie, and she quickly dug it out, grinning when she saw who it was.

"Rochester Library. Sophia speaking." Since her office door was open, she'd answered formally in case anyone happened to walk by.

"Hello. May I speak to the sexiest librarian on the planet?"

Shifting in her seat, she smiled and said, "I'm afraid we don't carry that book, sir."

"Ah. I get it. Somebody's nearby. Ok. Well, I just wanted to hear your voice and to ask you to dinner tonight."

"Yes. That can be arranged."

"And then, maybe after, we can strip naked and have hot, steamy…"

"Perhaps we can discuss this another time," she replied, squeezing her legs tightly together.

Drew chuckled, the rich sound of it traveling straight to her core. "I can hardly wait until tonight."

"Me too," she said, right as Eve poked her head around the corner. Sophia held a finger up, and Eve nodded and backed away.

"I'll let you get back to work, but first, where do you want to have dinner tonight?" he asked.

"My place?"

"Are you cooking?"

"We'll see."

He laughed again. "Ok. I'm in Detroit for a meeting, but I should be to your place by six o'clock. I'll call if I'm going to be any later."

"Sounds good." Perfect was more like it. That would give her plenty of time to set the stage for the evening.

"See you tonight, sweet Sophia."

After they hung up, she sat there for a moment in a lovestruck daze. She literally pinched herself to make sure she wasn't dreaming and then said, "Ow!"

Just then, Eve poked her head back in and said, "Are you ready for lunch?"

"Yes," Sophia replied, but as they walked out, all she could think about was dinner and what would happen after.

Chapter 31

On her way home from the library, Sophia made two stops, one at Victoria's Secret and the other at Whole Foods. Lucky for her, they were in the same plaza—go figure! At Victoria's Secret, she browsed through their latest collection of sexy bras and panties, looking for the perfect set to show off her assets. Plus, she had a coupon, and as a girl on a budget, she hated to have coupons go to waste.

"Looking for something special?" asked a young saleswoman.

"Well…yes, actually."

The woman nodded enthusiastically. "With your coloring, I would suggest something red. It will really pop against your skin."

If it made Drew *pop*, she was all for it! She perused the various options that the saleswoman showed her until she made her selection. Then she paid and left the store, giddily swinging her pink and white striped bag. After stowing the bag in her trunk, she went into the Whole Foods store, where she selected the items she needed to make dinner. Although she loved to eat, she wasn't a big fan of cooking, but she could certainly follow a recipe, and she wanted to do this for Drew.

When she got home, the first thing she did was change clothes. Since she was in a celebratory mood, she opted for a casual black t-shirt dress that she'd bought on sale at Old Navy. What she'd liked about it, besides the price, was the way it skimmed over her curves and swung around her legs when she walked. Plus, even though it was casual, it was still a dress, which was something she hardly ever wore. Surely, Drew would notice the extra effort she'd gone to, especially when he undressed her later and saw the sexy red lingerie she had on underneath. Her nipples hardened just thinking about it.

Once she was satisfied with her appearance, she went into the kitchen, where she plucked her mom's famous lasagna recipe out of a binder and went to work. Of course, she donned her apron first, since she had a habit of spilling things and didn't want to have to change again. Sophia danced and hummed as she moved around the kitchen, anticipating the moment when Drew would walk through the door and smell the meal she'd prepared. Maybe when he saw her, he'd want to postpone dinner until after they made love, even though the lasagna would taste better when it was still warm.

While the pasta was in the oven, she mixed up a salad and set in the refrigerator, and then she began to set the table. The battered table looked much better after she'd spread a floral tablecloth over it. She'd bought a bouquet of flowers at the store, and she placed them in a pretty crystal vase and set it in the center of the table. She added a pair of white candlesticks in matching crystal candle holders, and voilà! She was ready.

Now came the hard part—waiting! Feeling as prepared as she was going to be, Sophia took out her current book, curled up in her comfy (worn-in was more fitting) reading chair, and got lost in the story. It was an engaging World War II tale set in Italy, and the details were so vivid that she felt like she was transported to war-torn Europe instead of sitting in her cozy blue chair in the middle of her living room. She didn't look up until the buzzer rang on the oven, and she quickly went to take out the lasagna.

It was ten minutes until six, and Drew should be arriving at any moment. He hadn't called to say that he'd be late, so she assumed he'd be on time—which is why, when it became ten *after* six, she became concerned. Placing the lasagna back in the oven on the warm setting, she paced the kitchen for a few minutes, wondering whether she should call him. He already teased her plenty about being a stickler for schedules, so she hesitated. Besides, she didn't want to appear overanxious. He was probably caught up in traffic or on a business call, or he'd gotten stuck in a meeting and hadn't had a chance to call her yet.

Deciding that now would be a good opportunity to practice patience, she sat back down with her book and tried to delve back into the story. But even the raging war couldn't keep her from glancing at her watch, and at six thirty, she stood back up. It wasn't like Drew not to call her when he said he would, especially when he knew that she was making dinner. Now her impatience was turning into worry. She couldn't just sit there any longer, so she picked up her phone and dialed. The phone rang and rang until it finally transferred to voicemail. She tried to be soothed by his deep voice asking her to leave a message, but it was no use. Attempting to keep her voice steady, she left a message asking him to call her as soon as possible.

For the next twenty minutes, she paced through her small house and kept looking out the front window for his car. But nothing. When seven o'clock rolled around, she tried calling him again, and this time, her call went straight to voicemail as if his phone had been shut off. Why would he do that? And why couldn't he have at least sent her a text message even if he was in a meeting? Now her worry was turning into frustration with a touch of anger. The lasagna sat in the oven, probably congealing, and the salad was wilting in the fridge. She was seriously beginning to wonder if she'd gone to all this trouble for nothing.

Her imagination, being that of a reader's, carried her away into more troublesome thoughts. What if he were getting cold feet? What if he'd decided that they were moving too fast or that he didn't want a relationship with her after all? But no, that didn't make sense, because he'd called her earlier to say how much he was looking forward to the evening. What in the hell was going on?

And then her phone rang, and she experienced a pang of relief until she saw who it was.

"Hello?" she answered, her voice shaky.

"Sophia. Oh, thank God you're there."

"What is it? What's wrong?"

"It's Drew. He's been in an accident," Diane said, breaking into tears.

Heart pounding, Sophia clutched the phone tightly and said, "What happened? Where is he?"

"He's at Detroit Mercy Hospital. I just got the call a few minutes ago. I feel so helpless, Sophia. Can you go down there? Please?"

Sophia had already slipped on her shoes and was grabbing her purse and keys. "Of course. I'm leaving right now."

"Thank you so much. Mark and I feel terrible that we're not there. I hate to put you out, but..."

Sophia interrupted her. "You're not putting me out, Diane. He's my...best friend. Of course I want to be there. I...I...love him." And then she burst into tears too.

"Oh, sweetie. I know you do, and he loves you too. I'm sure of it. Are you going to be ok driving? Now I'm going to worry about you too."

Sophia swiped her tears away and trained her eyes on the road. She'd be no use to Drew if she crashed her car. "I'll be fine. What else can you tell me about the accident?"

"A nurse called to say that Drew had been taken there by ambulance after he was involved in a three-car accident on the expressway. She said he was conscious but shaken up, and they were checking him over for broken bones or a concussion. My God. I hate to think of him lying there all alone."

Sophia pressed down a little harder on the gas pedal. "He won't be alone for long. I'm hurrying to get there," she said.

"Don't you get in an accident too!"

It was just like Diane to treat her like one of her own children. She always had, and Sophia loved her for it. "I had a feeling that something bad had happened," Sophia admitted. "Drew was on his way to my house for dinner, and he was an hour late. I kept waiting for him to call..." She couldn't say anymore for fear of breaking down again.

"I know. He told me."

"He did?"

"Um-hum. He called me earlier today to ask for some advice. But I really shouldn't say anything else. It's not my place."

Sophia was flummoxed, but she knew better than to press. Whatever it was, Drew would tell her when he was ready. Right now, her main concern was his well-being. "I should probably go so I can concentrate on the road. But I promise to call you as soon as I know something."

"Ok. Thank you so much, Sophia. Give Drew our love and kiss him for me, please."

Kissing and hugging him was exactly what Sophia planned to do as soon as she possibly could. Right now, she'd settle for seeing him alive and in one piece, and then she'd smother him with affection.

Thankfully, traffic was lighter at that time of night, and she made it to the hospital in forty minutes. She was also grateful that she'd put on sneakers in her hurry to get there, and now she jogged through the parking lot and into the hospital, rushing up to the reception desk to inquire about Drew. The receptionist consulted her computer screen and gave Sophia directions as to which floor he was on.

"Thank you," Sophia called over her shoulder as she hurriedly walked to the elevator. Not having been in hospitals very often, she still should have known that she wouldn't be able to see him right away. The clerk at the floor desk directed her to a waiting room and said that someone would be with her shortly. Another hour went by, which she passed by making phone calls and pacing. First, she called Diane to let her know she'd arrived but had no news yet, and then she called her own mom just because she needed to hear another comforting voice.

The minute her mom said hello, Sophia burst into tears again. It took her a minute to calm down enough to tell what had happened, after which her mom offered to drive down there with her dad to keep Sophia company.

"Thanks, Mom, but I don't think it's a good idea. I know how you and Dad are about night driving, and there's nothing you can do here anyway. I just needed to talk to someone."

"Of course, Sophie. You know you can call us anytime, day or night. We'll always be here for you."

Her mom's sentiment made the tears flow even harder, but then a nurse stepped into the room, and Sophia hurriedly ended the call.

"Are you Sophia Russo?" the nurse asked.

"Yes."

"We were waiting to get permission from the patient's parents before we could give you any information."

Sophia hadn't even thought of that. Since she and Drew weren't married, naturally, they'd have to contact his relatives first. "Is he...ok?" she asked.

The nurse nodded. "He'll be fine. He has quite a few cuts, one of which required stitches, and he'll be sore for a while, but he's ok."

"Thank God," Sophia replied, placing a hand over her heart.

"You can come back and see him now, but visiting hours are over in a half an hour, so then you'll have to leave."

Sophia nodded and followed the nurse down a long corridor to a room near the end of the hall.

"There's another patient in the room, so please keep your voice down," the nurse said and waved her inside.

Sophia disliked hospitals almost as much as cooking, but right then, all she cared about was getting to Drew. There was a male patient sleeping on the right, and a curtain was pulled on the left, blocking her view of the other bed. She walked softly but quickly around the curtain, and there he was, the man that she loved. His eyes were closed, and he had a bandage over his right eyebrow. There were smaller cuts on his cheeks and chin, and he was wearing a blue hospital gown, but other than that, he looked as handsome as ever—at least to her.

She was afraid to wake him, yet they only had a half an hour, and she was dying to talk to him, to touch him...

Just then, almost as if he sensed her presence, his eyes popped open, and his face lit up with the sweetest smile she'd ever seen.

"Oh, Drew. Thank God you're ok." Forgetting that she was supposed to be quiet, she rushed over to the bed and bent down to kiss him, pausing because she didn't want to hurt him.

She was still trying to figure out the best angle when he laughed and said, "Just kiss me!"

She pressed her lips gently to his and sighed. All the anxiety drained out of her as he tenderly kissed her back. Even though the kiss lacked its usual energy, it was still intoxicating and comforting.

And then, feeling exhausted from the waiting and worrying, Sophia slumped down into the chair by his bed. "Tell me what happened," she said.

Clearing his throat, Drew relayed the story. "I was hurrying home because I didn't want to be late for our dinner when the guy in front of me slammed on his breaks to avoid hitting something in the road. I didn't have enough time to stop, which caused me to hit him, and then I was hit by the car behind me. My car's totaled, but at least nobody was seriously injured. It could have been a whole lot worse."

She didn't even want to imagine it. It had been bad enough driving down to the hospital knowing that he was ok. If something else had happened...

"Soph? You're crying."

She'd been so caught up in her thoughts that she hadn't even realized it, and she quickly swiped her tears away.

"Come up here. Sit with me."

"I probably shouldn't. You're hurt, and the nurse told me I couldn't stay long, and..."

"Soph. Please. I've just been in an accident, and I want to hold my girl."

My girl. She loved the sound of that. She carefully climbed up on the bed and curled her body against him. When she leaned her head against his shoulder, he said, "Ouch!" But then he immediately started laughing.

"Don't do that!" she said. "Do you know how scared I was? How scared we all were?"

Brushing her hair back, he said, "Who's we?"

"Your parents, my parents, me! In fact, I promised your mom I'd call her as soon as I knew something..."

"Not yet. Stay with me for a few more minutes."

She wasn't about to argue with him, not when he could have been killed. She shuddered just thinking about it, and he squeezed her tight.

"I'm sorry I missed our dinner," he whispered. "I was trying to get to you, and I was just about to call when the accident happened."

Laying her hand on his chest, she rubbed it soothingly. "It doesn't matter as long as you're ok."

"Just out of curiosity, what did you make us?"

"Lasagna and a salad. My mom's recipe."

"Stop. You're making my mouth water."

She smiled against his chest. "I never tasted it. I was waiting for you."

"Well, I'm sure it would have been delicious."

Glancing up at him, she said, "I'll make it for you again sometime."

"I'd love that."

And I love you. It was right on the tip of her tongue, but this time, she hesitated not because she was afraid, but because it wasn't exactly the perfect setting. A sterile hospital room with a snoring man in the next bed was a far cry from her cozy kitchen with the flowers and candles and the home-cooked meal. Tears gathered in her eyes again, threatening to spill over.

Just then, the nurse who had shown Sophia to the room poked her head around the curtain. "Five more minutes," she said and gave them a half-smile before walking back out.

It was now or never, and Sophia had to tell him. She simply couldn't hold it in any longer. Propping herself up on her elbow, she said, "Drew. I..."

"Wait. I have something to tell you first."

"You do?"

He nodded, and picking up one of her hands, he raised it to his lips and placed a gentle kiss on the back of it. "I've been thinking about this for a while, and after what happened tonight...well, I don't want to wait anymore."

Her heart was pounding so hard that she felt the pulsing in her ears. Gazing at him, she nodded, encouraging him to continue. But he didn't appear to need it.

"I love you, Sophia. I love you so much, and I was going to tell you at dinner, but then…"

She might have knocked the air out of him then, she hugged him so tight. And laughing and crying at the same time, she said, "I love you too. I love you too!"

"Ow," he said, and when he didn't follow it up with laughter, she pulled back. "It really hurt that time," he said, rubbing his shoulder. But he was still smiling, beaming really, and if she wasn't mistaken, his eyes were glistening too.

"I love you," he repeated, quieter that time as the man in the other bed was stirring.

"I love you too. So, so much."

And then the nurse reappeared, and in a firm voice, she said, "Time's up."

"They're keeping me overnight, but I should be released tomorrow morning," Drew said, reluctantly letting go of Sophia's hand.

"I'll come back in the morning. Early," she promised.

"I wouldn't come too early. It'll take a while before he's released," the nurse said.

"That's ok. I'll wait." And with that, she leaned in and gave Drew a quick kiss before hopping off the bed. She started to follow the nurse out but turned and glanced over her shoulder. Drew mouthed "I love you," and she quickly mouthed it back before following the nurse out the door.

On the drive home, Sophia called Diane and gave her an update on Drew's condition. Diane's relief was palpable, and by the end of the conversation, she was half-laughing, half-crying as she thanked Sophia repeatedly for being there.

"There's no place else I'd rather be," Sophia replied. "I take that back. I'd rather Drew was at home with me." *Oops.* That kind of slipped out before she could censor it.

Diane didn't miss a beat. "He's lucky to have you," she said.

"I feel lucky too."

After they hung up, Sophia called her mom. She hated to call so late, but she was certain her parents would want an update too. By the time she got home, she was thoroughly exhausted, yet she had a hard time falling asleep. The evening hadn't gone at all as planned, yet she would always remember it as one of the best nights of her life.

No flowers, candles, or dinner. Her in a dress and sneakers. Him in a faded blue hospital gown with a bandage on his forehead. An old man snoring in the bed across from them. Yet none of that mattered. Drew loved her, and she loved him, and from this moment on, she wouldn't hesitate to tell him. In fact, she planned to tell him so often that he'd probably get tired of hearing it. *But God, I hope not.*

And then she thought about his list, or his love note as she liked to think of it. He'd skipped a couple of items on the list, but she was so, so, glad he had. He'd told her that he loved her, and if he never went back to the other items, that was fine by her. Although, when she finally closed her eyes, she was envisioning numbers eight and nine...

Chapter 32

Sophia glanced out the car window at the passing scenery, and her excitement kicked up a notch. She hadn't been to Mackinac Island since she and Drew and their families had gone there years ago. But this time was different. This time, it was just the two of them, and they were travelling together not just as friends, but as lovers too. She could hardly wait to get there and to be alone with him without any distractions.

Since his car accident, they'd spent every free moment together; however, Drew had been working overtime training a new salesperson. He'd decided not to accept the promotion that he'd been offered based on the amount of travel that would be required. "I don't want to be away from you that much," he'd said. Therefore, he'd been charged with training someone to take over the territory that he would have been given.

Secretly, Sophia had been thrilled that he'd turned the position down, but she'd made sure that he'd done it for the right reasons and not just because of her. After a lengthy discussion, he'd convinced her of his decision, and then they'd followed it up with a vigorous lovemaking session as if to seal the deal. "I've known guys who travel a lot for work, and it doesn't always bode well for their marriages or their families. I don't want that to be me," Drew had insisted. That had been the first time he'd spoken so directly to her about the m-word, and she'd been pleasantly surprised.

When she'd relayed the conversation to Eve, Eve had insisted that he was whisking her off to Mackinac Island to propose, but Sophia had shrugged it off. "He just wants to do something nice for my birthday," Sophia had said, but Eve wasn't buying it. "I guarantee that you'll come back with a big rock on your left hand," Eve had said before she'd rushed off to meet Jake Owen for lunch.

Eve and Jake were now officially an item, and Sophia couldn't be happier for her. They were so sweet together, and along with Jake's daughter, they were like a ready-made family. Eve had insisted that they weren't heading down the aisle anytime soon, but based on the way Jake treated her, Sophia disagreed. Eve had attempted to make a wager over which one of them would get married first, but Sophia had declined. It wasn't that she didn't want to marry Drew; it was just that she was so happy that she didn't want to jinx things.

"So, are you happy that you wheedled it out of me where we're going?" Drew said, breaking into her thoughts.

She giggled. "I didn't *wheedle* it out of you."

"Ok. So, you tickled it out of me. Same thing."

"I never knew you were so ticklish."

"Well, now you do. And I'm sure you'll use it against me again."

She smirked at him. "As I recall, you didn't mind it so much."

Drew smirked back, and she knew he was recalling what had happened after. It seemed like their sexual appetites had exploded after his accident. For the first couple of days after he'd come home, she'd been cautious with him, thinking that he was still in pain. But after that, he'd insisted he was fine, and they'd resumed regular *activities*. Their lovemaking had taken on a new fervor, bolstered by their newfound admission of love for each other.

Sophia still hadn't told him that she'd seen his love note, and maybe she never would. One day, when she'd been in his kitchen getting them some drinks, she'd opened the junk drawer just enough to see if the notepad was still there. And it had been. Right on top, where she'd last seen it. Maybe Drew had wanted her to see it, or maybe he'd simply forgotten about it. In any case, it didn't really matter anymore, because she had everything she'd ever wanted—him!

"You still haven't told me where we're staying," she reminded him.

"Well, I wanted to keep some things a secret," he said, keeping his eyes on the road.

Some things? Interesting. But she decided not to try and wheedle any more out of him. Besides, she had some surprises of her own in store.

Driving through Mackinaw City on the way to catch the ferry to the island was like stepping back in time. Most of the city looked the same, with its quaint shops and restaurants and that small-town Up North feel. Since it was the end of June, tourists were out in force, strolling along on the city sidewalks, licking ice cream cones, or indulging in the famous Mackinaw fudge.

Sophia relished the air of expectancy as they waited in line to board the ferry that would take them across the straits to the island. Once on board, they went to the top deck, where they could enjoy the best views of the impressive Mackinac Bridge and the surrounding area.

"I forgot how beautiful this is," Sophia said, leaning her head back against Drew's chest. He was standing behind her at the rail, boxing her in with his arms, keeping her safe and warm. Even though it was seventy-two degrees, the winds off the water were strong and cool, and she'd felt a chill until he'd come up behind her.

"It's even more beautiful this time," he said and gave her a squeeze.

If they hadn't been on a boat full of people, she would have turned around and kissed him passionately, but she'd have the chance soon enough. For now, she'd enjoy the scenery with his arms wrapped around her.

Twenty minutes later, they disembarked onto the bustling island. Drew carried both of their duffel bags in one hand, grabbed her hand in the other, and led her to a waiting carriage. She loved that motor vehicles weren't permitted on the island and that people got around the old-fashioned way: on foot, in horse-drawn carriages, or by bicycle.

Drew gave her a hand up while the driver stowed their bags in the back.

"Where to, sir?" the driver asked as they got settled.

"The Grand Hotel," Drew said.

"Yes, sir."

As the horses sauntered down the middle of Main Street, Sophia squeezed his hand excitedly. "The Grand Hotel? Really?"

"Yes. That was one of my secrets."

She smiled so wide her cheeks hurt. "I've never stayed there before. Have you?"

"No, but I remembered how much you liked the look of it the last time we were here, and I wanted to take you there."

Since they were the only two in the carriage and nobody was looking, she leaned over and flung her arms around his neck. "Thank you, so much! I love you."

"I love you too, my sweet Sophia." With that, he leaned in for a kiss, and this time, she didn't hold back. As their tongues met, she felt the sizzle all the way down to her toes. As anxious as she was to explore the island again, she was more anxious to be alone with Drew. The Grand Hotel! It couldn't get any more romantic than that!

But she was wrong! Drew had booked them a sumptuous suite for the weekend, and when he closed the door behind them, she flung her arms around him again, and they fell laughing onto the cozy queen-sized bed. She kissed his lips in rapid succession while murmuring words of appreciation.

"You don't have to keep thanking me, although I'm enjoying the method you're using," he teased and playfully squeezed her behind.

She was lying on top of him, and suddenly, their playfulness morphed into urgent desire. They shed their clothes in record time, stopping only when Sophia's arms got trapped in her shirt, and Drew had to help her out of it. Once they were naked, he rolled her over onto her back and began a thorough exploration of her body, kissing her from her forehead all the way down to her pink polished toes.

And then she declared that it was her turn, and she gave him the same treatment, although she stopped short of his toes because, as hot he was, toes weren't really her thing. He didn't seem to mind, especially since she spent an inordinate amount of time in the area between his hips, licking and lapping at him until he moaned with pleasure.

"I need to get a condom. Now," he said, hurriedly sitting up.

"No, you don't," she said, sitting back on her haunches with a seductive smile on her face. Here was her first surprise.

"Soph?"

"I went on the pill, and besides, this is the least likely time in my cycle to get pregnant. We're safe."

"Are you sure?" he asked with a mixture of concern and hopefulness.

"I'm positive. I was waiting for this trip to tell you."

"My God, woman. Just when I think I can't possibly love you more..." With that, he pulled her over him and rubbed himself across her entrance a few times.

Glancing down at their combined wetness, Sophia helped guide him inside, and once he was fully rooted, they both sighed. Even though they'd done this many times before, there was no comparison to the feel of skin on skin, and as they moved together, she gazed deep into his spectacular eyes and smiled. "I love you, Drew."

His hands gripped her hips tightly, and his breathing had become labored, but he returned the sentiment right before they exploded together, rocking and panting until they'd expended every ounce of energy.

Afterwards, he pulled her close, and they lay there atop the covers, soaking each other in, absorbing the significance of their lovemaking. They had finally reached a point of trust and security, where Sophia wouldn't worry even if she were to become pregnant. She knew without a doubt that Drew would take care of her and their child if it should come to that. Of course, she'd rather do things in the proper order and become his wife first.

Drew's wife? Wow! A few months ago, if someone would have told her that she and Drew would become a couple, she would have scoffed at the idea. And now, here she was, lying naked in his arms, in the Grand Hotel no less, considering what it would be like to be married to him. If the past few months were any indication, she'd look forward to it. Heck, she'd known him for so long that they already had a marriage of sorts, only now they had added the physical union.

She'd discovered that he wasn't perfect, but he was perfect for her, and she'd like to believe it went both ways. They complimented each other, made each other better people, lifted each other up. They'd had a few spats since they'd officially become a couple, but nothing that couldn't be resolved with communication and compromise. She'd even chosen to ignore his unmade bed, recognizing that it was small potatoes in the scheme of things! Of course, he'd chosen to overlook some of her quirky habits as well, including her incessant list-making. More often than not, he'd gotten a kick out of it, but on a couple of occasions, he'd ripped up her lists right in front of her face. She supposed he was trying to teach her to be more spontaneous, but that might take a while.

"Soph?"

"Yeah?" She'd been so relaxed, so contented that she'd almost drifted off until he'd spoken.

"What do you say we get dressed and go exploring? There's only a few hours of daylight left, and then we can come right back here and pick up where we left off."

Leaning up on her elbow, she traced the outline of his lips with her fingertip. His lips looked slightly puffy from all the kissing and sucking, and she liked that she'd been the one to make them that way. "If you insist," she said.

Brushing her hair back, he said, "I dare say that the lady has surpassed me in terms of sexual appetite."

"I'm just enjoying this," she said.

"I am too, but it's not like it'll be our last time. C'mon. Let's get dressed." With that, he rolled off the bed and padded to the bathroom, picking up his discarded clothes on the way.

She lay there and enjoyed the view before finally forcing herself to get up too. *He's right. I am a bit of a hussy these days!*

After taking a stroll around the hotel grounds (all that she was missing was a gown with a hoop skirt and a parasol, and it could have been a scene from *Gone with the Wind*), they caught a carriage ride back into town. Holding hands, they meandered up and down Main Street, wandering into a few shops along the way. Of course, one couldn't go to Mackinac Island without buying fudge, and Sophia insisted they buy a few blocks of it—some for now and some for later.

They ate dinner at a pub overlooking Lake Huron and then took a carriage back to the hotel just as the sun was setting.

"This is so romantic," she gushed. "It's the best birthday present ever."

"It's not over yet," he said, wiggling his eyebrows at her.

"I know," she said suggestively. She had one more surprise in store for him before the night was over.

Once they'd returned to the hotel room, Sophia suggested that he get comfortable while she got ready for bed. Then she selected the items she needed from her duffel bag, wrapped them up in her pajamas, and hurried into the bathroom. She heard Drew climb into bed and turn on the television, but she locked the door anyway.

He'd never seen her sexy red bra and panties that she'd bought the day of his accident, so she'd saved them until now. She put up her hair into a hasty bun using several bobby pins and slipped on her glasses. The last item she removed from her balled-up pajamas was a silky red scarf that she'd bought specifically for the trip. She quickly brushed her teeth and then took a deep breath before opening the bathroom door.

Drew appeared to be riveted to the baseball game on TV; however, as she moved further into the room, he glanced toward her, and then he did a double-take. Fumbling for the remote, he flicked off the TV and stared some more.

"Holy…"

Smiling, she slowly turned around so he could appreciate the back of her panties, which showed much more than they covered.

When she came back to center, he swallowed hard and asked, "What's the scarf for?"

Stepping toward him, she replied, "Remember in Florida when I told you about my fantasy?"

"Oh yeah."

"And you told me about yours?"

Drew nodded.

"Well, we're not in the library, but I thought we could combine our fantasies and try them out here." And then she motioned to the desk in the opposite corner of the room. "If you're interested, that is."

But he'd already scrambled off the bed and was stalking toward her. "Oh, I'm interested," he replied, glancing down at the bulge in his shorts.

She leaned back against the desk, and he came to stand in front of her. The room was cool, dark, and quiet, adding to the seductive ambiance she'd hoped to create. Anticipating his touch, she thrust her breasts forward a little, and he immediately responded by cupping them and flicking his thumbs across her taut nipples.

"I like the red on you," he whispered, right before dipping his head down and nuzzling her cleavage.

And then he licked a path from her chest to her neck, where he nibbled on the sensitive skin there.

"Mmmm. Glad you like it," she said, her voice breathy.

Sliding his arms around her waist, he closed the remaining distance between them and rubbed up against her center. She tugged up on his t-shirt, and he quickly removed it and flung it across the room. Gliding her hands over his bare chest, she said, "Don't you want to take my hair down?"

Looking like the happiest man on earth, he lifted his hands to her hair and carefully removed the bobby pins one by one. Why was it that the simplest actions were so erotic with him? Maybe it was the way he gazed at her, like he couldn't believe his good fortune. Or maybe it was the way he touched her, like it was the very first time every single time. Whatever it was, he had her all hot and bothered before the last bobby pin was out and her hair came cascading down to brush her shoulders.

Cupping her face in his hands, Drew leaned in and kissed her tenderly yet passionately. She responded by digging her fingers into his shoulders and arching her hips against his, pulling him as close as he could be while they still had some clothes on.

During a break in the kiss, she said, "You might want to take my glasses off now."

"Good idea," he said, carefully removing them and setting them on the desk. She'd set the scarf on the desk too, and now he picked it up and ran his hands over the silky material.

"Are you ready for this?" he asked, his voice huskier than it had been a few minutes ago.

"So ready."

With that, he covered her eyes with the scarf and knotted it at the back, plunging her into total darkness. "Ok?"

She nodded, her heart in her throat. They say when one sense is compromised, the other senses take over, and it was true. She became hyperaware of his sounds and touch, which accelerated her arousal even more. He kissed her, lightly brushing his lips over hers and then tracing them with his tongue. Then he slid his hands around her back and unhooked her bra, pulling the straps down her shoulders and tossing it aside, the whoosh of cool air causing her nipples to pebble. He stilled for a few seconds, and her anticipation skyrocketed, causing her to squirm against the desk.

"You're so hot, Sophia," he said, the sound of his voice reverberating through her chest, making it heave under his gaze. Or at least she assumed he was gazing, since she couldn't see him. She'd been right about her fantasy—her desire for him was magnified, and she liked giving up control for once, opening herself up to whatever he wanted to do to her, because now she knew that he would never hurt her. That he loved her and cared for her without reservation or restrictions. It had been the most freeing experience of her life until now.

She smiled in response, and then she felt his fingertips graze over her sex before hooking into the sides of her panties and slowly pulling them down. Standing there bare before him, she should have felt vulnerable, but she didn't. She felt exhilarated, powerful, sexy, and strong. That was what his love did for her, and right now, she wanted more of it—all of it.

Feeling his warm breath on her inner thighs, she knew what was coming next, and she spread her legs, clutching the desk for support. The second his mouth covered her, she tipped her head back and moaned, desperately needing the contact, reveling in the heat of his mouth and tongue. After several minutes of him lavishing attention on her, he pulled back, and a cool whoosh of air brushed her heated skin.

"Drew?"

He didn't answer, but she heard him removing his shorts, and she shivered in anticipation. She extended a hand out to touch him, but he gently brushed it aside, and in a swift fluid motion, he picked her up in his arms and carried her across the room. He laid her in the middle of the bed, and then she felt the mattress sink as he came over her.

"I can't wait any longer. I need you, Sophia." And on the sound of her name from his lips, he entered her in one long, deep stroke. Clutching his backside in her hands, she arched her hips up and met him thrust for thrust. Just as they were getting close, Drew suddenly yanked up her blindfold.

"Need to see you..." he said in short gasps, and then gazing deep into each other's eyes, they came in a raucous symphony of sounds, bodies shimmering with sweat and heat, faces glowing with pleasure.

Afterwards, he rolled off to the side, and they lay there splayed out on the bed, holding hands until their breathing returned to normal and their skin cooled. Finally, Sophia said, "Like I said before, best birthday ever!"

"There's still tomorrow," he replied with a secretive gleam in his eye.

I want to spend all my tomorrows with you. But to avoid sounding greedy, she smiled and said, "I can't wait!"

Chapter 33

"We're a lot better at this than the first time we did it," Sophia said.

"Practice makes perfect," Drew replied.

They'd rented a tandem bicycle and were zipping around the bike path that rimmed Mackinac Island just like they'd done as teenagers. Their rhythm on the bike matched their rhythm with each other—they were truly in sync, so much so that Sophia didn't have to concentrate on keeping the bike steady and could glance out over the water that sparkled in the afternoon sunshine without the fear of falling.

After riding in comfortable silence for a while, Drew said, "Let's stop up here."

It was a halfway point around the island, and Sophia remembered stopping at the same spot when they were teens. Large boulders separated the bike trail from the soft white sand, providing a perfect perch to view the sprawling Mackinac Bridge. They'd passed several bikers on the trail, but at that moment, nobody was around, and it felt like they had the place to themselves.

Drew gave her a hand up and sat next to her atop a large rock.

"Gorgeous," Sophia murmured, looking out over the glistening water.

"I agree," Drew said softly.

Something in his voice made her turn to look at him, but it was her he seemed to be admiring instead of the view. Smiling at her, he took her hand and entwined their fingers together. "I remember the first time we were here at this very spot. I wanted to kiss you then, but I was afraid to."

"Why were you afraid?"

"I didn't want anything to change between us. I thought that if we became more than friends, there'd be the possibility of losing you someday, and I didn't want to risk it."

Shifting sideways, she peered straight into his eyes and said, "I felt the same way. I told myself that it was better to have you as a friend than to not have you at all. But I never really believed it. I always wanted this, always wanted you."

Drew brought her hand up to his mouth and placed a tender kiss on the back of it. "I'm so glad we took the risk."

"Me too."

He leaned forward and kissed her lips, soft and slow, lovingly, lingering until they heard the voices of oncoming cyclists and broke apart.

When they were alone again, Drew inhaled deeply, and his expression became more serious. "Sophia?"

"Yes?"

"I hope you know how much I love you. I've been trying to show you over these past several weeks, and…"

She couldn't bear to see him looking so uncomfortable and nervous. It wasn't like him, and she didn't want him to feel that way with her—ever.

Cupping his face in her hands, she said, "I do know, Drew. You don't have to keep trying to prove it to me."

Looking relieved, he briefly kissed her again, and then taking both of her hands in his, he said, "I brought you here for another reason."

"You did?"

"Um-hum. I thought it was symbolic that we've been on two islands together, here and Sanibel. And islands are circular, never-ending, just like my love for you."

Suddenly, Drew let go of her left hand, reached into the side pocket of his cargo shorts, and pulled out a jewelry box. Sophia recognized the name of the jewelry store in downtown Rochester, and her heart leapt to her throat.

Calm down, Soph. He already told you that he bought you something from there. It's probably a necklace or a bracelet. But with a box that size…

He opened the lid to reveal a sparkling round diamond ring on a white gold band, and her eyes instantly welled with tears. "Sophia Russo, you're my best friend and the love of my life. Will you make me the happiest man alive and marry me?"

There wasn't a flicker of hesitation. Not one. "Yes! Yes! Yes!"

Taking her trembling left hand in his, Drew slipped the ring on her finger, and then grabbing her around the waist, he lifted her up and hugged her tight, somehow managing to keep them balanced on the rock at the same time.

Once he'd set her back down, she took a good long look at the ring he'd chosen, glimmering in the sunlight. It was stunning, and once again, she felt guilty for doubting him that day she'd seen him outside the jewelry store.

"Do you like it? We can always go back and exchange it..."

"NO! I love it! It's perfect."

"Good. You had me worried for a minute there."

"I was just thinking back to the day that I saw you in front of the store. I feel horrible about doubting you, especially now that I know you were there picking out this beautiful ring."

Drew scratched the back of his head and cleared his throat. "Well, to be completely honest..."

Oh no. What now?

"I didn't buy you the ring that day."

"But..."

"I bought you the heart necklace. The one that we looked at when I was buying a gift for my mom, remember?"

"Yes, but..."

"After my car accident, I went back and exchanged the necklace for this. I knew that I wanted to marry you someday, but it wasn't until then that I decided someday was now. I didn't want to wait another minute to start the rest of our lives."

Touched by his openness, Sophia decided to reciprocate. "I have a confession too," she said.

"Uh-oh. Should I be worried?" he teased.

She shook her head. "It's nothing too bad. At least I hope not. But since we're getting married, I don't want there to be any secrets between us."

"Ok. With that lead-up, I'm really scared," he said, looking somewhat amused.

"I saw your list," she blurted.

"My list?"

"Well, I like to refer to it as a love note."

Eyebrows knit together, he said, "You've lost me."

"Number one: Feed her. Number two: Buy her something shiny. Number three…"

Dawning struck, and Drew's face lit up with a huge grin. "When did you see my *love note*?"

"It was the morning after I stayed over at your house for the first time."

"You mean the day after you called me an asshole?"

"Must you always remind me of that?"

"Yes. I think I must," he replied, laughing.

"So, you're not mad at me for reading your list?"

Smirking, he shook his head. "No. But I am curious about how you found it."

"Well, you didn't hide it very well! I was trying to put my breakfast tray away when I saw it in the junk drawer."

"And of course you had to read it because you love your lists!"

"Love note," she corrected.

"From now on, if I write any more *love notes*, I'll leave them right out where you can see them."

"Deal. I just have one question."

"Hit me."

"When are you going to get to number eight?"

Tipping his head back, Drew laughed heartily. (It was more of a guffaw, really!) And then he said, "Let's go back to the room, and I'll show you."

And as they rode their tandem bike the rest of the way around the island, she kept glancing down at her engagement ring, thinking about what Drew had said.

Their love had come full circle—the perfect blend of friendship and passion—with the promise of many more *love notes* to come.

THE END

Author's Note:

If you enjoyed *Love Notes*, please take a moment to leave a review on Amazon and/or Goodreads. And while you're there, check out my other sweet and sexy contemporary romance novels!

I love to connect with readers. Please visit my website (susancoventry.org) and follow me on Facebook (Susan Coventry, Author), Instagram (susancoventryauthor), and Twitter (@CoventrySusan).

Thanks for reading!

Made in the USA
Lexington, KY
20 February 2018